Holy Moly!

Rachel paused at the view. Mitchell stood shirtless at the water pump. Her mouth dried up faster than a drop of water in the Sahara Desert. She watched him splash his face and chest. His muscles glistened as the drops of water made a trail down his lean, sculptured body. This cowboy was hotter than any fireman calendar she'd ever seen.

She pinched herself. Nope. Wide awake. She fanned herself and cleared her parched throat. "Supper is hot," she stammered. "I mean supper is ready."

Mitchell's startled gaze settled on her. "I'll be in. I'm almost finished."

Rachel swung around and shut the door with a soft click. Leaning heavily against the hard wood, she closed her eyes and blocked out the vision of Mitchell without his shirt.

I0598319

All for the Love of a Cowboy

by

N. Jade Gray

All for the Love of a Cowboy

Cover Art by *Rae Monet, Inc. Design*

The Wild Rose Press, Inc.
PO Box 708
Adams Basin, NY 14410-0708
Visit us at www.thewildrosepress.com

Publishing History
First Cactus Rose Edition, 2017
Print ISBN 978-1-5092-1270-5
Digital ISBN 978-1-5092-1271-2

Published in the United States of America

Dedications

This book is dedicated to the many supporters
who've prodded me throughout the years:
God, Nathan, Blake, Mason, Mom, Dad, Theresa,
Nancy, Ornery Siblings, NOC chicks, WARA ladies,
and many others who played the Jiminy Cricket
on my shoulder, whispering to keep trying.

~*~

Thank you to my editor, Nicole, for accepting the
challenge of taking on my story and the patience of
dealing with this newbie. I couldn't have done it
without you. :)

~*~

In memory of my mother-in-law, Kay,
who also enjoyed a good chick read.

~*~

I would also like to add a thank you to my beta readers
(guinea pigs) Theresa, Angela, and Margret.

Chapter One

Durango, Colorado, present day

A soft moan escaped Rachel Morgan as firm lips trailed along her jaw line. She gasped as his tongue blazed a path to her right ear and caressed the tender shell. The erotic dance brought a dreamy smile to her lips. Hot currents sizzled down her spine as he stroked the curvature of her neck. She would never underestimate the power of nibbling.

Ever. Again.

Whimpering, she arched into the sensation. She frowned as his warm breath retreated from her body.

"No," she groaned.

She reached to draw the muscular body to the shelter of her arms. Nothing but air. Where had her brawny man gone?

A low-pitched noise intruded, and she blinked her eyes open. Gazing at the culprit, she cursed. Damn. Her stupid alarm clock had just interrupted, hands-down, the best interactive dream she had ever had.

The consistent buzz bounced off the walls until she whacked the snooze button. She rolled over and stretched her toes, dislodging her big toe from the tangled sheets.

Staring at the ceiling, she pondered her dream man. How could she lure him back to her warm sheets?

With a sigh, she swung her legs over the side of the bed. Seven o'clock. The big red numbers mocked her. She rubbed her eyes. A yawn escaped as she extended her arms above her head. The movement caused a resounding pop from her spine.

What a long week. She had finally resolved the bugs in the new computer program late the night before. By fall enrollment at Fort Lewis College, everything should be running smoothly.

Too bad the overtime pay would go to repairs her vintage Mustang required. Which if she didn't hurry she'd be late for the appointment with the garage.

She exited her bedroom after a quick shower. Why was the apartment so quiet?

"Angie?" No answer. Giving her roommate's door a quick rap, she turned the knob and peeked in. The bed lay undisturbed. The living room and kitchen were both empty as well. Where was her roommate? Spying a piece of paper on the counter she picked it up and sighed in relief. She wouldn't have to call nine-one-one after all.

Hey Chickie,

You've probably noticed I'm not there. You seemed to be having pleasant dreams when I peeked in earlier, so I didn't want to disturb you. I didn't see much of you this week. I have wonderful, exciting news to tell you! Meet Bruce and your favorite roommate at our favorite pizza place at 6:00.

Ang

Rachel didn't need a mirror to know a blush stained her cheeks. Pleasant dreams? What a laugh. More like erotic, but she wasn't going to confess. Not even to Angie.

Hmm…exciting news. Dread fluttered briefly in her stomach. Wedding bells? She would bet her overtime check that's where this was leading. Crap. She was going to lose the best roommate she ever had.

She was happy for Angie. Truly. But also a little envious. It wasn't Angie's fault she sucked at communication with the opposite sex. Angie just made interaction with the male species look so painless.

"Come on, Rachel, envy doesn't look good on you," she mumbled. Glancing at the kitchen clock, she grabbed her keys. She needed to spend her hard-earned money on car repairs.

****

At five forty-five, Rachel exited the apartment. A breeze ruffled her hair, and the fragrance of rain and pine hung heavily in the air. She loved that smell.

Settling into her car, she gazed into the rearview mirror. What if Angie confirmed her fear and she was getting married? Who would she talk to at home? Blinking, she muttered, "I could get a dog."

Oh, geez. How pitiful was that? The first type of companionship popping into her head was a four-legged variety, not the two-legged kind.

Minutes later, luck was on her side as she found a parking spot close to the pizza joint. Clutching her purse to her chest, she locked her car, dashed through the rain, and gained shelter under a store eave.

She smiled as she heard the Durango Silverton's whistle blow a few blocks away. The train chugged into the station, back from a day of visiting Silverton. She had been sixteen when she had first ridden. The train ride had helped her fall in love with Durango.

"Hey Rachel."

She turned to see Angie sprinting toward her with her boyfriend Bruce close behind. Cheerfully she accepted a quick hug. "Did you order this rain?"

Angie waved a dismissing hand. "I'm so happy. Guess what?"

Rachel chuckled as she watched Angie try unsuccessfully to contain her happiness. "You won Publishers Clearinghouse? Hey, ow." She rubbed her arm where she had received a punch.

"Quit being such a wise butt."

"I'm going to go out on a limb and say you've gotten engaged."

Giggling Angie hugged Bruce. "Close." Shoving her left hand forward she replied, "Engaged, no. Married, yes!"

"Wait. Wait. Married?" Rachel's mouth gaped for a second. She watched as the two lovebirds gazed at each other. Leaning in she gave both a hug. "Congratulations." She was going to have to get a dog.

"A little impulsive on our part, but we flew to Vegas and got hitched."

"Vegas. Hitched." She sounded like a parrot. Shock. That would explain it. She had prepared herself for engaged.

"Rachel? Are you okay?"

Snap. Out. Of. It. "Sure. I'm just a little surprised."

Angie placed a supportive arm around her shoulder. "Well, at least you aren't screaming at me. That's the reaction I got from Mom." With a snicker, she said, "But, I think Dad and his wallet were secretly relieved." A quick glance behind Rachel had her smile disappearing. "Uh-oh, batten down the hatches."

Rachel turned to see an unsmiling Peg Jones,

Angie's mom, barreling toward them with her dad, Burt, trailing behind.

"Rachel, how good it is to see you. You are looking well."

"Evening, Peg, Burt. How have you been?"

The older woman slanted an eye at Angie and Bruce. "Well, I was having a pretty good week. Until, I found out my only daughter up and got married without telling anyone."

Rachel peered over Angie's mom's shoulder to see her longtime friend roll her eyes in exasperation. With a calming hand on Peg's arm she replied, "I'm really happy for them, though, aren't you?"

She heard a sigh of gratitude and glanced at her roommate in time to catch a quick thumbs up sign. "Everyone ready for some pizza? I hear one calling my name."

Linking her arm through her friend's, she leaned in and whispered, "You are so in trouble. I predict a lot of sucking up before you're back in your mom's good graces."

Entering the restaurant, Angie murmured in her ear, "Bruce invited a friend from his work to join us tonight." She raised her eyebrows several times suggestively. "Major hunk."

A wave of heat traveled from Rachel's cheeks to the tips of her ears. "Oh, no you didn't."

Innocent shock registered on her buddy's face. "Hey, don't shoot the messenger. I can't control my other half's actions."

"Good to see you are adjusting so well to married life." She knew the sarcasm was wasted when Angie winked at her new husband.

She should have worn stretchy pants.

A few hours later Rachel groaned as she buckled her seatbelt. She couldn't remember an evening she had enjoyed so much. There had been a few sketchy moments as Peg pouted, but by the end of the night, everything smoothed itself out.

Bruce's friend, Todd, had even asked for her number. She smiled. She felt like doing a happy dance.

Rubbing a hand down her arm, she adjusted the heater in her car. Man, the rain was coming down like cats and dogs. Blast. She could barely make out the side of the road.

She glanced over her right shoulder for any sign of headlights before pulling into the next lane. She gasped when her gaze swung to the front of her car. Where had the dog come from? Swerving to miss the mutt, she hit a puddle and knew she was in trouble.

A tree. She'd not seen the obstacle there a moment before. She braced herself. This wasn't going to end well. She whacked her head on the steering wheel and stars danced in her head.

She opened her eyes. Her lids felt like they had anvils attached. Dizziness. Darkness. Was she dying? She tried shaking her head to clear the fog. She couldn't die. She hadn't had her date with Todd.

Chapter Two

Durango, Colorado—1892

Mitchell Reeves scanned the room as he stood outside the swinging doors of the Silver Spur Saloon. Where the hell was he? His nostrils flared as he reined in his temper. Finally, he found his prey. Sanders leaned against the bar with an arm around one of the bar maids.

The ornate mirror behind the bar gave away his approach. Jake Sanders turned to sneer at Mitchell as he crossed the room.

"Hey, Reeves. You look a little hot." With an evil chuckle he asked, "Woman trouble?"

Mitchell controlled the growl clawing its way up his throat. "You know good and well why I'm here Sanders." Silence filled the saloon like a fog hanging on the air. "I don't want you near my sister, ranch, or cattle again. Do you hear me?" He poked Jake in the chest as he fired off the last question.

Jake shifted his weight, drew up to his full height, and clenched his jaw. "You threaten me, Reeves? You'd better watch your tongue. Accidents happen. Then I would have that ranch of yours and your little sister right where I want her." Jake chuckled and smiled at a cowpoke standing nearby. "On her back."

Mitchell felt his outrage bubbling in his throat

mere seconds before his fist connected with his adversary's jaw. Jake's head whipped back from the force of the blow.

He wiped at the blood trickling from his lip. "You'll pay for that, Reeves." Lunging forward, he rammed his fist into Mitchell's stomach.

Breath expelled from his lips in a hiss as he staggered. Regaining his footing, he gave a quick strike to his opponent's nose.

Jake put a hand to his nose. "You sorry son of a..."

Mitchell braced himself but stumbled as Jake threw his body against his own. Losing his footing, he fell into a table and chair directly behind him. The men who had been playing poker scattered. Cards and chips went flying as he knocked the table over and landed hard on the floor.

He watched in a daze as Jake advanced and loomed over his sprawled position. He tried not to flinch as Jake grabbed his shirtfront and drew his fist back to land a blow to his face.

"Had enough?" A sinister look crossed the stubborn cowboy's features as he gritted his teeth and punched.

Hooking a leg behind Jake's, Mitchell jerked his legs out from under him. "I'll tell you when I'm done." Diving on top of Jake, he pummeled him in the ribs with fresh vigor.

The two locked in a bear hug and rolled a few feet, crashing into another table and chairs.

A shot rang out and echoed throughout the saloon. Both men stilled at the sound.

Bill Silver, the owner of the Silver Spur, held a smoking pistol in the air. "Enough! I'll not have my saloon busted up by the likes of you, Sanders. Take this scuffle outside."

Untangling himself from his grasp, Jake pulled to his feet and wiped at the blood seeping from his nose. "I was minding my own business!" Pointing an unsteady finger in Mitchell's direction he exclaimed, "He's the one that burst in here looking for trouble."

Bill's steady gaze drilled into Jake's. "I'm not asking who started it Jake. I'm saying it's over."

Turning, Jake eyed him. "This isn't the end of it Reeves!" He rammed his shoulder firmly against his arm as he turned and shuffled over to where his hat lay on the floor.

His gaze didn't leave Jake's retreating back until he gathered his hat, and his buddies had exited through the swinging doors. Slowly he let out a breath he hadn't realized he held.

The saloon owner patted him on the back. "You look like hell, son. Here. Have a drink on me."

"Thanks, Bill, I could use one." He grimaced as his swollen gaze peered around at the destruction he had caused. "I'll pay for the damages."

"I'll tally the cost. Sanders will pay as well." Filling two glasses, he shoved one toward Mitchell. "This should cure what ails ya."

Mitchell threw back his head and downed the whiskey. The liquor burnt a fiery trail down his throat. He closed his eyes and lowered the glass.

"What did Sanders do this time?"

Mitchell studied his puffy face in the mirror. Boy, he was going to have a shiner. "You know Sanders. He has this knack of knowing when I'm not around."

Bill slid the whiskey bottle toward him. He

uncorked the bottle and poured another for himself. "I was out checking the fence someone had cut when Jake paid a visit to the house. Want to wager a guess on who probably cut the fence to begin with?" Tossing the glass back, he downed the contents. "Becky claims he just gave her a chaste kiss on the cheek. But you and I both know Sanders. I don't trust him, especially with my little sister."

"Sanders isn't one you want to make your enemy. He's caused me a few worries in the past with my girls." Patting him on the back Bill asked, "Another?"

Mitchell contemplated Bill's question as he fingered his glass. "No, I think I should head back home. A storm's brewin' outside."

"You be careful. I'm sure Sanders is really going to be gunning for you now."

"Thanks, Bill, for the drink and the advice."

Turning, Mitchell noticed one of the saloon girls, Lucy, making her way toward him. Her gaze locked with his as she swung her hips suggestively from side to side.

Pausing, she ran a hand across his broad back. "Looking for some tender loving care, cowboy?" Her lower lip jutted out, pouting, "I know how to make a man feel better given half a chance." Her sly blue gaze studied his amber one intently. "Would you like to join me upstairs?" Her hand leisurely drew circles on his back, and she smiled as she felt his muscles bunch at her touch.

He eyed the bar maid's plunging neckline. What she was offering was mighty temptin'. But he needed to think of Becky. He didn't want to take the chance Jake would head to the ranch.

Clearing his throat, he said, "I'm sorry, Lucy, but I need to get back home."

Her eyelids fluttered down to hide what seemed like disappointment. Slowly drawing a finger up his chest to his bloody lip she murmured, "That's too bad, Mitchell. I was really looking forward to relieving you of all of your aches and pains." Rising to her tiptoes, she kissed his swollen lip.

He winced at the gentle pressure. She tossed him a saucy wink.

"Maybe next time, cowboy."

He watched her retreat up the stairs before crossing the room to exit the saloon.

Chapter Three

Outside the Spur, Mitchell pulled up his collar to ward off the frigid wind. Glancing at the threatening sky, he hoped the rain held until he reached home.

A flash of lightning lit the night. He scanned the street for any sign of trouble. Folks were scurrying to reach their destinations. Sanders didn't seem to be among them.

Making his way to the livery stable, his thoughts wandered to his sister. Becky had been upset when he had left the house. Her words had followed him as the door slammed, "Mitchell, it was a harmless kiss. On my cheek. Don't get so worked up."

He had turned in time to see his sister stamp her foot in frustration and cross her arms. She wasn't a baby anymore. Becky had grown into a beautiful young woman while his attention had been on ranch matters. Where had the years gone?

Mitchell shook his head. "I know you think you are old enough to take care of yourself. But I don't want Sanders hanging around. Do you hear?"

"Why? What is wrong with Jake?" Her innocent question had aggravated him. What was right about him? He wanted better for his sister.

"If you can't see what he's like for yourself, then you're not as grown up as you claim."

Becky uncrossed her arms and jutted out her chin

defiantly. "At least he notices me."

He combed an unsteady hand through his hair as he replied, "His kind of attention isn't the kind you want or need." She stomped her booted foot and stormed to her room.

Shaking away his errant thoughts, Mitchell focused on his surroundings. The shadows plaguing the sidewalk and street could easily hide someone. An unsettling feeling had his nerves on edge. Someone was watching.

Rebel, his horse, nickered at his approach. Was Jake the one watching his movements?

He untied the reins from the hitching post and flicked one last glance around before he settled into his saddle. Pulling his hat brim lower, he urged his mount down the street.

Jake eased from the darkness and glared at Mitchell as he retreated into the night. He rubbed his stomach. Anger still had it churning. "Far from over," he muttered.

****

Mitchell relaxed once he reached the outskirts of town. A quick look behind him proved no one followed. Fat raindrops soon released from the sky, and he urged his horse into a gallop. He sucked in a shallow breath as pain ricocheted from his bruised ribs.

Lightning exploded across the sky as he approached a grove of trees. His nerves tingled and sprang to full alert. Something had snagged his attention as the sky lit up. Was it Sanders lying in wait? Ready to gun him down?

Easing Rebel forward, he squinted. What had caught his attention? As the sky illuminated again, he spied something lying at the base of the biggest tree.

He dismounted and eased his rifle from the saddle. Was this some kind of trap? A quick scrutiny of the area didn't show any signs of an ambush.

With caution, he approached the object. Maybe Jake had hit him harder than he thought. A body?

Unease shimmied down his spine. If this were a trick, wouldn't Sanders have already made his move? He cast one last leery glance about before he squatted down to check for signs of life. A steady pulse met his fingertips. He sighed in relief. The person was alive.

He continued to examine the body's limbs for injuries. Seconds later, he froze and snatched his hands away. Breasts! A bolt of lightning lit the sky as his gaze flew to the mud-splattered face. A woman?

What had happened? Squinting he looked for any sign of a struggle. No broken tree limbs were nearby. A branch hadn't fallen from the storm and knocked the woman unconscious. No clues were visible, and the rain soaked earth didn't offer answers.

One thing for sure, he needed to get her out of the rain. She was drenched.

Rising he strode to his horse and replaced his rifle. Rebel shifted and glanced back toward Mitchell. He gave the horse a reassuring pat before making his way back to the unconscious figure.

He grimaced as he picked up the woman. His ribs felt like they were on fire. Her head gently rolled to rest against his chest. She sure was a tiny thing.

As he turned, his boot snagged on a pouch laying in a puddle at his feet. With a groan, he shifted his burden and grabbed a strap protruding from it. What a strange looking sack.

Hooking the strange object to the horn of his saddle, he considered heading back to town. The doctor was probably farther away than the ranch. He needed to get her out of the rain. If necessary, he would fetch the doctor later.

A bout of lightning lit the sky as he struggled to place the woman in the saddle. With a sigh, he drew himself up behind her and took up Rebel's reins. "Come on, boy, let's get home."

Chapter Four

Mitchell shivered as another raindrop trickled from his hat and snaked past his collar. He urged Rebel forward, the horse's hooves sank deep into the mud.

He cradled the woman in his arms. She hadn't moved or awakened. How badly was she hurt?

He sighed when the shadows of his ranch loomed a short distance away. A lamp's soft glow reflected through a window. Never had home felt so good.

As he dismounted, he moaned as a sharp pain knifed through his ribs. Sucking in a breath, he lifted the woman from atop his horse.

The cabin's door swung open, and Becky stood silhouetted in the dim light. "I was beginning to wonder…" she broke off abruptly. "Mitchell, what do you have?"

With a shift of his cargo, he started up the front steps. "It's a woman. I found her unconscious next to the grove of trees by the curve in the road."

"Do you know who she is?"

He gazed down. Rainwater had washed a trail down her mud-smeared cheek. "I'm not sure," he murmured. "We need to get her out of her wet clothes before she catches a chill."

Becky turned and called over her shoulder, "I'll get a dry nightgown and some water heating."

Mitchell stood dripping and undecided just inside

the doorway. Where should he place his burden?

"Mitchell, don't just stand there. You need to get out of your wet clothes too."

Becky opened the door to his bedroom. "Why don't we put her in here? I can make up the bed in Mom and Dad's room for you to bunk in."

"She's drenched. The sheets will be soaked."

Becky waved him off. "We will put dry bedding on once we've gotten her out of her wet clothes."

A groan sounded from the woman. Mitchell's expectant gaze studied her face. Was she coming around? "Ma'am? Can you hear me?" A small whimper emerged from her lips, and she snuggled deeper into his chest.

He waited a moment, but she remained unconscious. Leaning, he set his encumbrance down.

"I'll go fetch the warm water."

Mitchell watched Becky retreat from the room before his eyes rested back on the tiny form dwarfed in his bed. Why had she been out in such a storm?

She couldn't be more than a child. He shook his head. Her parents were probably worried sick about her.

Becky rushed in with a steaming bowl of water. She dipped the rag and rinsed the patient's face. "This should make her feel better. I also brought a dry gown for her to wear."

Mitchell watched his sister's progress with interest. Each swipe of the cloth displayed more of her features. A pert button nose emerged and next full lips. No. Definitely not a little girl.

"Mitchell, look at the size of the knot on her head."

He bent to examine the area Becky had uncovered. The lump was huge. By tomorrow, the bump would be as colorful as any rainbow he had ever witnessed. Whatever she had hit her head on, she'd smacked hard.

"Can you help me get this coat off?"

He went to the other side of the bed and helped his sister. He held up the item. The garment was a colorful piece with bright green buttons and cloth.

His gaze caught his sister's glare.

Becky scanned his disheveled appearance. "Were you able to get any punches in? Looks like Jake landed a few to your stubborn hide. Why couldn't you have left things well enough alone?"

Draping the sodden material onto a bedpost, he heaved a sigh and ran a hand over his sore and battered face. "Listen, Becky, I don't want to get into a fight again. Not tonight. Do you need my help putting on the gown?"

A shocked look crossed Becky's face. "Mitchell! I'm sure this young lady wouldn't be happy to discover a man helped her out of her wet clothing." Her eyes skipped over his face again. "I will check your injuries once I have her settled."

Waving his sister's concerns aside, he stated, "I'm sure I can manage to clean my own wounds. They probably look worse than they are."

Becky harrumphed. "Your supper is warming on the stove. Why don't you go ahead and wash up and get something to eat?"

Turning, Mitchell paused in the doorway. "I need to get Rebel settled for the night." He watched Becky fuss over the woman for a moment. "Thanks for keeping supper warm for me."

With a dramatic shrug of her shoulders Becky exclaimed, "Well, it's the least I could do since you went off to defend my honor now isn't it?" She turned back toward her patient. With a bite to her lip, she finished unbuttoning the woman's blouse.

What in heaven? She paused as her eyes encountered the woman's undergarments. The lacy deep green garment clung to her breasts. Had she ever seen the likes? What an odd piece of clothing. Several moments passed. How do you release the stupid thing?

After a careful study, she noticed what could be a small clasp in the front. She lifted on the material and finally freed her breasts.

Lifting the strange object, she examined it and draped the article over the nearby rocker. The woman's trousers were strange as well. After disposing of the denims, Becky gasped. She had thought the lacy object covering her breasts had been indecent. Her drawers were barely there!

Was this one of the town's painted ladies? If so, why would she be out in such weather?

She eased the patient up, grasped the gown, and slid it over the woman's head. Next, she dried her hair as best she could. Her quick movements hadn't caused the woman to stir.

She started at the soft knock on the bedroom door.

"Beck, do you need any help with anything?"

"Come on in. Can you lift her up while I change the bedding?"

Mitchell gazed down at the woman's face as Becky made short work of replacing the bedcovers. "She didn't wake up?"

Becky shook her head, "She didn't make so much as a peep." She paused as Mitchell placed the woman back on the bed. "Mitchell I'm worried about the bump on her forehead. It looks like a nasty one." Mitchell ran a hand through his already disheveled hair. "I'll fetch the doc in the morning if she hasn't come to." Shifting, he was startled as he felt something drop from his shoulder. He had forgotten the object he had slung over his arm. Bending he picked up the article by its long strap. "I brought in the saddlebag she had with her."

Becky ran a hand over the smooth leather pouch. "Are you sure that's what it is?"

Both startled as a low groan emitted from the bed. Anxiously they waited to see if the woman would awake. Her eyelids remained closed, but she began to mutter.

Mitchell leaned in closer to try to catch the mumbled words.

"What did she say?"

He rose and shook his head. He ran a hand over his scruffy chin. "I'm not sure. But it sounded like she said stupid dog."

"That's strange. I wonder what she meant." Becky turned and gathered the wet clothing lying about. "I'll just take these and put with my wash." With a quick look back at Mitchell she suggested, "Why don't you go ahead and give me your things as well." Shaking her head, she looked at the red stain on Mitchell's shirt. "Is the blood yours or Jake's?"

Mitchell grimaced as he unbuttoned and shrugged out of his shirt. "I believe it may be a little of both." He met Becky's unflinching glare as he handed over the garment. "Why don't you go ahead and go to bed." He made his way to his dresser to retrieve a fresh top from the upper drawer. "I'll stay and watch over our patient."

Glancing back at the sleeping form Becky asked,

"Are you sure? You have a big day tomorrow. You need a good night's rest."

"I'm sure. I'll sit with her while I eat my supper. I'll move the rocking chair closer to the bed. We'll be fine." He paused in moving the chair as he spied the lacy item draped across the back. The piece was unlike any undergarment or camisole he'd ever set eyes upon.

Becky followed his gaze. "Oh! Let me take that to wash as well." She snatched the item off the chair and added it to the load she held in her arms. "I'll just say good night. Call me if you need anything." She rushed from the room and quietly closed the door.

As the door clicked shut, Mitchell came out of his trance and glanced at the bed. He envisioned how the article of clothing would look on the woman lying in his bed. He swallowed hard as he realized the delicate lace wouldn't hide much of her body. He erased the image as he rubbed a hand across his face. The vision didn't immediately disappear.

He retrieved his supper and balanced the plate as he eased his large frame into the rocker. Oh, his ribs, they felt like they were on fire. A smile tipped his lips at the hope Sanders suffered as well.

He studied the features of the woman as he scooped a bite of beans onto his spoon. His gaze took in her auburn hair, dry now from Becky's administration. The curls softly framed her face. He would imagine her hair would light like a flame in sunlight.

Her dark eyelashes rested against her pale cheeks. Who was she? Placing his unfinished plate beside the chair, he lifted an extra quilt from the bed and covered his long body. With a heavy sigh, he closed his eyes.

Chapter Five

Mitchell jerked awake. What had roused him? With a glance to the nearby bed, he noticed the woman sitting straight up and whimpering. Sheer terror resonated from her features.

Mindful of his sore ribs, he eased out of the rocking chair and approached the bed. "Shhh, everything's okay." He placed a hand on her shoulder to calm her, but he started as she wrenched away from his touch.

With a wince, she lifted a hand to her forehead. A strangled cry escaped from her lips. "What happened?"

"You've had an accident. Do you remember what happened?"

"No." Her hand trembled as she rubbed at her eyes. "Where am I? Is this the hospital?"

The panic and confusion hadn't eased from the woman's face. "No ma'am, you are at my ranch."

Tears threatened as she settled against the feather pillow. Closing her eyes, she gulped in a mouthful of air. With a small hiccup she asked, "You're not a doctor?"

Mitchell felt helpless. Her voice was so small and frightened. "No ma'am."

"What's wrong with my eyes? Everything is hazy." Tears ran unchecked down her cheeks. She squeezed her eyes shut.

Mitchell hated tears. They made him feel helpless and unsure of how to handle the situation. He resigned himself and sat on the edge of the bed. He cleared his throat. "Now don't cry." He paused in lifting a calming hand. She hadn't liked his touch earlier. "I'm sure there isn't any cause for concern. I'll fetch the doc in the morning if you haven't improved."

Her eyelids drooped. "I'm just going to rest my eyes for a bit."

Mitchell studied the tear streaked face. He lifted her hair and scrutinized the bump on her forehead. The swelling had receded, but the bruise had spread across her brow in a colorful hue. Did she have serious damage? He shook his head and swore under his breath. He should have taken her straight away to the doctor. What had he been thinking? Somewhere a loved one had to be worried.

Turning, he dipped a washcloth in the nearby water basin. He applied the cool rag to the woman's temple and wiped away the trail of tears. He traced an old scar above her eyebrow, wondering what could have caused the mark. He startled as she reached for his hand in her sleep, her grasp tight upon his. She cuddled their clasped hands under her cheek, smiled, and sighed.

Her warm breath caressed his swollen knuckles. He watched in fascination as a dimple appeared in her cheek as she nuzzled his hand. Awareness crept up his spine. His fingers itched and stung.

What the hell? He tugged to loosen her grip. The tingle was turning into a steady burn. At last, her grasp went slack, and he pulled away.

He glanced down and rubbed his palm down the length of his leg. The burning sensation diminished.

With a slight stumble, he backed up a step before turning to open the bedroom door. Sleep wasn't coming any time soon; he might as well do some chores.

Chapter Six

The fingers of dawn had barely stretched across the sky as Becky eased into Mitchell's room. With a fleeting look, she realized the patient was alone. The rocker was empty except for an abandoned quilt.

Her brow puckered. Where was Mitchell? He must have already headed outside to tend to his chores. Fetching a fresh bowl of water, Becky swabbed the woman's face.

Raking her hands through the woman's curly hair she said softly, "You'll be okay. We'll take care of you." Examining the bump under the hairline, she noticed the swelling had gone down from the previous night and now represented a rainbow of green, purple, and yellow hues.

"Is she awake?"

With a squeal, she jumped and pivoted to spy her brother lounging against the bedroom doorframe. "Land sakes, Mitchell, you gave me a fright." Placing a hand on her racing heart, she shook her head. "No, she hasn't wakened."

With a frown, he approached the bed. "She did wake for a moment last night." He shook his head, "She was having problems with her eyes."

Becky glanced worriedly at her brother and bit her lower lip. "Do you think that will pass?"

Mitchell considered Becky's question as he stared

25

down at the sleeping woman. "I'll fetch the doc if I need to."

"I'm going to start breakfast."

Mitchell wearily sat in the nearby chair and laid aside the discarded quilt. His gaze settled on the woman in his bed.

Beams from the sun filtering between the curtains at the window danced upon her cheek. He remembered how his hand had burned at her touch. Would her lips have the same effect on his?

In disgust, he shook his head. He pitched the rocker and rocked back and forth. What was he thinking?

Mitchell leaned forward expectantly when he noticed her eyelids flutter. A moment later, she opened her eyes. "Good morning. Are you feeling better?"

She opened her mouth to speak, but nothing emerged. Clearing her parched throat, she tried again. "Thirsty"

Mitchell reached for the nearby glass and took great care to ease the woman's head up slowly as he held the cup against her full bottom lip. After a moment he asked, "Better?"

She nodded and leaned back against the feather pillow.

He set down the water before asking, "Are you still having trouble with your eyes?"

With a lift of her hand, she felt the bump on her forehead. "Better. Not as obscure as before." Her green gaze met his.

He shifted on his feet as a sigh of relief escaped. That was an improvement. "Can you tell me your name?"

Her eyelids drooped. "Rachel. Rachel Morgan."

He stared down at the sleeping woman. Her name was unfamiliar. He had lived long enough in the area to know most of the people who lived in the vicinity. Who was she?

His head throbbed. Lack of Sleep? Or repercussions from fighting with Sanders? He eased down into the rocker, leaned his head back, closed his eyes, and drifted into a light doze.

****

Rachel opened her eyes and realized her foggy vision had cleared. Thank God.

With a quick look about, she knew she wasn't in a hospital. She had hoped everything had been a dream. Rustic. That best described what she was seeing. From the quaint furniture to the small, unlit lamp by the bedside.

Her gaze landed on a tall man slumbering nearby in a rocker. The man sprawled was like the room, rugged. She studied the reddish blond hair falling across his forehead. One eye was swollen and black. Either he had run into something or recently been fighting. A matching mustache drooped over his lips. He leaned awkwardly in the chair.

"Oh good, you're awake."

Rachel's startled gaze flew to the door. A younger woman rushed into the room. A big smile graced her pretty face.

"Mitchell and I've been worried."

Rachel gave a fleeting look to the man the woman had indicated with a flick of her hand. "Where am I?"

The young woman sat on the edge of the bed. "My brother, Mitchell, found you last night on his way home from town. You're at our ranch. My name is Becky

Reeves. How are you feeling?"

Becky was so lively. Rachel's head pounded as she kept up with the conversation. She closed her eyes. Softly she asked, "Do you have any Tylenol?" As she opened her eyes, she saw the man and woman glance at each other. Their expressions mirrored slight confusion.

The man leaned forward in his chair. "Ma'am, I'm not sure what Tylenol is."

His resonant voice was deep and sexy. His eyes gave her a slight chill. They were the color of a lion's coat, and his amber gaze studied her intently. Rugged. Handsome. This man had appeal, in spades.

She frowned in confusion. Who didn't know what Tylenol was? She swallowed and found her voice. "No Tylenol? How about some Ibuprofen or Excedrin?" She rubbed her left temple with her fingers. At their blank questioning looks, she tried again, "Do you have anything for a whopper of a headache?"

Becky nodded in understanding. "You poor thing. I can only imagine. I have something in my room that should help. I'll fetch them." With a swish of her skirt, Becky exited the room in a rush.

What a mess. Angie had warned her to be careful. Who knows what predicament she'd landed herself. She peeked from under her lashes at Mitchell. With a small squirm she asked, "Can I have some water?"

She accepted the glass with a shy "Thank you."

Becky returned to the room shortly. She held out some tablets and placed them into Rachel's outstretched palm. "These should help."

Rachel swallowed the tablets swiftly before they could dissolve in her mouth and settled back onto the bed.

Both Mitchell and Becky were regarding her closely.

Mitchell cleared his throat and asked, "Can you tell us what happened last night? Why were you out in the middle of nowhere?"

Placing the glass on the table nearby, she shook her head. Middle of nowhere? She'd been in town eating pizza. "I was driving home when it started to pour. I lost control of my Mustang when a dog ran out in front of me. That's all she wrote when I collided with a tree."

Both wore a bewildered look and glanced at each other nervously. With a rub of his hand over his battered face, Mitchell stated, "Miss Morgan, I didn't see your horse anywhere near where I found you. It must have taken off after it got spooked."

Okay, the man's voice was to die for and he was as handsome as sin, but what was he talking about? She didn't have a horse that would have run off. She leaned back against the pillows. "I'm not sure how my Mustang could have taken off without me driving it."

"Driving?" Mitchell asked absentmindedly.

Was she talking a foreign language? Rachel didn't answer. First, they hadn't known what Tylenol was and now they believed her car was a horse. A weary sigh escaped. "I think I will rest for a little bit longer."

In minutes, she was sound asleep. Mitchell and Becky gazed at Rachel as she slept.

"I think she's a bit confused," Becky stated.

"I guess if I had a bump on my head that big I believe I would be as well." He turned from the bed. "I don't think we need to fetch the doc. I'm going to grab a bite to eat. I'll be out in the north pasture helping with the cattle. Can you handle taking care of Rachel by yourself?"

Becky waved a dismissive hand toward him, "She's resting. Go. I don't think we'll have any problems."

Chapter Seven

When Rachel next opened her eyes, her headache had receded. The lamp on the nearby nightstand put off a soft glow. Had she slept the day away?

Outside the window dusk had settled, but she could still see the shadows cast by the San Juan Mountains. A soft knock interrupted her reverie. The man from earlier entered in a blue chambray shirt stained with sweat and dirt. Her brow wrinkled as she tried to recall his name.

He stopped mid-room and smiled. "You're awake? How are you feeling?"

With a nervous swallow, she smiled shyly. "Better. I've been such a slug bug though and slept the day away."

"You needed the rest. We won't hold anything against you for staying in bed."

Rachel studied him from under her lashes as he crossed the room to the only dresser in the room.

"I just need to get a few fresh clothes." He grinned sheepishly. "Guess I should move my things into my folk's room. That way I don't trouble you."

He turned toward the dresser. Pulling out the top drawer, he shuffled around until he found what he was looking for.

She watched a moment while he shifted through the drawer. His things? Lordy, she was in the hunk's bed. "I'm sorry. I didn't mean to kick you out of your bed." A slow heat spread up her cheeks as a vision flashed in her mind. Her and the hunk entwined on said bed. Goldilocks eat your heart out; she'd gotten the better deal.

Even from across the room she could tell his amber eyes danced with merriment. Gracious, he couldn't know what she was thinking.

She tugged the quilt higher up her chest. "Well, um, I'm sorry. Why didn't you just take me to the hospital? Then you wouldn't be missing the comfort of your bed."

A flash of uncertainty crossed his face quickly and vanished. "I'm sorry. I should have taken you to Doc Brown last night. The rain was coming down so hard I just thought it would be safer to bring you back to the ranch. My home was closer."

Rachel stammered, "I didn't mean to sound ungrateful. I'm inconveniencing you and your sister." Her hand slid out from under the quilt and indicated the room.

"Ma'am, that's no problem at all. You take all the time you need to mend."

Mend? Something was rotten in Denmark. Who talks like that? Rachel bit her bottom lip. She had a more pressing problem than the words coming from the hunk's mouth.

"Um, I'm sorry. What was your name again?"

"Mitchell."

"Mitchell, I need to use the little girl's room. Can you point me in the right direction?"

Rachel almost giggled. Had she ever witnessed a man blush before? This was a first.

He swallowed visibly. "It would probably be easier

to use the pot under the bed. I'm not sure you're strong enough to go outside yet. I'll be back to check on you."

She watched as he retreated from the room as if the hounds of hell were nipping at his heels. The giggle she had been holding emerged. Had she ever had that effect on a man before?

He had to be joking! She leaned over and pulled the covers up to peer beneath the bed. A wave of dizziness overcame her as she sat up.

"He hadn't been kidding," she muttered. Putting her hand to her head, she silently willed the spinning to subside. That would be all she would need, to barf or pass out in front of the hunk.

She cringed. Her bladder couldn't wait. Slowly, she slid out of bed and waited another moment for the vertigo to fade. She felt awkward, but in no time she'd finished her business and slid back into the warm bed.

Wiggling further under the quilt, she pondered why Mitchell and his sister didn't have indoor plumbing. The idea was hard to fathom. She smiled. On a brighter note, she hadn't passed out on the pot.

As if on cue, a knock sounded at the door.

"Come in."

Mitchell slowly stuck his head around the door. "I thought you might like some coffee and something to eat."

Pinch me! A handsome man was waiting on her. Now she knew she had really cracked her head last night. She eyed the biscuits and her stomach growled. "It seems like forever since I ate pizza last night." Helping herself to the biscuits, she pointed toward the cup of coffee, "I hate to disappoint you, but I really don't care for coffee. My friend Angie can drink gallons of the stuff."

He laughed. "Probably wise not to drink the coffee, since I made it." He studied her with his warm amber eyes. "What's pizza?"

Rachel nearly choked on a bite of biscuit. Seriously? She searched his eyes and couldn't find any indication he was pulling her leg.

The unease she had experienced earlier crept up her spine. Placing the biscuit back on the tray, she said slowly, "Can I have my clothes? I'd like to go home."

"I don't believe Becky got your clothes washed." He eyed her silently and appeared to wrestle with something he wanted to say. Finally, he blurted, "Why were you running about in men's clothing? Do you not realize the dangers of being out alone?"

Rachel bristled at the sensor in Mitchell's voice. "Excuse me?"

"What if I hadn't been the one to find you?"

Shoving the quilt aside, she swung her legs out of bed and rose. Swaying slightly she flung out her arm to ward off his hand of support. "I've had enough! I'm going home." Who did he think he was to lecture her, on her clothing nonetheless?

The nightgown dragged the floor as she crossed the room. A few steps from the door, her head swam and she swayed unsteadily. She felt a strong pair of arms grasp her gently before she crumpled to the floor in a faint.

Chapter Eight

With a blink, she awoke as a stream of sunlight grazed her cheek. What happened? She groaned when she realized she fainted in front of the hunky cowboy. Leaning up on an elbow, she consoled herself. At least she hadn't tossed her cookies.

An odd feeling settled over her as she leaned back against the pillow. Something wasn't quite right.

"Good morning. How did you sleep?" Becky rushed into the room and stopped at the foot of the bed. "Mitchell said he had brought you some coffee and biscuits last night, but you didn't eat much. He also said you weren't fond of coffee. Wise choice, he doesn't make the best coffee in the world. Would you like some tea or maybe I could make some flapjacks." Becky finally paused for a breath.

Rachel eyed the young woman. She was probably a few years younger than herself with beautiful black hair and expressive dark eyes. She smiled as she waited on Rachel's response.

"I think I slept like a rock. Thanks for the offer of food, but I'm not hungry."

Becky tilted her head. "You sure have curly hair. I don't think I've ever seen hair as curly as yours."

Rachel reached up to feel her hair. "It's a perm. I know this trend is kind of out of style, but my hair is so lifeless and I wanted to give it a boost." At Becky's

35

confused look she continued, "You know. A perm. Rods are put in your hair and then a solution, and voila, it curls."

Becky shook her head. "I've never heard of such a thing. On special occasions I use the hot curling rod to curl my hair."

Was she on hidden camera? That had to be to be the case. They were just waiting for her to lose her mind. She asked nervously, "Becky can I ask you a strange question?"

"Sure."

"Am I being punked?"

"I'm sorry. I don't know what you mean."

At Becky's lost expression she continued, "I enjoy a joke as much as the next person. Really, I do, but I think you and Mitchell have carried this far enough."

"Rachel, I don't know what you are talking about."

"Can you tell me the date?"

She received another strange look from Becky, "It's June twentieth."

She sighed in exasperation. "And what is the year?"

"It's June twentieth, eighteen ninety-two."

Are you kidding me? Fingers of disbelief crept up Rachel's spine. She groaned and leaned back, shutting her eyes. "You mean the year is twenty sixteen don't you?" Reopening her eyes she watched as Becky shook her head. "This cannot be happening, this isn't real!"

"Rachel, I don't understand. What's not real?"

"Becky, where are we?"

"Don't you remember? Yesterday I told you we're at my brother's ranch." Becky nervously shifted.

She rubbed her temple and asked, "Where is your

home located?"

"What, our ranch?" At her nod Becky continued, "We're just north of town."

"Durango?"

"Yes. Isn't that where you're from?"

What should she say? Yes, but where I'm from is more than one hundred or more years in the future? "Originally, I'm from Oklahoma. But have been living in Durango ever since I graduated from Fort Lewis College."

Becky eyed her in disbelief. "You're telling me you went to school at Fort Lewis?" Rachel nodded her head in assent. "A Military Fort and Indian Boarding School? I'm not sure you can study there, can you?" Becky continued to stare at her strangely. "The Oklahoma Territory has only been settled for a few years, is the land as wild as I hear?"

Rachel wasn't the delusional one! She wasn't! She couldn't be. She shook her head and glanced away from Becky's inquisitive stare.

"Rachel? Are you sure you don't work at the Silver Spur and are just trying to get away from that life?"

Her eyes connected with Becky's. "Where?"

Becky rolled her eyes. "The saloon, the Silver Spur."

Waves of shock rolled over her. Did Becky just ask if she was a prostitute? "You think I'm a saloon girl," she stammered. "Good heavens, no! Why would you even assume something like that?"

Becky leaned in and whispered, "Those undergarments you had on were indecent. The most scandalous things I've ever seen in my life."

Heat crawled up her cheeks. Great. If Becky

thought she was a saloon girl, is that what Mitchell thought as well? Why should she care what these two lunatics think? Eighteen ninety-two. How absurd.

She felt a tentative touch to her hair. "I'm sorry, Rachel. I didn't mean to upset you. I'll leave you to rest, and maybe I can show you around the house later."

The bedroom door closed with a soft click as Becky left the room. Rachel rolled to her side and hugged her stomach. She'd rarely suffered from indigestion, but she did now. Heartburn on steroids!

The ache didn't recede. She was sure Mitchell and Becky didn't have a brown paper bag to hyperventilate into. They hadn't been invented, according to them. Or had they?

She shook her head, and it began to pound again. She ran a tentative hand over her forehead and winced at the soreness. What had happened? Surely, she couldn't have traveled back in time. Tears stung her eyes and slowly made a trail down her cheeks. She fought off her anxiety as her eyes grew heavy.

She'd died and was in purgatory. That had to be it. She thought of her family in the future. What would they think? Tucking her hand under her pillow, she gave in to her tears, and her body quaked as she cried herself to sleep.

Chapter Nine

Mitchell found his thoughts wondering to Rachel throughout the morning. He questioned where she came from and if there was anyone looking for her. She had to have concerned family and friends, or maybe even a husband worried about her.

A knot formed in his stomach at the thought of her being married. With an agitated shake of his head, he didn't want to define why that thought caused his stomach to churn.

By mid-morning, Mitchell gave up the pretense of working. He sighed in frustration. His mind was miles away from his daily chores. The repairs to the corral would just have to wait. Leaning against the top railing, he stared out toward the mountains deep in thought.

Should he investigate the area where he found Rachel? Maybe that would turn up some answers.

The sun burned brightly overhead as he rode leisurely on the road to town. A gentle summer breeze tickled his nose with the scents from the pines and the meadows. Peering into the distance, another scent came to mind as he breathed deeply, one that had been delicate, musky, and soft like the woman he had held.

With a pull on the reins, he eased Rebel to a standstill by the large tree in the bend of the road. Dismounting, he kneeled to the ground and ran his fingers through the grass. He wasn't sure what he was looking for, some sign as to what had happened to Rachel.

Had someone attacked Rachel as she had ridden by on her horse? Was she blocking that from her mind? Mitchell shuddered at the thought of someone physically hurting Rachel. Or had she been thrown from her horse when her horse became spooked?

Rising to his feet, he walked around the big tree slowly, looking intently for any sign of a struggle that may have taken place. He found nothing. Not even horse tracks. The hard rain must have washed whatever evidence he looked for away.

He walked back over to where Rebel grazed quietly by the road and reached for the dangling reins. "What do you think boy? Do you think we will find any answers in town?" Swinging his leg up and over the saddle, he gave his companion a gentle pat on his neck, "Let's ride into town, and see if we can't find out anything shall we?"

Durango was bustling with activity by the time Mitchell rode into town. Several men tipped their hats in welcome as he rode by on his way to the sheriff's office.

Easing down from his horse, he noticed the door to the jail was open. He stuck his head in and gazed about the empty room. "Is anyone here?"

A shuffling noise echoed from the cell area, and a few moments later Sheriff Wade appeared. "Morning Mitchell, what brings you to town?"

"Morning, Sheriff. I just had a little business to take care of and thought I would stop by to see if you have any leads on who's been cutting fences and running off cattle from the surrounding ranches."

The sheriff scratched his head and grimaced. "Whoever is doing this, they're getting to be a real pain in the backside. Pete Graves came to see me yesterday afternoon about some cattle gone missing from his place. He said he and his boys had been out looking for days. Guess we need to add rustling to the charges whenever we find who's causing all these problems."

Mitchell shook his head. "I still have my suspicions Mr. Waters is behind all of this somehow. I just don't have any evidence."

The sheriff shuffled behind his desk and lowered himself into his chair. "I tend to agree with you, Mitchell. But until we have proof, I can't arrest anyone."

Mitchell removed his Stetson and dragged a hand through his hair. "I hope we get a break soon." Turning toward the door to leave he paused.

"Is there something else on your mind, Mitchell?"

He dreaded the answer, but he needed to ask about Rachel. Placing his hat back on his head he turned to ask, "Has anyone reported a woman missing in these parts?"

With a rub to his potbelly he replied, "Can't say I've had anyone mention anything to me. Why do you ask?"

"A couple of days ago, I found an injured woman on my way home. She says her name is Rachel Morgan. I have her at my ranch. I just wanted to make sure no one is searching for her."

Sherriff Wade leaned over and spit a stream of tobacco into the nearby spittoon, "Was she hurt badly? Do you expect someone treated her unkindly?"

Mitchell gazed out the open doorway. "No, I don't

think so. She had a big bump on her head. But as far as Becky and I can tell, that was the only injury." Mitchell shuffled his feet. "Guess I'll ask at the saloon before heading home."

"Let me know if I can help with anything, Mitchell. I'll keep my eyes and ears open on our other problem."

"Thanks, Sheriff." Tipping his hat in farewell, he headed down the street to the Silver Spur.

Even though it was only early afternoon, the saloon was a hubbub of activity. Mitchell scanned the occupants until his gaze landed on the owner. Bill stood behind the bar wiping down glasses. Spotting Mitchell, he waved his free hand in greeting.

"Kind of early for you to be drinking isn't it, Mitchell?" Bill smiled. "Or is there something else we can do for you today?"

"I've come to see what I owe you for the damages I caused the other evening." He glanced around at the saloon. "I see you've already taken care of the mess. The place doesn't show any signs of the ruckus I caused."

Placing the glass he had been drying on the counter, Bill turned to shuffle through some papers stacked neatly on the counter. "Let's see here; this needs split by two." Bill quickly did some figuring in his head and quoted Mitchell a price.

Mitchell frowned. "Are you sure Bill, the amount doesn't sound right to me?"

Bill chuckled. "Well, it is Mitchell, I've given you the discount, and Sanders has to make up the rest."

Mitchell smiled and chuckled. "You do realize, Bill, I am the one who started the whole uproar."

"Yep."

"You're not going to make Jake too happy if he ever finds out you charged him more."

Bill chuckled. "Who's going to tell him? You? I doubt it."

Placing the required money on the bar, Mitchell smiled his appreciation. "Well, thanks, Bill. I'm not sure I deserve the partial treatment though."

Bill nodded his head in understanding. "I know Mitchell, but it's my way of getting payment for all the problems Sanders has caused in the past. Don't fret over it."

Mitchell tipped his hat to Bill. "Well, I appreciate the gesture." Turning he started across the room to the swinging doors. "Oh, Bill, I almost forgot. Have you heard of anyone missing a woman in these parts?"

Bill pondered the question for the moment. "You mean besides me?"

Mitchell shook his head and laughed. "Never mind Bill. I'll see you later."

Standing outside the Silver Spur, Mitchell scanned the people milling about. Why wasn't anyone looking for Rachel? She was a beautiful woman. Someone out there must be searching.

The sun was slowly descending by the time Mitchell arrived at the ranch. He swung his leg over the side of his black stallion. "Come on, Rebel, let's get you some oats and settled for the night."

"You talkin' to that horse again?"

Mitchell glanced up at his ranch hand, Toby. "Guess it's become a habit. He's the only one who doesn't argue or talk back."

Toby winked at Mitchell. "I know several ladies in town that would like to have the privilege of arguing with you."

Mitchell smiled and shook his head. "Now, Toby, you know better than to believe the gossip about town."

Toby took Rebel's reins from Mitchell. "Not gossip, but pure gospel. Go on, go have your supper. I'll take care of ol' Rebel here."

"Thanks Toby. Make sure you give him an extra scoop of oats for me will ya?" Mitchell opened the door and encountered a delicious smell wafting in the air. "Beck, something smells wonderful."

Becky wiped her hands on her apron and walked into the sitting room. "I hope you're hungry."

"I'm starving." Taking a quick peek about the room he questioned, "Rachel been up and about?"

"She's been awake most of the day, but I haven't checked on her lately."

Mitchell glanced down at his dirty clothes. "I need to get a shirt to change into and wash up before supper. I'll just go get fresh clothes from my room and check on her."

He knocked lightly. Not hearing any movement or sound, he opened the door. The room was dark as he walked in. He lit the lamp by the bed. The soft glow illuminated Rachel as she slept. He reached out and gently trailed a finger down her cheek where a tear had run down her face.

Her skin was soft to his touch. He turned to retrieve a clean set of clothes. What could have caused her tears?

"Dirty again, cowboy?"

Mitchell chuckled at the softly spoken question. Rachel's deep emerald eyes rested on him. "I'm sorry. I didn't mean to wake you." He settled himself on the edge of the bed. "I heard you slept most of the day. How are you feeling?"

He watched as Rachel blinked slowly. She scooted away from him and rose on the pillow. "Goodness, I didn't mean to snooze that much."

"That's all right, you probably needed the sleep. Are you hungry?"

Rachel's stomach growled as he asked the question. Grinning, Rachel glanced at Mitchell. "Well, if that didn't answer your question."

Mitchell stared at Rachel. The smile she had given him produced a dimple in each cheek, and her eyes danced with amusement. He cleared his throat. "Becky has supper ready. Do you feel up to coming to eat at the table, or would you like for me to bring a plate in here for you?"

Rachel glanced down at the thin cotton nightgown. "I don't believe I have appropriate dining apparel on."

Mitchell rose from the bed. "I'll go see if Becky has something you could borrow."

"What about my clothes? Surely they are clean by now."

Mitchell frowned. "I'll check, but I don't think that would be the proper clothing, either."

He returned in a few short minutes with a dark green dress draped over his muscular arm. "Becky didn't have time to launder your clothes, guess this will have to do for the time being."

Rachel eyed the dress. "I think your sister is a little taller than I am, but I guess the outfit will work better than running around in a nightgown."

Mitchell's gaze took in the little bit of nightgown showing above the quilt and visualized the body underneath. "Depends on the person that's doing the looking," he whispered under his breath as he left the room.

Chapter Ten

Rachel clearly hadn't heard what she thought she had. She climbed slowly out of bed. A giggle bubbled up and escaped. She swore she just caught Mitchell ogling her body. Now she knew she must be dreaming.

She peeled the nightgown over her head. Then noticed she had a slight dilemma. No bra. She eyed the dress Mitchell had laid on the bed. She didn't have that much in that area anyway, surely no one would notice if she went without.

She wished she had a mirror. Besides the dress dragging the floor, it fit perfectly. Looking down at the low neckline and her breasts, she smiled. Okay, maybe not perfect. The bodice lifted her breasts and made them look fuller. She actually had cleavage.

Opening the bedroom door, she caught her first glimpse of the rest of the cabin. The room beyond was just as rustic and as sparsely furnished. No television graced a wall, just a couple of kerosene lamps on matching end tables on either side of a couple of chairs.

A huge stone fireplace took up one entire wall and a picture window graced another. To her left Becky stood in front of a big wood cookstove softly humming. With a sigh and a lift of her dress, she bravely headed into the kitchen.

"Can I help you with anything?" Yeah, as if she knew the first thing about cooking on a wood burning stove.

"I have everything ready. I hope you're hungry."

"I think I'm hungry enough I might be able to eat a horse."

"Well, maybe I should tell Mitchell to keep you away from the corral tonight." Becky chuckled. "I'm glad you have an appetite. Could you go out back and see what's keeping Mitchell?" She pointed to a door at the back of the kitchen. "Just through there."

Holy Moly! Rachel paused at the view. Mitchell stood shirtless at the water pump. Her mouth dried up faster than a drop of water in the Sahara Desert. She watched him splash his face and chest. His muscles glistened as the drops of water made a trail down his lean, sculptured body. This cowboy was hotter than any fireman calendar she'd ever seen.

She pinched herself. Nope. Wide awake. She fanned herself and cleared her parched throat. "Supper is hot," she stammered. "I mean supper is ready."

Mitchell's startled gaze settled on her. "I'll be in. I'm almost finished."

Rachel swung around and shut the door with a soft click. Leaning heavily against the hard wood, she closed her eyes and blocked out the vision of Mitchell without his shirt.

"Are you feeling faint? Come over here and sit down, Rachel. I would hate for you to overdo the first time you've been out of bed." Becky held out a chair for her at the kitchen table.

Sinking down, Rachel fiddled briefly with the fork beside the plate before placing her hands in her lap. Seconds later, she heard the back door open.

She drew in a deep calming breath as Mitchell took

the chair to her right. With a glance from under her eyelashes, she took in his damp face and hair.

Becky sat across from her and held her hands out to Rachel and Mitchell. "Mitchell, would you say a word of grace, please?"

Grasping both hands, Rachel lowered her head. Mitchell's deep voice resonated with each word he spoke, but she didn't hear a single one. What was wrong with her? A bonk on the head and she's practically swooning over a hunky cowboy. This wasn't like her. Snap. Out. Of. It.

"I went and looked for your horse today."

Rachel's started gaze flew to meet Mitchell's amber stare. What was he saying?

"I wasn't able to find any tracks. I'm sorry, but your Mustang is probably long gone."

Oh. He was talking about her car. She took a roll from the breadbasket. "That's disappointing news. I was quite fond of my, um, horse. It had been a present from my parents."

Her parents. They must be worried sick about her. Was she dreaming? Or was she in a coma back in her time? Surely, what she was experiencing wasn't real. Someone was going to pop out at any moment and yell "Gotcha!"

Becky passed a bowl of potatoes. "Are your parents living?"

What do you say to a question like that? "Yes, it's just they seem so far away." Literally. Was it even feasible for her to believe she traveled back in time?

"Where do they live?" Mitchell's question interrupted her thoughts.

Thinking back to Becky and their earlier

49

conversation, she decided she had better be careful how she answered. "A few years back my dad and mom were part of the Oklahoma land run and have a small spread in the Oklahoma Territory."

Mitchell frowned, "Are you in Durango all by yourself? Visiting family?"

Rachel chose to ignore his questions. "How about you guys? Where are your parents?"

"They died five years ago of the fever." Becky's eyes were shadowed with sadness.

Rachel's brain whirled furiously. What fever were they describing? Typhoid? Cholera? Was the disease something she could catch while here? Dare she ask? "I'm sorry to hear that."

With pride in her voice Becky explained, "Mitchell continued to work the ranch after their deaths. Papa, I know would be proud of what he's made of it."

****

Mitchell sat quietly and observed Rachel. The neckline of the borrowed dress drew his gaze. The creamy flesh exposed was hard to ignore.

"Don't you think so, Mitchell?"

He jerked out of his revelry. "What?" He looked up to find both Becky and Rachel studying him.

Becky sighed. "I said if Rachel is feeling up to travel, I could take her home tomorrow."

He watched as a frown marred Rachel's brow and she bit her bottom lip. Didn't she want to go back to her place? "We would be happy to take you now you're on the mend."

"I don't think that will be possible."

"Why not?" Mitchell didn't understand. "Isn't there anyone worried about you? Family? Friends?" He paused. "A husband?" His eyes scanned her ringless finger.

Rachel adverted her eyes from his and muttered, "You wouldn't believe me if I told you."

He placed his fork down and steepled his hands. He had barely heard her softly spoken words. What wouldn't he believe? Leaning in close to her he asked, "Beck and I want to help you Rachel. Tell us. Are you in trouble?"

Rachel could feel the tears building. Trouble? That didn't even begin to explain the mess she was in. They had no idea. She pulled away from his closeness. Wiping her mouth with her napkin, she slowly eased to her feet. "If you both will excuse me, I want to get a bit of fresh air."

Exiting through what she assumed was the front door, she drew in a long breath of fresh air. She wanted to scream, *"I live at the Club Durango Apartments on Goeglein Gulch Road."* She was sure they would look at her as if she had lost her mind. Could she blame them? She had!

The moon peeked out from behind a cloud, casting an eerie shadow on the nearby San Juan Mountains. A chill skipped down her spine. She swiped at the tears cascading down her cheek. What was she going to do?

Leaning against the porch railing, she wondered if Becky and Mitchell would commit her if she told them the truth. A small hysterical laugh bubbled out. Heck, maybe she should order her own personal white straightjacket for herself.

Frantically she wiped at her tears as she heard the door open and close behind her. Oh please, let the interloper be Becky.

Inwardly she groaned as a male scent wafted under her nose. No. Luck still wasn't with her.

Leaning her head on her palm, she turned her head to observe the man leaning against the porch railing. Lines of concern creased his face.

"Tell me, Rachel. What's wrong?"

With a watery smile she asked, "What gave you the idea something's wrong?"

His lips quirked and he reached out a hand to brush a tear away from her cheek. "Lucky guess."

"You will just think I've gone crazy."

"Let me decide."

"You asked if I'm visiting family in Durango. The answer is no." She turned her head and stared out into the night. "I live there, but the year is twenty sixteen not eighteen ninety-two." Rachel held her breath. Why didn't he say something? "See. I knew you would think I've lost my ever loving mind."

****

Mitchell cringed. More tears. He moved closer and gathered Rachel into his shoulder and wordlessly let her sob. What had she meant she lived in twenty sixteen? Was she claiming she was from the future? That was ridiculous. Right?

Shifting, he stroked a calming hand over her hair. Her distress was real. He would take her to see the doctor tomorrow, just to make sure there were no serious injuries from her accident.

He felt Rachel stiffen and ease away. "I seem to have gotten your shirt wet."

Mitchell missed her warmth immediately. "This old thing will dry pretty quick." He turned to watch Rachel edge farther away from him. "Maybe you should go and rest."

Rachel opened the door. "Good night." With a quick glimpse back she muttered, "I'm not crazy."

As the door shut behind her he sighed and muttered, "Maybe not, but I'm beginning to wonder if I am." He shifted his position on the railing trying to ease his aching body. He had tightened up the minute he held her in his arms. The light scent from her hair still clung to his shirt. Maybe a walk would help before he called it a night.

Chapter Eleven

Rachel jolted awake as a rooster crowed outside her window. She hoped her situation had changed, and everything had been a dream. Disappointment bubbled up. No. As she looked about the room, she was still stuck in the past.

She covered her eyes. She had made such a fool of herself last night. Mitchell probably thought she was a certifiable basket case. Why should she care what he thought?

Climbing out of bed, she stretched her hands high over her head. She wasn't fond of using the pot under the bed, but she didn't think her bladder wanted to wait. She would venture outside later to find the privy.

Clad in the dress from the evening before, she ran her fingers through her hair and sauntered out to find Becky or Mitchell.

Her stomach growled as her nose encountered the smell of breakfast. She hadn't eaten much the night before. Becky stood in front of the stove once again. She asked cheerfully, "Can I help with anything? I don't know how to operate this stove, but I could give it a shot."

"You look better today." Becky waved her hands at the table. "I'm almost done."

"Maybe later you can give me a cooking lesson on this beast."

"I'd be happy to show you anything you would like."

Rachel chuckled. "You may regret that. Especially after you sample my cooking." Sneaking a biscuit she asked, "Where's Mitchell?"

Becky lifted the pan off the burner. "He's out talking to the hired hands about the chores for the day."

She nibbled on the flaky pastry a moment before asking, "You have quite a bit of land?"

Becky shrugged her shoulders. "Dad built up a decent spread before he passed. Mitchell has grown the cattle herd to about one hundred head and wants to start breeding horses."

Rachel was impressed. "Sounds like he has big plans."

"The Flying W next to our ranch is bigger, and they've been bugging Mitchell to sell." Becky glanced out the window as she rinsed a glass in the washbasin. "Strange things been happening around here. Mitchell and I think the Flying W is behind most of the problems because they want him to sell to them so badly."

"What kind of bad things have been happening?"

"Mostly downed fences and a few missing cattle."

Finishing off the biscuit, Rachel wiped her palms. "You think the owner of this ranch would stoop that low to get your land?"

"We don't know. Our ranch isn't the only one being hit. The sheriff is trying his best, but has no proof so far on who could be behind the problems."

The sound of boots echoed on the porch. Rachel watched Mitchell enter and place his Stetson on a peg by the door.

"Mornin' ladies." His amber eyes ran a quick scan

over her before he turned away.

Rachel felt the heat of a blush spread to her cheeks as she murmured a reply.

"Mitchell, are you taking Rachel and me into town today?"

"Planned to. Thought I could pick up the supplies I ordered and swing by to have Doc Brown check Rachel's bump."

Great. The first step in being committed. She inwardly groaned. She knew she shouldn't have confided in him. Well, why not pacify him. She smiled and fluttered her lashes. "I did hit my head pretty hard. Maybe I should see the doctor. Just to be on the safe side." Could they tell she was irritated?

Becky interrupted her thoughts. "Do you think I could pick out some fabric to make a dress for the July Fourth dance?"

Mitchell sneaked a biscuit. "I don't see why not."

Becky squealed and clapped her hands. "Rachel, there is this yellow fabric that would make a wonderful dress for the celebration." Becky stopped and eyed Rachel. "Of course you will need a dress for the dance as well."

"Oh, that's not necessary." She hoped she was safely home in her own time by July Fourth.

Mitchell shook her concern aside. "Of course you will need something to wear. You can't wear Becky's dress."

Should she ask about her own clothes? She was sure she would be told, once again, how inappropriate they were. "I don't have any money."

Becky waved her objection aside. "Help me with my chores, and we'll be even."

"Thanks Becky, but I still feel strange about accepting handouts."

"It won't be if you help me with gathering eggs and milking the cow."

Rachel bit her lower lip, "But, Becky, I've never milked a cow before."

Flipping a hand in the air Becky replied, "You'll get the hang of helping with the chores. Let's eat so we can be off to town." Becky plunked down in a chair, reached for a biscuit, and lathered it with jam.

Mitchell grinned at Rachel's expression. "It's not as bad as it sounds."

Distressing is what it was. Computers she could handle, milking cows was unknown territory.

****

After breakfast, Rachel helped Becky put the kitchen back in order before donning her boots to visit town. The hem of her borrowed dress dragged as she stepped outside. In the front yard sat a wooden wagon. She inwardly groaned. Her buns didn't have enough padding for such torture.

A shaggy dog trotted toward her. She stared. The accident had happened so quickly the other night, but she could swear the pooch looked exactly like the mutt that had caused her dilemma. Guilty by canine association?

Becky stopped to pet the scraggly beast. "Are you coming, Rachel?"

With a shaking finger, she pointed. "Is that your dog?"

Becky looked from Rachel to the dog. "His name is Chet. Don't you like dogs?"

Giving the canine a wide berth, she walked toward

the wagon. "I used to." She could swear Chet was grinning as he cocked his head at her. What was she thinking? Maybe a visit to check her noggin wasn't a bad idea after all.

An older man stood holding the reins of the horses hitched to the wagon.

Mitchell took the reins from the man. "Thanks Toby."

Rachel was aware of the ranch hands eyes upon her.

"Ma'am, can I help you with a hand up?"

Rachel suddenly felt like Half Pint from *Little House on the Prairie*. The only difference was she wasn't going into town with Pa. Looking at the creaky wagon, she decided a little help probably wouldn't hurt. She smiled. "Yes. That would be wonderful."

"Toby, this is Miss Rachel Morgan. She's a distant relative on my mother's side. She'll be visiting for a while."

Rachel stared at Mitchell. A relative? Is that the only way he could explain her existence? She was surprised he was claiming the crazy lady as a family member. Her lips quirked. Guess it was a good thing he had said the relationship was faint. Otherwise, how would they explain her having the hots for him?

With a wink Toby murmured, "A pleasure, miss."

"Ahem. Toby, what about me?"

Toby broke into a wide grin. "Miss Becky, of course I can't pass up helping two beautiful women in one morning."

As they set out for town, Rachel found herself positioned between Becky and Mitchell. The buckboard seat didn't seem as wide as when she had first sat down.

Mitchell's thigh brushed against hers. Her heart did a silent flip-flop. This was going to be a long ride into town. No. She definitely wasn't Half Pint.

The steady pace and rocking motion constantly threw Rachel up against either Becky or Mitchell. Of course, she would prefer Becky. That option was less threatening. The countryside was gorgeous, as usual. Nothing had changed that fact in her little time travel excursion.

The summer flowers were in bloom, and their fragrance filled the air. Curiously turning her head from one side of the road to the other, she tried to make out where exactly they were. Time and buildings sure changed things. She wasn't sure if she really recognized any landmarks.

As they hit another rut, Rachel bumped against Mitchell again. "How far did you say the drive into town is?" Even to her ears the question sounded like, "Are we there yet?" Angie sure would have gotten a kick out of the situation she found herself.

Flicking the reins Mitchell replied, "It's just a couple of miles into town. Won't take long."

His amber gaze burned into hers. She quickly averted her eyes. Her thigh tingled where she had brushed against his. At the rate they were traveling, the journey was going to take forever.

Becky interrupted her tormented thoughts. "We will have to get you some pretty ribbons for your hair while we are shopping for fabric."

She reached up and touched her curls. She probably looked a mess. She wished she had her pick. If Becky thought she needed something, her hair must really look a sight.

****

Mitchell silently studied Rachel as she spoke with Becky. Her curly hair hung down past her shoulders. As the sun bounced off the tresses, it brought out a vibrant flame just as he imagined. He gripped the reins a little tighter. He would love to run his hands through those flaming tresses. Struggling with getting his desire under control, he had to agree with Becky, some green ribbons in Rachel's hair would look good. Dark green ones would be the best. They would match her eyes perfectly.

"Here we are, ladies." He slowed the horses as they approached the edge of town.

Chapter Twelve

Any delusions Rachel entertained about being punked or part of an elaborate joke burst. This wasn't a dream. Dust rose as travelers passed by in wagons and on horseback. This was beyond the twilight zone. She couldn't begin to describe what she was seeing.

She'd really traveled back in time! She tried not to choke as her anxiety level skyrocketed. What in the hell was she supposed to do? This wasn't a click your heel three times and wish she was back home situation. She was in deep trouble here.

I will not hyperventilate! I will not hyperventilate! If she chanted the phrase enough maybe she could convince herself not too.

She took a deep breath. Spots of light twinkled behind her closed eyes. Please don't faint.

"Are you all right?"

Opening her eyes, her gaze met Becky's concerned stare. She needed to pull herself together. She smiled. "Fine." She cleared her throat. "I'm fine."

Did she sound convincing? As she looked from Becky to Mitchell, she realized she didn't. Doubt, with a splash of pity. That's what she saw in their eyes.

Dodging their stares. She observed the structures. She frowned. Why weren't the buildings made of wood? Weren't buildings in the old west wooden? Without thinking, she asked about the buildings.

Mitchell shot her a strange look from under the brim of his hat. "After the fire in eighty-nine most of the buildings were rebuilt out of stone or brick." Pulling on the reins, he maneuvered the team out of the way of another wagon. His confused gaze swung back to rest on her. "You weren't living in Durango then?"

Of course, he meant eighteen eighty-nine. No, she hadn't been living here then. Ignoring his question, she sat up straighter as she recognized several buildings. The Strater Hotel sat proudly on Main Street, just as the building did in her time, only newer. What year was it constructed? She couldn't remember.

As she pondered the question, she heard a familiar sound that made her smile. A short whistle from the Silverton Narrow-gauge railroad reverberated throughout the town. Of course. Silverton would be a booming mining town during this time

She was fascinated. The streets and boardwalks were crowded with people as they went about their daily routines. A quick look to her right, she noticed a saloon with women hanging over the balcony. They were taunting and calling out to people as they strode or rode by.

A dark-haired scantily clad woman pointed at their wagon and nudged the girl standing beside her. Leaning over the wooden railing further, she yelled a greeting, "Hi Mitchell! Beautiful morning, ain't it?" She rose up and raised her hand in a big wave above her head stretching the tight bodice even tighter. "Come on by before you leave town."

Her mouth, she was sure, hung open. She snuck a peek at Mitchell. He must be a regular.

Mitchell took a hand from the reins and tipped his

hat toward the saloon girl, but kept the wagon moving down the street, not pausing to say hello.

She turned in the seat to stare at the gorgeous girl. Her breasts almost fell from her top as she leaned farther over the railing. Would he visit her before they left town? Could the unflattering flutter in her stomach be jealousy? She glanced briefly away in confusion before her gaze settled back on him and studied him unobserved.

His black Stetson was low over his brow, and his mustache looked recently trimmed. Overall, a very nice looking man. Why wouldn't he have several women vying for his attention? But a saloon girl? Really?

She couldn't see his wonderful amber eyes. He had them diverted and trained on the road ahead. With a sigh, she turned her head to take in more sites.

****

"Dammit!" Jake Sanders exploded as he exited the Silver Spur. He grabbed his hat from his head and slapped it against his leg. What the hell? Of all the fool things. Bill Silver wanted him to pay for half of the damages from the other night before he would serve him a drink. He felt like punching something. Or someone. This was Reeve's fault. His eyes narrowed. Speaking of Reeves. His angry gaze studied the threesome passing by in the wagon. Well, well, well, what do we have here?

His fury diminished. Becky looked as lovely as usual, but the auburn haired beauty sitting between the Reeves held his attention. He placed his hat back on top of his head, his lips quirking into a semi-smile. He believed his luck just changed. Maybe coming to town today wasn't going to be so bad after all.

****

An uneasy tingle raced down Rachel's backbone. Nothing out of the ordinary caught her attention as she scanned the street. What could have caused her discomfort?

Upon closer scrutiny, she noticed a cowboy staring intently at her from the wooden boardwalk. What could his deal be? He pushed his hat up high on his forehead and didn't hide the fact his eyes were raking over her form in obvious appreciation. Not a bad looking man, but an unexplained hardness about him had another shiver racking her spine.

"We're here." Mitchell descended from the wagon and tied the reins.

"Mr. Jones's store has a lot of material to choose from. Have you ever shopped in his store?" At Rachel's negative shake of her head, Becky continued, "We should find what you need to make a dress." Becky slid down from the wagon seat with a graceful flounce.

Becky had made her exit from the wagon look so easy. Rachel eyed the ground. Before executing the jump, a hand appeared to help her down. She smiled down at Mitchell. "Thank you." The warmth from his work-roughened palm had her body humming in a strange way.

"I have errands to tend to. You ladies have fun shopping." He tipped his hat. "I'll meet you back here. Then we will take Rachel to see Doc Brown."

Oh, let's not forget the crazy lady's noggin'! Rachel's lips tightened, but just as suddenly softened. With a tilt of her head, she watched Mitchell's backside as he strode away. Now that was a derriere to admire. Too bad those cowboy buns weren't encased in a pair of Wranglers.

"Rachel, are you coming?" Becky tapped her foot impatiently on the wooded boardwalk.

Soooo Busted! She fanned her flaming face and followed Becky into the general store.

A man in his late twenties, maybe early thirties looked up from behind the counter. "Morning, Miss Reeves. How are you doing this fine June morning?"

Rachel considered him unnoticed. His blue gaze hadn't strayed from Becky. He had a firm clean shaved jaw with nicely trimmed hair. He wasn't as rugged and virile as Mitchell, but very nice. His eyes finally swung to Rachel, and his hand dragged his bangs away in what she thought looked like a nervous gesture. He nodded and smiled, "Miss."

"We're fine, Mr. Jones. This is Rachel Morgan. She's a friend of the family and visiting for a spell."

"Nice to meet you." Rachel extended her hand for a polite handshake. Turning she stared about the shop in wonder.

"Have you any new fabric since I was in last?" Becky did a quick scan of the display on a nearby table.

Mr. Jones pointed a finger toward a back wall. "I did get in a few new items." He paused a moment and shot Becky a smoldering look. "The pretty yellow piece is still here, as well."

Becky squealed with delight. "Let me show you, Rachel."

Rachel stared at the items displayed as she slowly followed Becky. The store wasn't like any super store where she had ever shopped. She trailed her hands along some of the cans on the shelves.

Becky stopped and ran her fingers over a pale

yellow and blue flower fabric. "What do you think?"

"Perfect. The color will look wonderful on you. A good choice for your celebration dress."

"Now to find something for you."

Rachel still felt bad. A shopping trip and she was unable to pay her way. How was she going to reimburse Becky and Mitchell before she found her way back home? She hated to think of herself as a freeloader. "Couldn't we just pin up the hem on this dress?"

"Don't be silly." Becky pointed to a light green print. "How about this?"

Rachel smiled. She could picture her mom picking the precise same piece. If the material had polka dots, then this shopping trip would be identical to her last expedition with her mom. A sudden wave of sadness threatened. Would she ever shop again with her mother?

Becky leaned in close. "Of course you need new undergarments. It's not decent what you're wearing."

Heat blossomed across her cheeks. She quickly glanced to make sure Mr. Jones hadn't heard. This morning before leaving for town, she asked Becky for her bra and panties. Becky had given them back reluctantly, muttering the whole time about their indecency.

"Becky. Let's not go overboard. Remember, I don't have any money."

Becky waved off her arguments. "You can't keep running around in my things."

Rachel watched in despair as Becky piled stockings, cotton underwear, shoes, shirt, skirt, and a nightgown on the counter. There wasn't going to be anything left in the store if she didn't stop her. "Becky.

Enough," she whispered fiercely.

Amused male eyes met her own. Mr. Jones cleared his throat and began writing down the items in his ledger. Casually he asked, "You ladies attending the Independence celebration in a couple of weeks?"

"We'll be there. I just love to dance. Don't you Mr. Jones?" Becky exclaimed. "How about you? Are you attending?"

Mr. Jones eyed Becky. "Yes. I enjoy listening to the music and taking a turn about the floor. Could I ask you to save a dance for me Miss Reeves and please call me Jim?"

Rachel placed a hand over her mouth to cover her merriment. Obviously, Becky had an admirer, and she was so clueless.

Becky continued to gush. "I would love to." Picking up the purchased items off the counter, she turned toward the door. "We'll see you in a couple of weeks, Mr. Jones. I mean Jim."

Rachel elbowed Becky as they left the store. "He has the hots for you."

Becky glanced at her in puzzlement. "Excuse me?"

Hiking a thumb over her shoulder, she smirked. "What I'm trying to say is your Mr. Jones is interested in you."

Becky glanced through the window of the store. "Whatever would give you that idea?"

Rachel rolled her eyes. "Oh please. Save a dance for me was my second or third clue."

"Clue?" Becky's blue gaze stared at her as if she had two heads instead of one.

Rachel was fascinated. Was this how she had acted around men? Wondering around with no idea the opposite sex may have been interested in getting to know her better. She shook her head. "It means." She waved her hand dramatically while she thought of what she could say. "You know." She stopped at Becky's confused look. Sighing heavily, she gave up.

"Excuse me, ladies. I don't want to intrude. Could I lend a hand with your purchases?"

The smooth question had come from a cowboy leaning casually against their wagon. His voice had been smooth, confident, and resonant.

"Why Jake Sanders. What brings you to town?" Becky snickered like a schoolgirl.

Rachel recognized the cowboy. He had been the one who had studied her so intently. Had he been waiting for them to emerge from the store? He looked at her suddenly. His unnerving black eyes twinkled as they roamed over her features. Lingering a little too long on her revealing square neckline. Up close, she noticed the cowboy's nose was bruised and swollen. Had it been recently broken?

His attention didn't waver as he answered Becky. "Oh, this and that." Straightening from the wagon he asked, "Aren't you going to introduce me to your pretty friend?"

"Oh. Where are my manners?" Uncertainty crossed Becky's face before she continued. "Jake Sanders this is Rachel Morgan. A friend of the family."

Jake tipped his hat. "Pleasure, ma'am."

Here was a proverbial bad boy down to his bones. His picture would be in the dictionary under the definition. Rachel secretly shuddered. He had dark black hair that curled slightly at the ends, and dark stubble graced his face. The smile he sent her didn't quite reach his eyes. She finally murmured, "Nice to meet you, Mr. Sanders."

He leaned in close and turned up the wattage on his smile. "Oh, ma'am, call me Jake. No need to stand on ceremony."

Forcing a smile, she nodded. "Jake"

"Here, Jake, help us load the packages into the back of our wagon." Becky shoved an armload of packages into his arms.

"I don't get to be of such service to two beautiful ladies every day."

Add smooth to the list. Rachel was troubled by the way Becky ate up all of his malarkey. Couldn't she see he was full of bull?

Rachel watched closely as Jake placed their items in the back of the wagon. His gaze bounced back to her and roamed from the top of her head to her feet. His lips twitched, and a genuine smile appeared.

What was so funny? Rachel peeked down to see what amused Jake. She was standing on top of Becky's hem. She kicked the dress out from under her feet. Okay, so she wasn't the Jolly Green Giant.

She jumped as a low growl immerged from behind her. Twisting, she encountered Mitchell's fierce stare. He squinted, and his nostrils flared as his gaze bounced from her to Becky before finally landing on Jake. "Sanders! I thought I told you to stay away from my sister."

Mitchell with hands on hips and jaw clenched glared at Jake.

Rachel took a tiny step back as she witnessed Jake's hardening gaze.

"Well, Reeves, looks like you don't look any worse

for wear after the beating I gave you." Jake jerked his hand toward Becky and Rachel. "I was just being a gentleman and helping your sister and Miss Morgan with their packages."

Rachel could swear she could see steam coming from Mitchell's nostrils.

Mitchell's angry eyes sought out Becky. "Wonder where you got the idea they needed help?"

Becky squirmed and stammered, "I'll wait in the wagon."

Rachel picked up her hem and without a word sauntered to the wagon. She peeked back. Mitchell stood rigid staring at Jake. If Mitchell didn't like the cowboy, her instincts couldn't be far off. Right? She made a few awkward attempts, but she finally managed to climb up on the buckboard.

Becky leaned over to whisper in Rachel's ear, "Mitchell thinks Jake is trying to get under my skirt. I've told him I can take care of myself, but he refuses to listen to me."

"Becky, I think I would listen to your brother in this matter." She considered the two men. "He seems to know Mr. Sanders very well."

"Oh. Not you, too!"

Mitchell said a few more words to Jake, but they were low and Rachel couldn't make them out. Abruptly he turned and grabbed the reins. In one fluid motion, he was in the wagon. He frowned at Becky. "Did you listen to anything I told you?"

"Really, Mitchell, Jake was just helping with our packages."

He sat silent for a moment. His amber gaze snagged Rachel's. "Was he behaving improperly?"

"No." How did she say he gave her the heebie-jeebies though? "He was nothing but polite."

Mitchell nodded in understanding. "Sanders can be charming when he wants to be." His arms bunched as he flicked the reins. "Let's check to see if the doc's in."

Rachel wiggled awkwardly. Drat. He still thought she was a loon.

Jake shifted his weight as he watched the buckboard pull away. He smiled. Miss Morgan was quite appealing from a distance, but up close more so. Yes, a tasty morsel indeed. Whistling, he strode toward his horse.

Chapter Thirteen

The doctor's house was a small, white building located at the edge of town. Rachel studied the bold letters on the sign posted on the side, Doctor Stanley Brown. Once again, Mitchell turned to help her down from the wagon. Should she be getting used to his helpful touch?

The front room was empty as they entered. The area was sparsely furnished with a desk in the far corner. A bookshelf against the adjacent wall held a collection of leather bound books.

"Hello. Doc Brown?" Mitchell's voice boomed.

An older gentleman shuffled into the room from a doorway to their left. "Mornin'. Sorry, I didn't hear you come in. What can I do for you?"

"Good morning. Do you have time to check Miss Morgan? She fell and bumped her head. We just want to make sure nothing serious occurred from the accident."

"Well, let's have a look shall we Miss Morgan?" The doctor's hands shook as he pulled back her hair covering her forehead. "My. You did bang yourself good. Let's go on back to the exam room and look you over proper."

Rachel sat down on the table the doctor indicated and started to swing her legs back and forth. She gazed about the room in silent wonder. The atmosphere was pure doctor's office, but the tools and books were quite different from her regular doctor's. She smiled to herself. The doctor would be amazed at the information he could have at a touch of his fingertips.

Dr. Brown shut the door. "Now then young lady, let's start at the beginning. Why don't you tell me how this happened?"

"I was driving home in the storm we had a couple of nights ago. A stupid dog ran out in front of my car, and I bumped my head on my steering wheel when I hit a tree." She stopped suddenly. What was she doing? Sign her up for a padded cell right this instant. With a glance from under her lashes, she thought she better revise her story. "The storm spooked my horse, and she threw me. I really don't know what collided with my hard head."

The doctor patted her hand reassuringly and eyed her carefully. "Sounds like you've had a trying time. Let's just take a look, shall we?"

The examination took only a few minutes. "I really don't see any damage other than the big goose egg you're wearing on your forehead. Have you had any dizzy spells or blurred vision?"

Rachel nodded. "Yes, the first day after the accident. Everything seems to be getting back to normal since then."

As they walked out of the examination room, Mitchell and Becky rose to their feet. "Well, Doc, what do you think? Any concerns we should be worried about?" A look of worry briefly crossed Mitchell's face before he masked the expression.

Had she imagined his apprehension? The look had come and gone so quickly.

The doctor removed his spectacles and wiped them with a cloth from his vest pocket. "She'll be right as rain in a few days. She just needs to take it easy." Turning toward Rachel, the doctor said in a stern voice, "You will have to refrain from riding your horse young lady at least for a week." He turned back toward Mitchell and Becky. "You make sure she follows those instructions."

Rachel felt a hysterical bubble of laughter waiting to make its escape. With a swallow, she placed a hand on the doctor's sleeve. "I don't think that will be a problem. My Mustang seems to be missing. So I won't even be tempted to go for a ride."

"Oh, I'm sorry my dear." The doctor returned a kind pat to her hand. "You let me know if you should have any problems."

Mitchell pulled some coins from his pocket. "How much do we owe you for today's visit?"

The doctor's eyes twinkled as he studied them. He scratched his chin. "I believe a dance from each of the young ladies at the upcoming social should cover the charges."

Rachel glanced at Becky then studied Mitchell's profile. Was the doctor joking? Would she still be here to take a twirl with the good doctor? Bestowing a quick smile, she replied, "Seems more than fair. Don't you think, Becky?"

"Yes, Rachel, a fair price indeed."

The sun was high in the sky as the wagon rumbled out of town. Rachel's stomach growled. The little amount of breakfast she had earlier had definitely disappeared.

Becky giggled. "Good thing I packed a lunch."

Rachel rubbed her tummy. "That was almost louder than a buzz saw."

Becky eyed her quizzically. "What's a buzz saw?" She shook her head. "You say the strangest things sometimes."

Flicking her wrist with nonchalance she murmured, "Never mind. I can't explain what I mean." She gazed about. "Mitchell? Where did you stumble across me the other night?"

"Just up ahead. A nice shady area should be perfect for us to enjoy the basket Becky packed."

She pondered a moment. Would she be able to find a way back to her own time? Pressed once again between Becky and Mitchell, she found it hard to concentrate on her surroundings.

She drew in a deep breath of the fresh mountain air. This was one of her favorite things. The mingled smells of pine and meadow wafting on the slight breeze delighted her nose.

Lost in her thoughts a minute passed before she realized Mitchell was slowing the wagon.

He pointed to a huge tree in the bend of the road. "I found you at the base of that tree. Does anything look familiar?"

Rachel stood as the horses stilled. No. Nothing made sense. Had she ever felt this lost before?

"Let me give you a hand down." She waited for Mitchell to descend from the wagon. He surprised her by reaching up and grabbing her about the waist and lifted her down.

She could feel the heat of a blush stain her cheeks. "Um…thank you."

"You're welcome."

With a step backward, she eased from his embrace. A quick scan of the area brought on a feeling of dread. How exactly did she go about finding her way home?

She ran her fingers over the bark and pondered her dilemma. Did the conditions need to be the same? She started at Becky's voice close behind her.

"I don't think you will be able to find your horse Rachel. The hard rain washed away any tracks your horse would have made."

She shrugged with a casualness she didn't feel. "Yes, I'm sure my horse is long gone by now." She stared unseeingly across the meadow. "Mitchell? Do you remember anything unusual about the evening you found me?"

He shook his head. "Besides you dressed in men's clothing?"

What was with them and her clothes? She tempered a groan of frustration. "Yes. Well, anything besides that little matter."

"No. Nothing pops into my head." He stared off into the distance in concentration. "When I lifted you to place you on Rebel your saddlebag dropped from your shoulder."

Her heart leaped in anticipation. "My what?"

Mitchell lifted his hands to describe what he had found. "It was a leather pouch that had several funny looking pockets." He moved his hands about a foot apart. "About this big. I just figured it fell off your horse when your mount took off."

Her purse! She wanted to shout with glee. That had to be what he was describing. Oh, to have that small connection to her time would be wonderful. She contained her excitement as she asked, "Where did you put my pur…um, saddlebag? I haven't seen my pouch the last few days."

Pushing the brim of his hat up, he wrinkled his forehead in thought. "I remember bringing it into the house. You'll find your satchel somewhere in the bedroom."

Jumping in pleasure, she grabbed his arm and tried leading him back to the wagon. "Come on, let's get back to the ranch."

Becky frowned and paused in unpacking the food, "Don't you want to eat lunch first, Rachel?"

Rachel dropped Mitchell's arm. She needed to contain the bubble of excitement wanting to burst forth from her body. Dragging the toe of her boot through the grass, she stammered, "Of course. We probably should eat before we start back."

Sitting down reluctantly, Rachel pulled a piece of chicken from the plate and took a bite. The chicken was probably delicious, but she wanted to get back to the ranch. She couldn't have told anyone what she had consumed. Whether the meat had been chicken or a burnt hot dog. A few moments later, she finished chewing with a flourish and sprang to her feet. "I'll help pack up the remains."

It took forever to reach the ranch. As soon as Mitchell halted the wagon, Rachel prodded Becky from her seat. She jumped down and practically ran into the house, but not before she heard Mitchell ask Becky, "Doc did say she was okay, right?"

"That's what I heard him say. Makes you wonder if the doctor knew what he was talking about." She turned back toward the wagon. "Could you help me bring in the packages?"

Mitchell brought a hand up to restrain Becky from following Rachel into the house. A frown marred his brow. "Becky, something I've been thinking about. Rachel says she's been living in Durango, but today when we were in town she looked about like she had never seen the town before and didn't even ask for us to take her by her home before coming back to the ranch."

Becky worried her bottom lip. "I hadn't thought about that. Do you think the bump on her head has caused her to forget those things?"

Mitchell turned to pick up the packages from the back of the wagon. "I just don't know Beck. I just don't know."

Chapter Fourteen

Running into the bedroom Rachel stopped suddenly. Where should she begin to look? Her gaze scanned the few items in the room. She rushed over and looked behind the rocker; that's where Mitchell had been sitting when she first woke up. Finding nothing, she spun around to eye the dresser. Oh, where could he have put the confounded thing? The only other big object in the room was the bed. Squatting down, she lifted the colorful quilt. The pot was there, she leaned a little farther over. A strap! Her purse was under the bed. Crawling down onto her stomach, she slowly inched her way under.

****

Mitchell entered the room to see Rachel's backside wiggling from under the bed. He cleared his throat. "I hope you don't get stuck." All he could hear was some mumbled reply. Crossing the room, he took off his hat, laid it on the bed, and put down the packages he had brought in. Leaning over, he glanced under the bed from the other side. He contained his amusement at the picture she painted. "Can I ask what you're doing?"

He saw her blow a curl from her eye. "I'm trying to get my purse."

"Here let me help. I have longer arms." He reached and grabbed the leather strap easily. He rose to his feet. What was so exciting about this saddlebag? No, wait.

That isn't what she had called it. A purse, that's what she had said.

He grinned as he heard another murmur come from under the bed. "I can't understand what you're saying."

"I said I think I'm stuck. Can you help me out from under here?" Her muffled voice rose and carried a little louder this time enough for him to hear.

Skirting around the bed, he found her backside wiggling invitingly. He swallowed hard. What a tempting sight. He flung the purse in the nearby rocker and leaned over. Grabbing her by the ankles, he slowly slid her out from her predicament. His left hand accidently slipped above her boot and touched silky smooth skin. What would it feel like to run his hands up farther on her leg? He dropped her feet suddenly as if they had burned his hands. Those types of thoughts could get him into a lot of trouble.

Rachel drew herself up to her knees and grimaced at the sight of the dust coating her borrowed dress. She brushed the dirt from her breasts. "Thanks. The opening didn't seem all that small when I started under there."

Mitchell stood mesmerized as he watched her hands innocently brushing her chest. In his mind he replaced her hands with his own. How soft and smooth would her skin feel under his callused palms? His body became taunt at the thought. Clearing his throat, he spoke softly, "I'm glad I could be of assistance. I need to go unhook the horses from the wagon." He reached across the bed to grab his Stetson and beat a hasty retreat out of the room, breathing out a sigh as he firmly closed the door to the bedroom and to his thoughts.

Rachel stared at the door as Mitchell exited with some force. Now, what was that all about? Had she made him mad somehow? With a shrug, she turned her attention to her purse. She was such a packrat. What would she find?

Sitting down carefully on the bed, she trailed her hands over the soft leather. She pulled on the tab to unzip the main compartment and turned the purse upside down to dump the contents onto the bed. Tears sprang to her eyes. Amid all the usual stuff, she spied the letter she had gotten from her mom earlier in the week. She opened the envelope to reread the cherished words that had been written by her mother. She scanned over the usual chitchat about the farm duties and chores. Next were the precious words about what had been going on in the community and church. Her hand shook as she placed her fingers against her trembling lips. Tears flowed down her cheeks unchecked. She had always been susceptible to being homesick. Her situation was worse than being a state or two away from home. She folded the letter with reverence. Placing the envelope to her chest, she vowed to protect the correspondence no matter what she encountered.

Next, she picked up a packet that had pictures enclosed she had recently printed. She opened the flap and smiled. Inside was a photo of her and her Mustang Angie had taken. Flipping through them, she gasped. Her mom and dad smiled back at her. They had come out the month before for a visit. For once, she was glad she was such a packrat.

Her hands shook slightly as she looked over the items displayed before her. A hair pick, compact mirror, container of Tylenol, a package of Dentyne, a hair scrunchy, tube of Blistex, calendar planner, checkbook, and wallet.

She unsnapped the fastener on the billfold and opened it up. She ran a finger over her driver's license. Finally, a good picture and no one would appreciate it. Unzipping another compartment on her purse, she spied a few feminine hygiene items, her cell phone, a small bottle of her favorite perfume, the latest romance novel she had purchased, a small can of pepper spray, and a Snickers bar.

She gave the chocolate wrapper a sniff of appreciation. She'd save the treat for a special occasion. Briefly, she reread the book blurb and snorted. Pirates. She loved stories about swashbuckling buccaneers.

Her cell phone's black screen was daunting. She sighed heavily, what had she expected? Five bars to make a precious call? "You can't hear me now," she mumbled.

She replaced all the beloved items into her purse. Making her way across the room, she opened the top drawer of the dresser. Peering inside, she trailed a hand over the men's shirts Mitchell hadn't removed yet from the drawer. Moving aside the shirts, she placed her purse at the bottom of the drawer and covered it up.

She smoothed down her freshly combed hair and exited the bedroom. Becky sat on the couch in front of the fireplace looking at the material they had purchased in town.

"The dance is next week. We will need to get started on our dresses if they're going to be done on time." Becky looked into Rachel's eyes. "Is something wrong?"

She held back a small sniffle. "I'm just missing my mom and dad." She waved Becky's concern aside. "I hope you know what you're doing when it comes to sewing. I've got to admit I haven't done any since high school home economics class."

Becky studied her strangely for a moment. "You had a class at school where they taught you how to sew? Your mom didn't teach you?"

"Of course my mom showed me how to sew, but we also had classes at school. We even had boys in our class, because they were required to have so many hours of cooking and sewing." Rachel watched Becky break into laughter. "What's so funny?"

"I just had a vision of my brother with a needle and thread sewing a new dress for me."

"What's so amusing?" A deep voice questioned from the doorway. The girls looked up as Mitchell joined them in the sitting room, glanced at each other, and pealed with laughter.

Becky dabbed at her eyes. "Oh, nothing, we were just talking women talk."

Mitchell inched toward the door. "I'm going to go check with Toby on how the branding went today."

"Go ahead. Rachel and I have a lot of work to do if we're going to have these dresses ready for the Fourth of July festivities." She folded the material. "First we need to get supper started."

"Becky, do you feed the ranch hands as well?"

"No. Thank goodness. Toby is responsible for feeding them."

Rachel rose from the couch. "Let me help you out."

"I still have some chicken I didn't fry up earlier."

A thought formed in Rachel's mind. "Would you mind if I tried making chicken and noodles tonight?" She hadn't prepared the dish in quite awhile, but the therapeutic kneading of dough should work wonders for her morale.

Becky's eyes took on a faraway look before she smiled. "Mom used to make the best noodles." She frowned. "Are you sure you're up to it? The doctor did say to take it easy for a few days."

"I don't think cooking will be too exerting. I need to feel like I'm being useful around here."

Becky grinned. "That will give me time to think of a pattern for our dresses. You've got a deal. Do you need my help in getting started?"

"I'm not sure I'm ready to tackle the wood stove just yet. Could you put the chicken on to boil?"

"I'll give you a quick lesson."

She eyed the stove wearily. "Thanks." Excitement bubbled in her stomach. She was going to prove she wasn't useless after all.

Becky's lesson was quick, and in no time the water boiled. She cut up the chicken and placed the meat in the hot water. Shooing Becky out of the kitchen, she raided the pantry for flour, salt, and pepper. Next, she found the eggs and added a dash of milk in a big bowl.

Soon the ingredients were forming a ball of dough. A calmness she hadn't felt in days settled over her. The stress worked out of her body as she wielded the sticky mass. Many happy memories flooded her mind as she thought back to her grandma showing her how to make the noodles. She couldn't have been much older than seven at the time. Her mother had dropped her off at her grandma's for the day. The kitchen had smelled of fresh baked apple pie. Grandma Morgan had the patience of a saint. Flour had been everywhere, but Grandma had claimed after she'd finished they were the best noodles she had ever tasted. Rachel grinned at the memory. She was sure her grandma hadn't been showing a bias at all.

Not finding a rolling pin, she improvised with a tin cup sitting nearby on a shelf. She liked her noodles a little thick. Would Mitchell like them fat or a little thinner? She jerked to a stop as she realized what she was thinking. Was she really trying to impress him with her cooking? Grinning, she admitted maybe she was just a little. How better to impress a man but through his stomach?

She hummed one of her favorite old rock and roll tunes as she rolled the cup back and forth over the dough. Man, she wished she had her iPod. A few minutes later, the words poured out as she continued working.

She started to wiggle her hips and body to the beat playing through her head.

"What are you doing?"

Rachel jumped and dropped the cup as her gaze connected with Becky's blue gaze. She could feel a wave of heat rising in her cheeks. "I'm sorry. Was I was singing too loud? Guess I got carried away."

Becky stood deep in thought for a moment. "What's Rock and Roll, and why do you love it?" She frowned in confusion. "I don't think I've ever heard that song."

"I know Joan Jett sings it better than I do." She could have kicked herself. When was she going to think before she spoke?

Becky cocked her head. "Joan Jett? Is she a singer from the east?"

Oh, Angie would have gotten a kick out of this conversation. "I think she's from the east. I'm not sure."

"Well, you have a nice singing voice."

"Thank you, Becky. I don't think I'll go on the road though." She glanced down at the rolled dough. "These noodles need to dry a bit." She busied herself cleaning up her mess. "Do you think I could possibly have a bath?" It seemed like weeks since she had stood under her steaming showerhead, instead of just a few days.

"I'll ask Mitchell to haul the tub in and you can take a bath before going to bed tonight. If you wish."

"Do we have to bother Mitchell? Surely, we can handle the tub. Couldn't we?"

Becky stared at her. "That tub is heavy! Besides, you're not supposed to be doing anything hard. Doctor's orders."

Speaking of the devil, Mitchell entered the kitchen through the back door. She wiped flour off her hands onto the apron tied about her waist.

His gaze swept Rachel before asking, "Everything okay?"

She shrugged and placed her flour-covered hands behind her back. They instantly stuck together. "Just giving a helping hand in making supper."

Mitchell chuckled. Striding across the room, he stopped in front of Rachel. His hand grazed her cheek lightly. "Are you making it or wearing it? You have a bit of flour on your face."

She felt his touch down to her toes. She lowered her eyes. "I guess I got carried away."

"I can't wait to sample." He cleared his throat. "Dinner that is." Shuffling backward he stated, "I'll be in the barn."

"Mitchell, Rachel would like to take a bath. Could

you bring in the tub later?"

Rachel squirmed as his gaze settled on her. He looked so serious. What was he thinking?

He cleared his throat again. "That shouldn't be a problem."

She watched Mitchell exit before turning to cut the dough on the table. Slow heat spread through her cheeks as she remembered his touch as he wiped the flour from her face. So soft, like a flutter of a butterfly's wing.

"Rachel? Do you need help with anything else?"

She jumped guiltily. She had forgotten Becky was in the room. "I think I have everything under control."

Becky removed the boiling pot from the stove. "Rachel? Can I ask you something?"

Pausing with the knife in the air Rachel studied Becky's serious look on her face. She hoped it wasn't a question on some of the odd things she had said or done. "Sure. What's the problem?"

"How do you truly know if a man likes you?" Becky paused in her task and turned inquisitive blue eyes in her direction.

Oh, Lordy. How did she answer when she didn't know the answer herself? She stalled by tapping a flour-coated finger against her bottom lip. "Well, I think one way is how they act around you." She gestured with her hand. "You know. Do they go out of their way to make you happy? Do they enjoy your company?" She shook her head. "I'll admit I'm not good at understanding men."

"Do you really think Mr. Jones, that is Jim, likes me?"

She smiled. "Girl, I do believe the man has it bad.

But, once again, I'm not an expert. Maybe you should play it by ear."

Becky frowned. "Play it by ear, huh? Is it easy?"

She blew a curl away from her eyes. "You'll just have to wait and see what happens."

"What if nothing ever happens?" A small whine entered into Becky's tone.

This she knew something about. "My best friend told me once you have to be patient. One day your prince will come."

They fell silent as they started putting noodles in the hot water with the chicken. They worked well together. After the chicken and noodles were back on the stove, Becky showed Rachel how to make biscuits.

"Can you fetch Mitchell from the barn? I'll just put the dishes on the table."

Why was Becky always sending her after Mitchell? She inhaled deeply as she stepped out onto the front porch. The smell of rain hung heavily in the air.

Like a light bulb going off, she wondered if she could travel home if it was raining. She had arrived when the sky had poured cats and dogs. Is that how this whole crazy thing worked?

Could she travel back to her own time under the right circumstances? How would she get back to the tree, the scene of the original crime? Would the walk take her just over an hour? Would it be possible to sneak away to attempt? She shook her head to clear her errant wonderings.

She stared about curiously. She'd not taken the opportunity earlier to study the ranch. A small barn stood adjacent to the house with a wooden corral jutting from the structure. Another building stood a small distance away. That must be the bunkhouse.

With a turn, she gazed at the house in the fading evening light. The structure shone with the foundation of love in which it had been built. Truly rustic, but beautiful.

Crossing the yard, she paused as she saw the scraggly dog lounging near the barn door. Kneeling to the ground, she peered into the dog's eyes. "You're the reason I'm here aren't you?"

How stupid was that thought? She scratched the dog tentatively behind his ear. "What power do you wield if you're the cause of my time travel?" Staring into the dark eyes, she shook her head. "I know. I've totally lost my mind."

Rising, she opened the barn door. Slowly she moved down the stalls following the sound of Mitchell's voice.

"What do you think, Rebel? Would you like that?" The horse's ears twitched back as if considering every word spoken.

Rachel giggled. "Does he answer you?" She propped her arms on the half door of the stall where Mitchell groomed a huge black horse.

His amused eyes met hers. "Sometimes."

"Supper is almost done." Taking a calming breath, she took a hesitant step through the door. Extending her hand, she brushed the soft velvety nose. "What is your name, pretty boy?" She tilted her head to the side. "When does he reply?"

He smiled. "He doesn't talk to people he's not familiar with. He has to get to know you first."

She nodded. "That's smart to teach him stranger danger."

"Stranger danger?" He frowned. His hand paused in stroking the horse's coat. "His name is Rebel." He watched her pet the horse's nose. "If you comb him, you'll become acquainted."

A tingle coursed through her fingers at his touch when he passed her the currycomb. "You're such a pretty thing. Aren't you?" Her hands glided over the horse in soft sure strokes.

"Bet you miss your horse."

She glanced at Mitchell. How did she tell him she had never had a horse and never ridden one in her life? She held her tongue. Things were complicated enough.

After a few quite moments, he cleared his throat. "Guess we should wash up. Thanks for the help."

The night sky twinkled as they made their way to the house. "Would you still like for me to bring in the tub?"

"Please. If it's not too much trouble."

A slight tinge graced his cheeks as his gaze met hers briefly before darting away.

She stared in wonder at his blush. "Mitchell?"

"No, problem at all."

Chapter Fifteen

Mitchell leaned away from his plate and patted his stomach. "I'm impressed. Some of the best noodles I've ever eaten."

His intense gaze made Rachel fidget. "Thank you."

Scooting the chair away from the table, he stood up. "I'll go get the tub. Becky can help you get some water started."

"What is your saying?" Becky winked from over her shoulder as she placed dishes in the sink. "I think he has the hots for you."

"Oh Becky…" She stammered to a stop. "I really don't think so." Who could like a crazy woman claiming to have travelled through time?

Only a few minutes passed as they washed dishes and got water heating on the stove.

Becky hid a yawn behind her hand. "I'm going to go on to bed. I've had a long day. We'll work on our dresses tomorrow."

Rachel watched as Becky leaned over the soft glowing lamp in the front room and blew the flame out on her way to her bedroom.

A shuffling noise from the back door drew her attention. Mitchell opened the door hauling a portable tub. Her eyes widened. No wonder Becky balked at bringing the thing in. The contraption looked awkward to carry.

"Let me give you a hand with the water." Rachel lifted the first bucket off the stove and poured it in.

Steam rose from the tub less than ten minutes later. She drew a hand through the water and sighed. The temperature was just right.

"Let me know if you need anything."

Rachel reached out and grabbed his arm before he exited the room. "Wait. Do you have soap, shampoo, and a towel?"

"The soap is on a shelf in the pantry. I'll get a washcloth and towel."

As Mitchell made his way from the room, he visualized Rachel with soap and water glistening like dew on her skin. He swallowed hard. He had been too long without a woman's touch.

He avoided looking into her eyes as he reentered the kitchen. He handed over the items and beat a hasty retreat back to his room. He sat on his bed and ran a trembling hand threw his hair.

He could stand to have a bath. Maybe he should put more water on before Rachel got undressed. He realized his mistake the moment he entered the room.

He had underestimated how quickly Rachel would undress. She hadn't noticed him yet, but he froze and came to a standstill. She stood by the tub in the skimpiest pair of drawers he had ever seen and nothing else. She turned from folding her borrowed dress to find him gaping at her. She gasped and grabbed for the towel lying nearby.

"What do you want?" Her voice rose, bordering on hysteria.

He tried to answer. What had he come to tell her? "I'm sorry. I didn't think you would be undressed already. I'll put on a bucket of water so I can take a bath after you're finished."

She motioned to the stove. She stuttered, "Go ahead."

He couldn't pump water into the bucket fast enough. He found himself stumbling for words. "Um. Let me know when you're finished."

Rachel stared after him. Had that really just happened? A mortified chuckle escaped. He was the first man to view her near naked body. Had he found her attractive?

She glanced down at the towel clasped in front of her bare breasts. Her nipples had hardened when she had caught sight of him staring at her. Whether he found her attractive or not, her body was letting her know how she felt about him.

She smiled. What had he thought of her unsuitable lace boy shorts? Peeking at the dark hallway, she lowered the towel and finished undressing.

Her body tingled as she settled in the water. A deep sigh emerged travelling all the way from her big toe. She leaned her head back and studied the log ceiling. This felt divine.

A quiver coursed the length of her body as she caressed her limbs with the rag. Every nerve ending danced in the cloth's wake. She hadn't ever felt this way before. Was this because of Mitchell's attention? What had he awakened within her?

Closing her eyes, she submerged her head. The water soothed her tired body. A few moments later, she almost groaned as she lathered up her hair. It had been years, literally, since her last shower.

Unsure how long she had lingered in the tub, she

noticed steam rising from the bucket of water on the stove. She'd be a prune if she didn't emerge soon.

Cautiously she rose and grabbed the nearby towel. She made quick work of drying herself. She pulled her new underwear on and dragged a light blue nightgown over her damp head.

Nibbling on her lower lip, she realized she had forgotten the robe or wrapper thing in her room. She retrieved her discarded clothes and clutched them to her chest. A few moments later, she paused in front of the room where Mitchell was staying. Her cheeks heated as she recalled his stare from earlier. With a lift of her hand, she rapped hesitantly. She gasped and jumped back as the door swung open.

His intense amber gaze scanned her from the top of her wet head to the toes peeping from under the gown's hem. The sensual look he shot her had her backing further away.

"The tub is all yours." She turned and slipped into her room. Leaning against the closed door, she placed a hand over her heart, inhaled, and tried to calm the pounding. It wasn't her imagination! He just looked at her like the big bad wolf ogled Little Red Riding Hood.

With a shiver, she flipped back the quilt and sank onto the bed. Yanking the covers up to her chin, she groaned. Complications! Who needed them? Closing her eyes, she silently said a small prayer before drifting to sleep.

Chapter Sixteen

What a mess. Rachel sat on the front room floor with Becky, surrounded by material, thread, and buttons strewn about. Her butt went numb at least thirty minutes ago. She had concentrated on Becky's ramblings, but her focus had been on the missing Mitchell. He hadn't been there when they sat down for breakfast.

Trying for a nonchalant approach, she cleared her throat. "Is Mitchell not going to eat breakfast this morning?"

Becky finished threading a needle before answering. "He ate earlier. One of the ranch hands rode in this morning to tell him fences on the north side of the ranch were down. They will probably be gone a few days mending fences."

A bubble of disappointment churned her stomach. Her sleep had been fitful in anticipation of seeing him this morning. With a shake of her head, she directed her attention to the project before her. "Okay, tell me once more how I'm supposed to cut this out?" She held up the material expectantly as Becky calmly explained again, what needed to be done.

A couple of hours later Rachel stretched her legs and eyed her project. Becky was a good teacher. The pinned material resembled a dress.

"I need to take a break. Mother Nature is calling."

Becky rose and gave her long legs a shake. "Yeah, I could use a good stretch. Are you hungry?"

On cue, Rachel's stomach growled. The small breakfast from earlier was long gone. "I could manage a bite."

A soft summer breeze greeted her as she opened the front door. The privy was behind the house. She finally worked up the nerve the day before to ask where the outhouse was located.

Indoor plumbing. What year did that become popular? Opening the door, she gazed into the dim space. She missed her well-lighted apartment bathroom. She smiled at the dime novel on the shelf.

As she exited, Chet's agitated bark startled her. The sound of a horse approaching had her heart leaping with excitement. Was Mitchell back? The eager smile vanished once she recognized the rider.

"Morning, pretty lady. How are you this fine morning?"

Rachel shielded her eyes from the sun to glance up at Jake Sanders. Now what was he doing here? "I'm fine."

Jake's gaze raked her from the top of her head to her small booted feet. He pushed back his hat and leaned back in his saddle. His lips twitched then lifted into a charming smile.

Rachel squirmed under his scrutiny. She shuffled her feet. Now she knew how a bug felt being studied under a magnifying glass.

"Well, Jake what brings you out this way today?"

Rachel released a huge sigh of relief as she turned to see Becky standing on the porch watching them intently.

"Mornin', Becky, you're looking mighty pretty this morning as well."

Rachel expected a girlish giggle from Becky, but one wasn't forthcoming. She tilted her head. Had Becky finally taken Mitchell's warnings to heart?

Becky smiled, stepped down off the porch, and came to stand by Rachel.

Jake took his hat off and wiped the sweat from his brow with his arm. "I was out checking the fence line and decided to check in on you ladies since I wasn't far away. I figured it was the hospitable thing to do. Us being neighbors and all."

A new thought wormed into Rachel's head. Did he know Mitchell wasn't here? She studied his dark eyes intently. A small spark of something appeared and disappeared. In that brief flicker, she had her answer.

She battled a wave of panic. She thought of her pepper spray tucked away in her purse. Maybe she should start carrying the container in her pocket. She lifted her chin in defiance. He wasn't going to intimidate her.

"Do you ladies mind if I get down and water my horse in your trough?"

Rachel wished Becky would be rude and say no, but she knew that wasn't going to happen.

"Sure Jake. Would you like something to quench your thirst?"

He cast a sly glance toward Rachel. "Sounds good, Becky. Do you have any cookies?" He winked at Rachel.

She cringed. This little visit wasn't going to be over anytime soon.

Jake settled in a chair on the porch. "Rachel, where

are you from?"

His smile directed at her had the hairs on her arms standing at attention. Smoothing a hand over her limb, she slowly lowered herself onto the first step and leaned against the porch post. "I'm from the Oklahoma Territory." There was no need to tell him she had been living in Durango recently. Or not so recently, however you wanted to look at the fact. She grinned.

Jake stared at her with a strange heat glinting in his eyes. "What put the smile on your face, pretty lady?" His voice had grown husky.

She shifted. His look and tone made her uneasy. Her smile disappeared. "How about yourself? Where are you from Mr. Sanders?"

The dog trotted across the yard and jumped up the two steps to where Rachel sat. He positioned himself on his belly and laid his head in her lap. His soulful eyes captured hers. She lifted a hand and pet the mangy dog. Was Chet aware of the unnerving feelings arising in her at Jake's presence?

"Looks like you've made a friend there." Clearing his throat, he stated, "You know, I've asked you to call me Jake." He frowned at her as he thought over her question. "Originally, I guess I'm from Texas."

"I gather you travel around quite a bit."

He shrugged. "I've been around. I've worked for Mr. Waters at the Flying W the longest. Been with him going on two years."

Where had she heard Flying W? She pondered a moment. Then she remembered Becky had mentioned the name a few days ago. The neighboring ranch she felt was the root of their problems.

"What do you do for Mr. Waters?"

His chest puffed up with pride. "I'm the foreman."

"A huge responsibility. Is the place a big spread?"

"Largest around these parts."

Relief spread up Rachel's spine as Becky emerged from the house with a plate of cookies and a glass of water for Jake.

"Are these your famous oatmeal raisin, Becky?"

"Of course. Would I offer any other type?"

Rachel watched the exchange wordlessly. How often did he come around for cookies? Was Mitchell always away when he did?

"Rachel, would you like one?"

Her mouth watered as she chose a medium sized cookie.

Jake grinned. "I haven't had anything this good since the last church social in town. Becky always has the best meals."

What a relief. That explained a lot. She nibbled a bite and frowned. She lowered the soft morsel. The flavor was familiar. The taste was just like her friend Angie's grandmother's recipe. Now that was weird.

Jake took his sweet time chit-chatting. Rachel clenched a tuft of Chet's hair willing Jake to leave. She controlled a sigh when he finally rose. She stood up to let him pass.

"I guess I need to get back to work." Jake passed by and grazed her breast as he descended the steps.

She suppressed a shiver and leaned harder against the porch railing. Chet sidled closer and growled low in his throat. Had the graze been on purpose?

Jake took his time untying his horse's reins. Turning, he threaded the leather straps through his fingers. "Thank you, lovely ladies, for the company and cookies." With a tip of his hat, he smiled and winked at Rachel. "I'll be seeing you soon."

Oh, he was smooth. Rachel crossed her arms over her chest and absently rubbed her arm. She controlled the quiver that threatened. She'd done a lot of that during this visit. Her nerves were shot.

Becky and Rachel stood silently as they watched horse and rider retreat from the yard.

"You know I'm beginning to think Mitchell's right."

She turned to Becky and looked at her questioningly.

"I do believe Jake wants to get under someone's skirt, but I don't think I have anything to worry about anymore."

A wave of dread filled her. "What do you mean?"

"I mean Jake hardly even looked at me this morning. His eyes followed your every move."

Her gaze swung back to Jake's retreating figure. He cast a look back and tipped his hat again. Okay, that clinched it. The pepper spray would be in her pocket from now on.

Chapter Seventeen

Mitchell was weary. A few days of repair turned into three. He lifted his Stetson and swiped a forearm across his sweaty brow. He hadn't planned on being gone from home this long. The fence along the west side of his property had been destroyed.

It had taken a day and a half for him and Toby to hunt down cattle and some were still missing. The other hands had stayed behind to repair fence.

"Let's take a break, Toby." Picking up his canteen, he took a long drink.

"Someone sure made a mess of things didn't they boss?"

He nodded. "Days like these I wonder if I shouldn't sell to Mr. Waters, Toby. Maybe I should take him up on his offer." Glancing down the line of fence they had worked on throughout the morning, he mumbled, "Even though I suspect Waters is the one who's causing these problems in the first place."

Toby studied him for a moment. "This ranch is worth it. I've seen what you've done over the last few years to make this place grow. This spread makes you and little Becky happy. Your mother and father would have been proud of you."

"Don't let Becky hear you call her little." He gazed into the distance at his other men repairing fence farther up the line. "Dad would have liked what the place has become." He took another swig from the canteen and recapped the lid. "I've thought about breeding horses."

Toby grinned. "Is that what you've been talking to ol' Rebel about? Bringing in a few women?"

Mitchell chuckled. "You've heard my conversations with him, huh?"

"It's hard to miss those heart-to-hearts when the barn is so quiet." Toby scratched his chin. "Is that why you've been so silent this week? You've been thinking about changes you want to make on the ranch?"

He shook his head. "Naw. I guess you could say I've had a woman on my mind."

Toby spit a stream of tobacco as he studied his face. "I knew it. The female is Miss Morgan? I could tell there were sparks flying off the two of you the other day."

"I'm not sure what you thought you saw. Sparks, maybe from me, but I'm not so sure about Rachel. That is Miss Morgan." He studied the mountains in the distance. He recalled the frightened look she had given him before running to her room after her bath. Her look had haunted him for three long days.

He had let the bath water get cold in hopes of cooling his body's urges. He couldn't remember a woman affecting his mind and body quite like this before.

Even thinking about her now had his body reacting with a gut wrenching emotion he couldn't name. "Let's get back to work, Toby. I need to be home before the dance. If I'm not back in time, Becky will have my hide!"

Chapter Eighteen

She. Was. Going. Crazy. If she had to look at another button, she was going to scream. She tied off the last one and sighed. Done.

She sat cross-legged in the front room in her old jeans and shirt. She'd finally convinced Becky to let her wear them around the ranch. Becky hadn't been happy, but Rachel needed the comfort.

Mitchell wasn't back. Becky didn't seem concerned. She put aside her sewing and rose. "I need some exercise. Is there a chore I can help with?" She had already gathered the eggs and milked the cow. Ol' Bessy, as she had started calling her, looked forward to seeing her every morning. She felt like she talked more to the cow than to Becky.

Becky had become quite and preoccupied the last couple of days. Not like the chatterbox she'd been when she had first arrived. Something was on her mind, but she hadn't shared with Rachel what was troubling her.

"You've already helped clean the house. I'm not sure what else you could help with."

"There has to be something. How about outside?"

Becky looked out the window. She wrinkled her nose. "With the guys gone, the barn stalls haven't been mucked. I doubt you want to do that."

A dose of dirty hard labor. She'd helped her dad many times cleaning the pig barn and the chicken coop on their farm in Oklahoma. Maybe that was just what the doctor ordered. "Is everything I need in the barn?"

Becky stared at her in horror. "You're not serious."

"Yes. I think I am."

"If you're determined. The tools and fresh straw are at the front of the barn in a little room."

The barn door squeaked as she opened it. The scent of hay and other earthy smells tickled her nose. Each were familiar smells from days on her parents' farm. Many times she had helped her father with chores around the farm. They'd had a few cattle, pigs, and chickens. Tears pooled as she wondered if she would ever see her parents again.

Wiping a tear from her cheek, she searched the area. The wheelbarrow, pitchfork, and shovel were propped along the front wall. Bringing the tools to the first stall, she smiled. Rebel will be happy to have a clean stall whenever they finally made it back to the ranch.

She worked steadily for a few hours. The first two stalls were finished, and she had started on the third. Searching her memory, she recalled a rock tune to sing. With a wipe of her brow, she sang into the rake handle. There was no one around to hear her so she sang with as much gusto and enthusiasm as she could muster.

Mitchell slowly lowered himself out of the saddle. "Well, boy, let's get you settled in." He slowed his approach as he neared the barn. A loud female voice echoed from inside. Was someone singing?

He paused in midstride. With a flick of his wrist, he tied Rebel's reins to the corral. He patted the horse's neck. "I'll be right back fella, just need to check out what's going on inside your home." He eased the barn door open.

He wasn't sure what he expected, but the sight that greeted his eyes stole his breath. Rachel was in one of the stalls wiggling her hips suggestively and singing loudly. He leaned his arm against the stall wall and watched as Rachel made another turn and rotated her hips in a gyrating motion.

He straightened abruptly. A strange heat unfurled in his belly. Her hips were mesmerizing. The tight fitting jeans showed her form to perfection. Was she wearing the lacy underclothing she'd worn the other night?

The words she sang were provocative, even though he didn't fully understand them. He growled low in his throat. "What do you think you're doing?"

Rachel squealed, jumped, and spun around at the gruff question. "Oh, Mitchell, you scared me to death. What are you doing here?"

"Last time I checked I live here."

Rachel stood with her hand on her chest. She waved her hand. "I know silly. What I meant to say is you're back."

"You know I could ask you the same thing. What are you doing here? You do realize I have men that do this kind of work for me." His eyes shifted to the jeans molded to her frame. The image of her behind wiggling as she had danced around the stall with the rake etched firmly into his mind.

"Well, all your men were with you, weren't they?" Her pert little nose lifted into the air.

She had a valid point. Boy, she was filthy. Dirt and sweat trails were visible on her face. "Want a hand finishing this stall? The men won't be back until later."

He grabbed the shovel leaning against the wall. "That is if you don't mind the help."

They worked in a comfortable silence. Rachel pulled the rake up and leaned on the handle. "Had you planned on being gone as long as you were?"

He teased gently, "Did you miss me?" He watched as a red hue spread across her cheeks. His pulse leaped at the thought of her possibly missing him while he had been away. "When we got out to the west side of our property the fence line had been torn down. We had to hunt down cattle and make some repairs before we came home."

"Becky had mentioned you've been having trouble with someone tearing down fences. Do you think it's the same person?"

He shook his head. "I think so, but don't know for sure."

Rachel scraped the rake across the floor. "Jake Sanders came by this week while you were away."

What the hell? His gaze tried to meet her downcast eyes. "What did Sanders want?" Unease settled in his bones. He whipped his hat off his head and raked a hand through his hair. Had Jake known he wasn't around to watch the women? Maybe the idea of taking all his men with him hadn't been his best decision. Becky knew how to handle a rifle. Did Rachel?

She shrugged her shoulders. "He claimed he was in the area checking fence and just stopped by to say hello. Plus, he was looking for a handout of Becky's cookies. Guess she has quite the reputation for her oatmeal raisin ones."

He reached out and stilled her movements. "He didn't make a nuisance of himself. Did he?"

"No. He behaved himself." She bent to hide her face and began raking again. She chuckled nervously. "The thing is Becky now has this crazy idea Jake is really into me instead of her." She glanced at him, "Ridiculous, huh?"

Jealousy slammed his gut. Dammit! Anger burned in his stomach. His irritation with Jake over Becky seemed like child's play compared to his feelings at the moment.

Did she like Sanders? He watched her eyes widen as he gravitated closer. His gaze dropped to her full pouty lips. "Not so crazy." He had fought the pull for days. He aligned her body to his and lowered his head. The moment his lips touched hers he was lost.

Rachel's eyes drifted shut as she felt fireworks and a familiarity that surprised her. The slight tickle of his mustache caused awareness to creep up her spine. Her eyes snapped open as cool air touched her damp lips. She stared into his twinkling amber gaze.

He leaned further into the embrace and eased her against the stall wall. A soft sigh escaped her lips before he claimed them again. The intensity grew as he sampled her sweetness.

Pure molten heat flowed through her veins. She felt so alive. The simple kiss had turned into a flame she wasn't prepared to handle. His arousal became apparent. Should she be afraid?

She nibbled innocently at his bottom lip. He groaned at the soft caress. His lips nibbled a trail to the soft shell of her ear. His hot breath caressed her lobe as he shifted closer.

The memory of her dream flickered and replayed in her mind. Mitchell was her dream man. The same sensations she had experienced from her fantasy were coming true. Was this just another one of her dreams? The damn dog wasn't what brought her here, but this man.

Her thoughts shattered as his hands touched bare skin. How had her shirt come untucked? No, not untucked, unbuttoned. His soft, whispering touch along her ribcage had her straining to get closer to the sweet torture. His hand finally settled on her breast and began circling her nipple in a slow, sensual dance through her bra.

She arched her body into his roaming hands as his lips captured her own. Oh, this cowboy had a talented mouth.

She meowed in denial as she felt him withdraw. "No," she gasped. She wasn't ready for this wonder to end. They had felt so right. She'd been searching her whole life to be awakened by a man's touch. This man's touch.

Mitchell gazed down at her swollen mouth. His mind barely registered she had said no. He'd never taken advantage of a woman who didn't want his caresses. What had he been thinking?

His palm rested against her right breast, and he could see the aroused nipple through her underclothes. He swallowed hard. Withdrawing his body from hers, he put some much needed distance between them. Why had he let himself get so carried away? Should he apologize for the most incredible kiss he had ever experienced in his life? He bent to pick up his hat from the floor. He dusted the hat off against his leg as he took a moment to gain control of his breath.

Chapter Nineteen

Rachel blinked. The heat was gone. What had just happened? Her eyes searched for Mitchell's, but his amber gaze instead was focused on the stall door.

Straightening, she buttoned her shirt and glared. Had he not felt anything? Men! She retrieved the forgotten tool from the floor. Slowly the cloud of passion dissipated.

Fine! If he could pretend nothing out of the usual just happened than so could she. She just needed to convince her trembling body.

"Mitchell?"

"Back here, Beck."

Rachel had been so busy fuming she had missed the squeak of the barn door opening. Was that the reason Mitchell had stopped his seduction? He had heard someone approaching. She still couldn't understand how he could turn off his passion so quickly.

Seconds later, Becky appeared in the front of the stall. Her nose wrinkled as she took both of them in. "Whew, you both smell awful."

Mitchell shoveled a load of manure into the wheelbarrow and glanced at Becky. "What? I don't receive a welcome home hug from my loving sister?" He chuckled at the look of distaste appearing on Becky's face. He winked at his sister as he leaned against the handle of the shovel. "We would be finished in no time if you would lend a helping hand."

Rachel's angry stare focused on Mitchell's back. Couldn't he act just a little befuddled? Like she was? His arousal proved he hadn't been unaffected. Didn't it? She blushed at the memory. Maybe he wasn't as immune to the encounter as his actions indicated.

"Well, both of you will need a bath before you come in for supper. I'm getting ready to start cooking."

Visions of a previous bath flashed in Rachel's head. She tampered down the image quickly.

"We're almost through in here. I'll tell Rachel how to get to the swimming hole so she can get cleaned up."

Becky backed away from the smelly stall. "I'll put fresh clothes out on the porch for both of you."

Mitchell grinned and looked at her for the first time since the kiss. "Beck has a slight aversion to horse manure and sweat."

She gave a husky laugh. "You don't say."

"I'll have the men finish this job tomorrow. I'm sure you're ready to call it quits for the day." He averted his eyes as he finished, "I'm hot and sure could use a swim."

Rachel was sizzling, but the sensation wasn't from cleaning the stall. She could use a cooling down. Her thoughts didn't chill, though, as they turned to skinny-dipping with a hunky cowboy. She fanned herself. One steamy encounter had corrupted her.

She watched as Mitchell led Rebel into his stall and removed the saddle. The horse munched noisily on the fresh bucket of oats provided. Was he just going to ignore her? "Um, I'll just go and get a change of clothes." She glanced down and grimaced.

Not meeting Rachel's eyes, he continued to stroke Rebel as he timidly indicated with his other hand. "The swimming hole isn't too far over the hill in a grove of trees behind the barn. I don't think you can miss the lake. I'll let you get cleaned up first."

Well, so much for her skinny-dipping fantasy. He just burst that bubble. With a sigh, she made her way to the porch where Becky had left some clothes, soap, and towel. She held the pile carefully away from her filthy body as she found the path Mitchell had indicated.

The trail was on a slight incline, and she found the climb robbed her breath. She hadn't realized how out of shape she'd become. Turning a corner, she gasped as she caught her first glimpse of the pond. The setting was so serene. Aspens and pines lined the far shore. She drew in a deep breath and let the scents invade her senses. A slight breeze caused a ripple to graze the water and erase the reflection of the mountains looming in the distance.

To her left a boulder jutted out into the water. A natural diving board. She smiled at the thought of Becky and Mitchell jumping off the rock into the water as young children.

She placed her bathing items on the rock and made a quick study of the area. Trepidation crept down her spine. The spot was secluded, but how comfortable was she shedding her clothes?

After a few moments arguing the pros and cons, she took off her dirty jeans and stained shirt. A cool breeze had her gasping as she paused in her green bra and underwear. Dipping a big toe into the water, she squealed. Holy cow! The water was downright chilly.

Taking a brave breath, she waded out waist deep

into the water and plunged under. An icy chill invaded her limbs instantly. Resurfacing she puffed as the air hit her wet skin. This was crazy.

A few laps across the small pond had her body invigorated by the cool water. Flipping to her back she slowly backstroked toward the boulder. She loved the feel of the cool water caressing her body. She felt so alive and sensual. Mitchell had caused this awareness.

Back at the boulder, she grabbed the bar of soap and lathered her body and hair. Sinking down into the water, she rinsed the soap hastily from her body. The breeze chilled her as she stepped from the lake. She quickly dried off and wrapped the towel about her body. The lingering sun danced along her skin and warmed her further.

She wrinkled her nose as she lifted her filthy clothes and leaned down to dunk them into the pond. As she scrubbed, peacefulness settled within her. Soon her clothes were drying and she stretched out, flipped open the towel and let the sun's rays dry her undergarments. Closing her eyes, she sighed as the warmth from the sun kissed her skin.

Waking abruptly, Rachel leaned up on her elbows. Had she been snoring? Is that what had disturbed her catnap? Fear raced down her backbone. She reached for her fresh blouse and fumbled with the buttons in her haste. Someone was watching.

Standing, she grabbed her skirt and quickly pulled it on. Sitting back down, she made short work of pulling her socks and boots on. Grabbing the discarded towel and her now clean clothes, she turned to trot down the trail. Hastily she peeked over her shoulder back toward the pond as she turned the bend in the trail.

Nothing appeared to be amiss. Rolling her shoulders, she tried to calm her unsettled nerves.

Intent eyes watched Rachel's retreating figure from the safety of the trees. He smiled as he relished his good fortune. When he had begun his silent vigil, he hadn't expected to see what he had witnessed. The vivid small green undergarments Rachel had revealed barely covered a body as lush as he had imagined. As soon as she unbuttoned her shirt, he had been like a statue, afraid to move or make a noise that would alert her to his presence. Even though she hadn't revealed her entire body to his watchful eyes, a wave of lust had hit his gut so hard he had hardly breathed the whole time he had watched her bathe. Once he saw she had dozed off while soaking up the sun, he had quietly moved closer to observe and drink his fill of her lush body.

He waved a bug away from his brow. She was going to be his. Reeves wasn't claiming this prize. Shaking his head, he slowly rose to his feet. His legs protested. He'd been crouched too long. Making his way back to where he had tied his horse, he grabbed the reins and swung gracefully into the saddle. One last glance toward the lake brought another smile to his face as he slowly swung his mount around and left the peaceful pond.

Chapter Twenty

Holding the romance novel she had retrieved from her purse, Rachel sat on the porch. The last few minutes she had stared at the book, not reading a single line. She kept imagining Mitchell bathing at the pond. She peeked at the path. He'd been gone for quite awhile.

Her gaze skimmed the handsome pirate and his beautiful captive on the cover. Mentally, she visualized Mitchell as the pirate and herself as the imprisoned damsel.

"What are you doing?" Mitchell stood on the top step observing her.

Rachel squeaked and jumped. "Boy, you scared me. I didn't hear you." She shifted and hid the book from his gaze.

He leaned over and snatched the paperback from her hands. "What is this?"

She peeped at the scantily dressed woman in the bright yellow dress and half clad man. "A book."

He quirked an eyebrow, held the paper book up, and opened his mouth to speak. Becky chose that moment to open the door to announce supper.

Becky studied first Mitchell then Rachel. "I'm glad both of you are looking a little cleaner than I last saw you. I'm not sure I could have handled any more manure smell."

Rachel rose from the chair and snatched the book

from Mitchell's grasp. "I'll be in the kitchen in just a moment." She hurried down the hall to store the book. She jumped as she caught a movement from the corner of her eye. Mitchell leaned in the doorway with his arms crossed.

He wasn't having a problem meeting her gaze as he had earlier. "You never answered my question. What type of book was that?"

She fingered her skirt. "A romance novel. I enjoy reading them when I have the time."

"A dime novel? I've never seen a cover quite like that. Where did you get it?"

She hid her frustration. "I've told you I'm from the future, but you choose not to believe me. I had the paperback in my purse when I traveled in time." She could see the skepticism radiating from him. Why had she said anything?

Mitchell shoved himself away from the doorframe and announced, "Supper's getting cold. Let's go eat."

The funk Becky had been in the last few days wasn't evident during supper. She kept up most of the conversation as they sat around the table. If she noticed Rachel and Mitchell didn't say much, she didn't let on. "Mitchell, could we practice dancing tonight? I don't want to make a fool of myself tomorrow at the dance."

Rachel grinned. "She just doesn't want to make a fool of herself in front of a certain gentleman."

Mitchell's questioning gaze bounced between both women. Becky sat blushing and speechless. "Is this true Beck, are you sweet on someone?"

If possible, Becky's cheeks became a little brighter at Mitchell's question. "Well, Jim did ask me to save him a dance."

Confusion creased his forehead. Turning to Rachel, he lifted his brow in question.

Wiping her mouth with her napkin Rachel answered his silent question. "Jim. Mr. Jones asked Becky to save him a dance when we were purchasing material at his store."

He was silent for a moment until recognition registered. "You mean Mr. Jones who owns the mercantile?"

Becky's chest puffed up in anger and she pointed a finger at her brother. "Don't you dare tell me you don't approve of Jim!"

He held up his hands in self-defense. "I didn't say that, I'm just surprised." He smiled. "I'll be happy to help you dust off your dancing shoes and polish your skills."

Becky squealed and jumped to her feet. "I'll just go clear an area for us to move around."

Mitchell watched as Becky rushed from the room. "Well, I wasn't expecting that."

Rachel chuckled. "What, she likes a man? Or a man likes her?"

His eyes glittered in amusement and he chuckled, "Both!"

She fingered her napkin and placed it beside her plate. "Um, Mitchell, I need to ask a favor of you, as well." At his questioning look she continued, "I need a little help learning how to dance." Of course, she knew how to dance, but the dancing she knew was sure to raise a few brows if she was to demonstrate her moves tomorrow night. She tried not to giggle at the thought.

Mitchell sat a moment in silence and just stared at her in wonder. "How old are you?"

Rachel frowned and squirmed as he stared at her. What did her age have to do with anything? "I'm twenty-four. Why?"

His gaze bounced off her features a moment before he answered, "I find it amazing such a beautiful young woman doesn't know how to dance. Or you've never been asked to dance."

Had he just described her as beautiful? "I didn't say I've never been asked to dance or I don't know how." Crossing her arms across her chest she huffed. "I just don't know how to do the dances from your time."

He stiffened. "What do you mean? In my time? He shrugged his shoulders as he asked, "Dancing is dancing, isn't it?"

She smirked. Oh what she wouldn't give to do a little dirty dancing or salsa with the specimen sitting across from her. Then what would he think?

Becky rushed back into the kitchen and motioned for them to get up from the table. "Come on. I have everything moved out of the way."

As Rachel snuggled later in bed, she smiled as she recalled Mitchell teaching her to waltz. When she had felt his hand upon her waist, she had blindly stepped on his booted foot. By the end of the lesson, she had mastered the waltz. She hoped he would save a dance for her tomorrow night. Becky had told her that her brother was quite popular with the ladies.

Chapter Twenty-One

Rachel awoke alarmed. Unlike recent dreams of her fantasy man, this one worried her. She glanced around the bedroom and shivered. The images had seemed so real, as if Jake had been in the room with her.

He had loomed over her, trying to steal kisses and he hadn't been gentle. She shook her head trying to dislodge the vision.

Moments later, she exited the bedroom. The house was quiet as she crossed the front room. Opening the door, she glanced at the sky as the sun began ascending into the sky. Taking a deep breath of the brisk air, her mind finally cleared. She studied the diminishing morning shadows hovering over the yard.

This time of day had been a favorite of Angie's and hers. They had spent several dawns watching the sunrise.

She missed Angie like crazy, her confidant and best friend. If only she could call her mom to get her motherly advice as well. What a mess. She'd debated on confiding in Becky over the last few day, but her brother didn't believe her, why would she?

Her thoughts turned to Mitchell and the kiss they had shared in the barn yesterday. Those feelings had been so unexpected. What would Angie say about the situation she found herself?

Was Mitchell the man she had been searching for to share her life? How could her special someone be from the past and not from the present where she belonged? Should she continue to search for a way to get back or should she accept her situation and just live? Shifting her chin to her other knee she wondered if she could be happy here if she didn't find her way home.

Would she ever see Angie again? The longer she was here the more she was convinced getting back to her time wasn't in the cards.

She angrily brushed away the tears trailing down her cheeks. What if Mitchell never cared for her? The way she was beginning to feel for him. She couldn't live on Becky and Mitchell's generosity forever. Would a day come when she was no longer welcome to stay? Then what would she do? Where would she go?

Lost in her thoughts, she didn't hear Becky open the front door and approach.

"You have such a serious look on your face. You look miles away."

"Try years away," Rachel muttered.

"Can I join you?" Becky studied her after she sat down. "Have you been crying?"

She shrugged her shoulders. "I had a small case of feeling sorry for myself. I'm better now." She swiped the remaining tears away. "I couldn't sleep. How about you?"

"No. Too excited about today I guess. I've always liked the Independence Day celebration."

They sat silently for a moment. Becky sighed. "I'm a good listener if you need to talk about what's bothering you. I know I talk a lot, but I can also listen."

Rachel watched as Chet crossed the yard and padded up the steps. "I may take you up on the offer Becky, but probably not this morning."

Becky gave the dog a pat on the head. "I guess we should be preparing our lunches for the church's box auction today."

"What are you talking about?"

"Did I forget to tell you about the church box auction? Silly me. That is just as much fun as the dance. All the women make a picnic lunch and decorate the box. The highest bidder wins lunch with you. The event is a lot of fun."

Heaving a frustrated sigh, she exclaimed, "Becky why didn't you tell me this before today? What am I supposed to cook for a picnic?"

"Don't panic! We will keep the meal simple. Some fried chicken, biscuits, and something for the sweet tooth."

"Glad you have a plan." Observing the sun, she asked, "Don't you think we need to get started if we're going to get the food prepared in time?"

The aroma of fried chicken filled the kitchen. Rachel's earlier melancholy had disappeared. "What should I make for dessert? I'm sure you're making your famous cookies?"

Becky grinned cheekily. "That's what everyone expects me to bring. I'm kind of well-known for them. Do you want to make a pie?"

She tapped her finger to her lip. "Do you have any canned peaches?"

"I think we have some in the pantry. Are you going to make a peach pie?"

"I'm going to make my mother's peach cobbler

recipe."

Twenty minutes later, she placed her dessert into the cook stove. Becky entered the kitchen carrying two boxes big enough for their meals. "I brought some scrap material to decorate our boxes."

Rachel surveyed the different colored ginghams and chose a light blue print. Laying the material on the table, she wondered why Mitchell hadn't made an appearance. "Where's Mitchell?"

Becky paused in decorating. "Oh, he was up before dawn. He left early for town to help set up for the day's activities. Toby will drive us into town." She examined Rachel's finished box. "Why don't you get dressed. I'll bring your cobbler out when it's ready."

Holding her handheld mirror from her purse, she studied her reflection. The dark green fabric of her dress deepened the color of her eyes, which shimmered with excitement. Smoothing a hand down the soft fabric, she had to admit she hadn't done a bad job of sewing the dress with Becky's help. Placing her hands in her pockets, she swung around gently to watch the hem swirl about her soft leather boots. Would Mitchell like how she looked?

She saw a small brown wrapped package with her name written on it. Gently lifting the parcel, she untied the twine that held the present together.

She revealed a dark green ribbon nestled softly in the paper. Mitchell must have left it for her. She smiled softly as she lifted her hair off her neck and slipped the ribbon underneath. She tugged gently, finished the bow, and picked up the mirror again to inspect her hair. Of course, the style exposed her elf ears, which she was self-conscience about, but the ribbon went perfectly with her dress.

In the process of placing the mirror in her purse, a vision of her disturbing dream from the morning had her grabbing the small container of pepper spray and placing the tube in her dress pocket. Boy scouts weren't the only ones who were always prepared.

A knock sounded. "Are you ready, Rachel? Toby has the wagon pulled up front."

Toby bestowed a smile to each as they descended the front steps. "I get the pleasure of driving the two prettiest ladies into town. I'm a lucky man."

Becky chuckled and tapped Toby on his arm. "You are such a flirt."

"Flirt or not, I'm still a lucky man. Let me give you a hand up Miss Becky, Miss Rachel." Taking their decorated boxes from each lady, he held them up and took a delighted whiff. "Both of these smell delicious. I might have to bid on both just so I can have lunch with the prettiest women in town."

Rachel glanced down from the seat to see Toby wink up at her before he climbed into the wagon seat beside her.

Becky smiled. "Thank you, Toby, but I'm sure the widow Peterson would be very disappointed if you didn't buy her lunch."

Toby picked up the reins and clicked his tongue. "Well, I wouldn't want to disappoint Mrs. Peterson now would I?" He tossed another wink at both of the women as they started toward town.

A light breeze brought a pleasant fragrance of pine and flowers from the meadow to her nose as the wagon rattled into town. Toby and Becky carried most of the conversation. She just listened in amusement.

The big tree stood proud as they passed. She wanted to stick out her tongue. Shifting in her seat, she shoved her predicament into the back of her mind. The day was too gorgeous to let her worry ruin everything.

Durango was bursting with activity when they arrived. People were in their best clothing and had come out in droves for the Independence celebration. Men greeted friends and neighbors while mothers kept a watchful eye on their children. Everyone's cares and troubles were on hold, just for a few hours if not the full day.

Toby pulled the wagon to a stop in front of a small white church. Rachel watched as women rushed about placing boxes of many different sizes, shapes, and colors on the tables set up on the lawn under a huge shade tree. The display was as pretty as a vibrant rainbow.

After assisting Rachel and Becky down from the wagon, Toby retrieved their lunches. "You ladies have a wonderful time today." He glanced up at the clear blue sky. "It's a beautiful day!"

The aromas coming from each of the containers had Rachel's mouth watering as she placed her box on the table. "I'm not sure my lunch smells as good as some of these. The men are going to have a hard time deciding which one they want to bid on."

Smiling Becky looped her arm through hers. "I'm sure you will have a pleasant lunch with whoever wins." Glancing about the lawn, Becky asked, "Do you want to go see what kind of activities the town has planned for the day?"

"Is there some kind of flier with a list of activities?"

Becky nodded. "They usually have them posted around town.

They found a poster attached to a post outside the churchyard. A few events looked interesting. Smiling, she turned to Becky. "I would like to see someone kiss a pig. How do they pick the participants?"

Becky worried her lip in concentration. "The citizens choose them. You place coins in the jar of the person you want to win. The person with the most change in their jar at the end of the contest wins the privilege of kissing the pig. Do you want to go see who has been chosen for the contest?"

She smiled. "Let's go."

A few minutes later, she studied the four jars lined up on a table. "Do you know all of these people?"

Becky scanned the name written on a piece of paper in front of the first container. "Bill Silver, he is the owner of the Silver Spur Saloon." Becky studied the rest of the jars. "Doc Brown. He's the one who checked out your bump. I'm not sure who this Travis McCloud is, but we both know who Jake Sanders is." She turned and giggled. "I would love to see Jake kiss a pig. Let's put our money in his jar, shall we?"

She smothered a giggle. "Too bad I don't have spare change. I would fill that puppy up."

Becky stared at her in confusion, her brow furrowed. "Puppy. What puppy?"

With a flip of her hand, she tried to explain. "Oh, you know. I would fill the jar clear to the top. It's just an expression," she finished quietly.

Nodding in understanding Becky reached into her handbag. "Well, we are in luck. I just happened to bring some extra change I can spare."

As the coins clinked against the sides of Jake's jar, both girls laughed.

Becky controlled her mirth. "Let's find Mitchell. We need to wish him and Rebel good luck in the race."

On their way to find Mitchell, they paused to watch a pie-eating contest. Rachel chuckled as she watched a young man stuff almost a whole pie into his mouth. She shook her head at his antics and prayed he didn't choke. His opponent grabbed his mouth and disappeared from the table suddenly. The young man grinned with his cheeks bulging as his hand was risen in victory by one of the judges.

A short distance away, Mitchell paused in readying Rebel as he spied Rachel in the crowd. He watched her laugh with his sister. His eyes roamed over her features. Her curls stirred from the slight breeze. A quick image of Rachel, her hair mussed as he held her in his arms yesterday in the barn, entered his mind. Both of them had seemed to be enjoying the moment, but as he had drawn away, Rachel had murmured *no*. Had she not enjoyed the kiss at all? Shaking his head, he pulled his Stetson off and ran a frustrated hand through his hair. That single word, no, had replayed repeatedly in his mind last night. Sleep had not come easily.

He jumped slightly as a hand ran up the length of his back and down to wrap around his waist. Turning slightly, he glanced down to encounter a steady blue stare. Lucy from the Silver Spur didn't blink as she studied him intently.

A coy smile graced her lips. "Good morning, Mitchell. You're looking none the worse for wear after your little tussle with Sanders the other night." Her heavy lidded gaze began a slow journey up from

Mitchell's booted feet, over his chest to peer into his amber eyes. Drawing a finger over his lips, she murmured, "Such a shame. I believe I would have liked to play nurse if you would only have asked."

He cleared his throat. "Good morning, Lucy. No, as you can see no permanent damage. I'm almost back to my old self."

"Well, I'm sorry to hear that, Mitchell." Her lip protruded as she pouted. Trailing a fingertip down his chest, she said, "You know where to find me if you have a relapse and are in need of any nursing."

He watched her saunter away. Lucy was a very attractive woman. For over a year she had been hinting she would like for him to visit her, and he knew she wasn't looking for conversation. Why didn't he feel any attraction toward her? Rachel, on the other hand, made him feel like he was out of control and on fire whenever he got near. He sighed heavily in frustration. Women!

Rachel spied Mitchell with a scantily clad saloon girl. Was that the same girl from the other day? She watched as the girl drew her hand down Mitchell's chest, turned, and saucily swung her hips as she walked away. Rachel frowned and twisted away from the scene in confusion. Slivers of jealousy raced down her spine as she drew in a deep breath. She had hoped after the shared kiss in the barn Mitchell had developed some feelings. He was such a charming, nice looking man. He had his pick of women according to Becky. Why would he settle for someone he thought was crazy?

Rachel felt his presence before he spoke.

"You know Becky I'm disappointed there isn't a pie throwing contest. You would make a wonderful target."

Becky turned to deliver a slug to her brother's arm. "The only way that would happen is if I had the chance to return the favor and throw a few pies at your face."

Rachel watched the exchange through lowered lashes. She cleared her suddenly parched throat. "Morning, Mitchell. Becky tells me you have entered Rebel in a horse race."

He nodded. "Are you ladies planning on coming over to watch? We line up in about half an hour."

She chuckled lightly. "Oh, I don't know. Becky and I had our hearts set on watching the women over at the church quilt instead of watching a dull and boring horse race." She grinned and winked.

Mitchell sucked in his breath and swallowed hard as he watched her dimples appear and disappear. He took in the amusement shining from her eyes before he cleared his throat and answered, "Is that so? Have you told Rebel your plans? I think his feelings will be hurt if you are not there to cheer him on."

"Well, I guess we wouldn't want to hurt Rebel's feelings now would we, Becky? I guess we could take a minute out of our busy schedule to come watch."

"Rebel appreciates the support." He turned and looked over the crowd. "What activities have you seen this morning?"

Becky reached up to stifle a giggle with her hand. "Oh, Mitchell, have you ever seen the kiss the pig contest? We put some coins in the jar of who we thought deserved to win. I just wish I had more coins to put in."

He arched his brow. "Whose jar did you choose?"

Two sets of eyes sparkled with glee as he heard them both say simultaneously, "Jake's!"

Mitchell's deep laugh drew a few eyes from people passing by. "Oh, I can't think of a more deserving person." Scanning the crowd, he noticed participants preparing their horses. "The race will be starting shortly. I need to finish getting Rebel ready. I'll see you ladies later at the church box luncheon." As Mitchell turned to leave, he paused and looked back toward Becky. "Can I have a word with you?"

Taking a few steps away from Rachel's questioning gaze, Mitchell turned and leaned in to ask Becky softly, "How did Rachel decorate her lunch box? Can you give me a hint? I want to know which box to bid on at the auction?"

"Why Mr. Reeves wouldn't that be cheating?"

He let a frustrated growl escape. "Becky!"

Becky grinned. Pushing up to her toes, she whispered into his ear.

Mitchell kissed his sister's forehead and murmured, "Thanks Becky, I owe you one." Smiling, he tipped his hat to Rachel and walked away.

Rachel fanned herself as she ogled Mitchell's retreating backside. What that man did to a pair of pants should be illegal. She tilted her head and eyed Becky. "What was that all about?"

Becky smiled brightly and tapped a finger on Rachel's shoulder. "You will just have to wait and see. Let's go find a place to watch the race. I hope there is a good spot close to the finish line."

As they wove through the gathering crowd, a small cloud of dust arose amongst the riders as they jockeyed their horses into position at the starting line.

Rachel was jostled slightly as she viewed the various horses and riders. Both exuded an anticipation that was barely contained. She gasped as her eyes collided with Jake Sanders' intent gaze.

He casually leaned across his saddle horn and stared at her unflinchingly. Suddenly his lips quirked into a small smile and he lifted a hand to tip his hat in her direction. Rachel gazed about distractedly, was he tipping his hat at her? Glancing back, she nodded her head reluctantly in acknowledgement and shifted her eyes away from his dark intent gaze. She bit her lip uncertainly. She hoped he hadn't thought she was seeking his attention.

Mitchell sat erect and tall in his saddle talking to a young cowboy a few feet away. He held Rebel in check with an easy steady grace. Even from this distance, she could sense a male power radiating from him.

A nudge from Becky's elbow brought her out of her revelry. "I think the race is about to begin. There's the mayor."

Becky pointed, indicating a portly man who stood to the side of the starting line. He held a small pistol in his hand. He pulled a pocket watch from his waistcoat and consulted the time. Raising his voice, he yelled above the excited crowd. "Gentlemen, we've been blessed with a mighty fine day. I want everyone to run a clean race today." He paused in his speech as he waited for the riders to nod in ascent.

"The course we have laid out is simple. Yellow ribbons mark the path. You will ride a mile out of town, turn around at Edwards bend, and head back into town where the starting line will also serve as the finish line. Does everyone understand?" He backed away from the racers and lifted the pistol into the air. "Ready? Set. Go!"

Rachel jumped at the loud discharge. The riders spurred their horses simultaneously at the loud report. She watched as Mitchell gently urged Rebel into an easy run. "Come on, Rebel, go," she silently encouraged under her breath.

Rachel watched as they disappeared from view. She turned to Becky. "How long will the race take?"

"Not long at all."

Chapter Twenty-Two

Dust swirled and hung heavy in the air as the riders made their way out of town. Mitchell squinted and pulled a bandana up to cover his mouth. The rider in front of the pack was in view. Slowly he edged past another rider. The cowboy cursed, and his mount's labored breath pounded in his ears. Leaning down, he whispered encouraging words into Rebel's ears. The horse tweaked his ears listening intently.

A loud snort from his left drew his attention. Giving a quick glance toward the rider, Mitchell realized Sanders was getting ready to pass. He smiled behind his bandana as he watched Sanders ease past. He wasn't too concerned. He would bide his time. Rebel was in his element, and he had yet to give him his lead.

In the distance, a large yellow flag flapped lively in the breeze. Giving a quick glance over his shoulder, he noted Sanders and himself were a good distance from the other riders. As they approached the one-mile mark, Jake turned his mount easily around the flag, and he followed with just as much ease.

The distance between Jake's horse and his own dissipated as he slowly eased Rebel forward. He noted Jake's horse was tiring, probably from running full out from the beginning of the race. Taking advantage of that exertion, he slowly let Rebel have his lead. The stallion's muscles bunched powerfully under him as he maneuvered past Sanders.

A loud curse reached his ears as he pulled ahead of Jake just on the outskirts of town.

A cheer burst forth from the crowd as Mitchell and Jake raced back into town. The finish was going to be close. Within inches of the ribbon, Rebel inched forward and crossed first. He'd won! By a nose.

Mitchell reined Rebel in, yanked down the bandana covering his mouth, gave a loud shout, and threw his Stetson into the air. Dismounting quickly, he leaned in to pick up his hat and gave another whoop of joy. Giving Rebel a celebrative pat along his sweat-covered neck, he glanced about the crowd looking for Rachel.

He shook hands with the crowd as they congratulated him, as he continued to keep an eye out for Rachel and Becky.

He turned in expectation as he felt a possessive hand run the length of his arm. He froze in shock as Lucy from the Silver Spur grabbed his neck, a fistful of his shirt and brought his lips down to her own. She gently sucked on his lower lip as she pulled away.

"Let me be the first to congratulate you appropriately, Cowboy." Slowly she dropped her arm from around his neck and gave him a sly look. Flicking her hair over her shoulder, she smiled coyly, turned, and sauntered off.

Rachel froze. That lip lock had looked serious.

"Come on, Rachel. We've got to congratulate Mitchell and Rebel."

She followed slowly behind and fumed. He'd already received his good wishes.

"Good race, Reeves."

Mitchell eyed Jake's outstretched hand for a

moment before clasping it grudgingly. "You too, Sanders. A very good race."

His sister broke through the crowd and launched herself at him. Wrapping her arms about her brother, she gave him a huge hug. "You did it! Oh, that was exciting!"

Rachel hung back. She chewed on her lower lip as she replayed in her mind the saloon girl's kiss. Had he enjoyed her attention more than what they'd shared in the barn?

"Good morning, Rachel. How are you this fine morning?"

She startled and turned to see Jake with his hat in his hands studying her intently. She had been so deep in thought she hadn't noticed him standing nearby. Her gaze shifted to Jake's dark fixed stare. "Good morning, Jake." She shifted away slightly from his body. He invaded her personal space. "That was an exciting race."

"Yes. A thrilling ride." His eyes flickered with some hidden message she couldn't decipher.

She shivered as his gaze left her own and scanned her body.

"You are looking rather lovely today, Rachel. Is that a new dress?"

She glanced down to assure herself a wardrobe malfunction hadn't happened. The way Jake was staring at her bosom she thought something might be exposed. "Thank you, Jake. Yes, it is a new dress."

He opened his mouth to reply but was interrupted by the mayor.

"Ladies and gentlemen, may I have your attention please?" The gathering quieted as they turned to where the mayor stood on a raised platform. "I would like to present the reward to the winner of the horse race at this time. Young man come on up and join me."

Mitchell handed Rebel's reins to a smiling Becky and threaded through the crowd to climb onto the stand.

The mayor reached out and shook Mitchell's hand. "Congratulations, young man. As Mayor of Durango I present you with your cash prize."

As Mitchell exited the stage, the mayor cleared his throat and shouted over the rising voices.

"Before everyone takes off for other activities, I would like to announce the winner of the kiss the pig contest." Reaching into his pants pocket, he pulled a piece of paper. "Our winner is Jake Sanders."

Jake had been in the process of handing over his horse to a stable boy when he heard his name. "What the hell?"

The mayor pointed. "Are you Jake Sanders? Congratulations, son, you've won the kiss the pig contest. You need to be over at the booth in half an hour."

Jake's eyes narrowed dangerously as he watched the mayor waddle away. He turned and cleared his throat. "Rachel would you do me the honor of accompanying me over to the booth where I get to kiss a pig?" He extended his arm. "I've won the good fortune of doing so."

Rachel wrestled with the bubble of laughter wanting to emerge. She glanced up to see amusement in Jake's gaze. Not the cold hard stare she'd witnessed before.

Jake extended his arm again. "Shall we?"

With a fleeting glance over her shoulder, she

observed Mitchell in deep conversation with someone. He didn't even seem aware of her existence. Apparently, the saloon girl had more of a lasting impression than she had. She didn't even have the chance to congratulate him. If he could pretend she didn't exist, then so could she. Lifting her chin, she placed her arm through Jakes and turned to Becky.

"Becky, Jake is escorting me to the pig kissing booth. We are in the midst of the winner of the contest. Would you like to walk over with us?"

"Well congratulations, Jake." Becky's eyes gleamed with merriment. "I think I will wait on Mitchell. You go ahead, and I will meet you shortly."

Out of the corner of his eye, Mitchell saw Jake lead Rachel away. He broke off his conversation abruptly. Was Sanders making a move on his woman right in front of him? He seethed inwardly. Why would Rachel even go with Sanders? The impression she had led him to believe was she didn't care for Jake or the attention he paid her. His gaze flew to Becky's as she gently touched his arm.

"Jake doesn't mean anything to Rachel, you know."

His stare followed Rachel's retreating form. She laughed at something Jake said, and the light husky sound carried softly on the breeze. He grumbled, "Doesn't look that way from where I'm standing."

Becky reached up and brushed his upper lip.

"What are you doing?"

"I didn't know red was a lip rouge you preferred?"

Oh damn. Lucy. Had Rachel seen the kiss? He ran a frustrated hand down his face.

"You wouldn't be in this pickle if you would just

tell her how you feel."

He frowned. "Exactly how do you know how I feel?"

Becky shrugged her shoulders. "Mitchell, your behavior is obvious to me because I'm your sister. Who knows you better than I do?" Pulling on his arm, she tried leading him in the direction Rachel had taken. "I believe we'll find Jake kissing a pig quite entertaining. Come on. Walk with me. Watching the smooch will be fun." Lifting his hand, he took a moment to massage his taut neck muscles before he answered, "I'll be along in a moment. I need to find Toby. He was going to make sure Rebel was taken care of at the stable for me."

Becky slowly backed away. "Well, you had better not be late to the lunch auction. Because if you don't bid on Rachel's box, I know who will be eating fried chicken with her instead of you."

He growled low in his throat. "That's not going to happen. Don't worry. I'll be there! Sanders isn't going to have the opportunity to enjoy the lunch or the company I've been looking forward to all morning!"

Becky shook her head and suddenly bumped into someone. "Oh, excuse me. I'm sorry." Looking up she found herself peering into the blue eyes of Jim Jones.

He placed his hands on her arms to steady her. "Whoa. Are you okay?"

Why hadn't she ever noticed how blue his eyes were before? He was holding her arms gently, and the warmth from his grasp sent a slight tremor up her arms. "I'm sorry, Mr. Jones. I didn't mean to run you down."

He seemed reluctant to release her. "No harm done, at least to me anyway."

"Oh, I'm fine, Mr. Jones." She missed the warmth

from his hands the minute he drew them away.

He smiled. "Are you enjoying the festivities?"

"Why, yes. Did you see my brother win the horse race?"

"I wasn't able to see the race. I bet your brother was pretty excited about winning."

She nodded. "The end was exciting. I was just on my way to see Jake Sanders kiss a pig."

"Mind if I escort you? But only if you call me Jim."

"I will let you if you call me Becky…Jim." She shyly lowered her lashes and accepted his offered arm.

"You look very becoming in your new dress, Becky."

She felt her cheeks heat at the compliment. "Thank you."

Rachel stood off to the side of the pen where the mayor had led Jake. He had been a perfect gentleman on the walk over. As well as pleasant and amusing. Nonthreatening. Tilting her head, she studied him unobserved from the small distance that separated them. What unseen force made her uneasy? His charm was only surface deep. Something about the man didn't ring true. No matter how charming and funny he tried to be.

Not wanting to be caught observing him, she scanned the citizens waiting. She spied Becky approaching on Mr. Jones' arm. She hid a smile with her hand. Becky was radiant. The right man brings out a certain glow in a woman.

Speaking of the right man, where was Mitchell? She scrutinized the crowd but didn't spot him. Jealousy reared. He's probably off with his saloon woman celebrating. She shook her head. What was happening?

Bitterness didn't suit her.

Becky grinned at Rachel as they approached. "Guess the donation we placed in the jar paid off."

Rachel shook off her melancholy thoughts and joined Becky in laughter.

Rachel wiped tears from her eyes. The laughter felt good. She'd needed that bit of fun. She felt better.

Amusement rumbled through the gathering as a small pig ran into the enclosure where Jake stood expectantly.

"Oh, how cute." Rachel observed the adorable piglet with a huge pink bow tied around its neck. The animal smacked its lips and grunted as he gazed at the crowd.

A loud squeal rent the air as Jake sneaked up and grabbed the pig from behind. He struggled with the squirming bundle for a moment before planting a smack on its snout.

Jake's eyes briefly caught hers before releasing his prisoner. Amid the cheers and clapping, Jake took a low bow.

From the back of the crowd a boisterous cowboy yelled, "Well done."

Jake swaggered over to where Rachel waited. Tipping his black hat upward he smoothly asked, "Can I interest you into having lunch with me?"

She smiled. "Uh, Jake, you have a small amount of dirt on your lip." She indicated with her hand where on her own lips.

He watched as her fingers brushed her lips before he reached into a pocket for a bandana. Quirking his mouth, he asked, "Better?"

Oh, Jake Sanders had charisma. No wonder Becky

had been confused about Mitchell's opinion of Jake. Sometimes he was charm personified.

"Yes, much better. I'm sorry, Jake, but I can't have lunch with you. I made a box lunch for the church auction."

He winked and caressed an imaginary mustache. "Well, tell me which one is yours and I will buy it."

Becky tapped him on the arm. "That's cheating, Jake. You'll just have to see if you can't figure it out. Come on, Rachel, we probably should go see if the ladies need any help getting ready for the picnic."

His eyes darkened and narrowed briefly, before he tipped his hat and smiled. "Until lunch then, ladies."

Before Rachel had taken a few steps to follow Becky, Mr. Jones halted her progress.

"A word Miss Morgan."

"What can I do for you Mr. Jones?"

"I don't want to be accused of being a cheat, but can you give me a hint on which box is Becky's?"

Rachel watched as a smiling Mr. Jones walked away whistling a soft tune. She didn't feel guilty about giving a blossoming romance a hand.

"What was that about?"

"Mr. Jones was just making sure you had prepared a box for him to purchase."

The churchyard bustled with activity. After inquiring on what they could do to help, they assisted in serving drinks to the people waiting.

Rachel handed a young man a cup of water and looked over the people milling about. Where was Mitchell?

"What's the matter, Rachel?"

Nibbling on her lower lip, she glanced at Becky.

"Oh, nothing really." She turned to ladle some water into a cup held out by a little girl. "I just thought Mitchell was coming to the lunch, but I haven't seen him."

"He had to go find Toby and take care of Rebel after the race. Don't worry he will be here." Becky paused and then stumbled ahead. "Rachel, do you have feelings for my brother?"

Oh boy! Did she have feelings? Or was her reaction a craving? She shrugged her shoulders. "Yes, I guess you could call it that. I'm not sure he feels the same." She sighed. "Did you see the PDOA after the race with the saloon girl?"

"PDOA?"

"You know. Public display of affection." At Becky's blank look she explained, "The kiss."

Before Becky had the chance to reply, someone was banging a pan getting everyone's attention. The auction was about to begin.

"Ladies and gentlemen, I'm glad you could come out today for the festivities. I hope everyone is having a pleasant day so far. I'm going to say a brief prayer, and then I will turn the auction over to Mr. Clement."

Mr. Clement stopped in front of the table laden with boxes. "There are some most pleasing smells coming from these boxes gentlemen. I hope everyone has come hungry and ready to participate. The money from today's auction will help pay for new books needed for the school." He picked up a brightly decorated box from the table. "We'll start with this pretty one right here. Who wants to start the bidding?"

The boxes disappeared off the table at a fast rate. Soon Mr. Clement held Becky's box in his hands.

"Well now, this one smells delicious. I may just have to bid on this one myself." He smiled at the crowd as they voiced their disapproval. "Let's start this box at two bits."

Rachel watched Becky anxiously glance around at the crowd. Voices bounced about until she heard Mr. Clement say sold.

A smiling Mr. Jones approached to claim his box and his lunch date.

A small bubble of envy churned in Rachel's stomach as she watched the smiling couple step away arm in arm. She was pleased Jim was able to buy Becky's box. The hint she had given him had paid off.

Chapter Twenty-Three

Mitchell leaned against a tree and observed his sister as she walked off with Mr. Jones. She laughed at something her companion said, and her cheeks took on a rosy hue. He smiled. Mom and Dad would have liked Mr. Jones. He was a nice young man. His gaze swung back to the front of the crowd where Rachel fidgeted. He wanted to believe his mom and dad would have liked Rachel too.

Becky had told Mitchell the fabric used to decorate Rachel's box. Gazing at the containers left on the table he realized hers was a couple away from being, auctioned. He looked quickly for Sanders. Finally, his eyes made contact with Jake's guarded stare.

He smiled and tipped his hat to Jake. Sanders wasn't going to win this round. He straightened from the tree as Mr. Clement held the next box into the air. Mitchell raised a hand. "One bit."

"Anxious are you, son?"

The crowd chuckled at the question.

Jake raised his hand to up the bid.

Mitchell's gaze slid to where Rachel stood. Her mouth agape and eyes wide, she stared at him as if he had lost his mind. He kept a straight face and held in the chuckle that wanted to emerge.

"Gentlemen, the current bid is one dollar, do I hear one and a half?" Mr. Clement glanced from Mitchell to

Jake. At Mitchell's shake of his head, Mr. Clement said, "Sold for one dollar!"

Jake's dark eyes flashed in triumph, and he smirked victoriously at Mitchell.

A giggling young woman sprinted to the table to claim her box and glanced shyly at Jake.

Jake paused, stared at the waiting woman before turning to glower at Mitchell. He recovered quickly, smiled at the young woman, and offered his arm.

Whew, dodged a bullet there. Rachel didn't know what she would have talked about with Jake if he had won the bid on her lunch. She tapped her foot impatiently and heaved a sigh when her box was finally lifted into the air.

Before Mr. Clement had a chance to start the bidding a voice yelled out, "Two dollars!"

Rachel swung around to see Mitchell smiling like a cat who had been treated to some cream. A satisfied tingle scooted along her spine.

Mr. Clement cleared his throat. "Well, does anyone give more than two dollars?" At the crowd's silence he yelled, "Sold!"

If Rachel thought watching Mitchell from behind was something, the front held just as much appeal. His hips rolled with an easy gate as he strode up to her. That kind of action would make any girl's heart race. Right? Tipping his hat, he offered his arm. "Let's find a spot under a tree and enjoy the picnic you've packed."

A few yards away a blanket lay spread out. The full limbs gave off ample shade. Rachel shook her head. "Pretty sure of yourself weren't you, Cowboy?"

He flashed a cocky grin. "I had a little help."

Rachel gently punched him on the arm. "You

cheated. Becky told you which one was mine. Didn't she?" She frowned. "If you knew which one was mine, why did you bid on the other box?"

"That was to throw off the competition." His eyes twinkled back at her as he pointed to the blanket. "Shall we?"

She crouched down and opened the box to lay out their lunch. She was aware of his silent scrutiny. What was he thinking?

"Your new dress looks lovely on you."

Did everyone take their charm pill this morning? She timidly peeked into his amber eyes. "Thank you." She reached a hand up to touch the ribbon in her hair. "Thank you for the ribbon also. The color goes well with my dress."

"You're welcome." He leaned on his elbow and continued to watch her intently.

She felt the heat of a blush creeping up her neck to her cheeks. She reached a hand to her nose. "Do I have something on my face?"

He shook his head but didn't answer for a moment. "I was just thinking I don't really know much about you."

A stab of anger rose quickly. She'd told him a little about herself, but he had refused to believe a word she said. Why would he believe her now?

He reached out a hand and touched her arm. "Please. Tell me about yourself."

She bit her bottom lip trying to choose her words. "You're willing to hear what I have to say?"

He broke his eye contact and looked at some of the other couples enjoying their picnics. His gaze swung back to scrutinize her. "I'll listen."

"Okay." She titled her chin defensively. "You already know I'm originally from Oklahoma, and I'm twenty-four years old." She paused to observe his nod. "I was born in the year nineteen ninety-two, and I went to college at the Fort Lewis College in Durango and received a Bachelor's Degree in Computer Information Systems. Guess you could say I'm a computer nerd." She chuckled and glanced back at Mitchell. "You don't have a clue as to what I'm talking about and probably don't believe me either."

Mitchell brought a chicken leg he held up to his lips to nibble off a small bite and observed her watchfully. He chewed before answering, "I'm not saying I don't believe you, but the idea of you traveling back to the past is a notion I'm having problems with." Taking another bite, he pointed at her. "Go ahead and tell me more of this future of yours."

She leaned forward on her knees and started gesturing with her hands. "The inventions would astound you! There are cell phones. That is a means of communicating with friends and family. They are portable, and you can carry the phone around with you." Pausing she tapped a finger against her lower lip. "Then there are computers. I work on a computer every day. Making sure the system works for the college correctly. I just upgraded the system for the fall term." She stopped suddenly and glanced briefly at him. "I don't think I can begin to explain what the computer has done for people in the future."

He watched as Rachel became more animated the longer she talked. Either she had an astonishing imagination, or she was actually telling him the truth. Or what she truly believed was the truth. He shook his head. Was he ready to accept what she was saying? But one thing was for certain. He was very fond of the woman kneeling in front of him, and he didn't want her to disappear as suddenly as she had appeared in his life.

She suddenly stopped mid speech to catch her breath. "Sorry, I guess I got a little carried away. I hope I didn't bore you to tears."

He placed his empty plate aside. "Is there any dessert hidden in that box somewhere?" His eyes roamed over her face and studied her lips as her tongue jetted out to wet her lips. "What did you make?"

"I made one of my mom's favorite recipes. Peach cobbler. I hope I did the recipe justice."

He gave an appreciate whiff of the air as Rachel uncovered the dessert. "Ma'am, your cobbler smells delicious."

Rachel beamed at his compliment. "Well, I hope you enjoy the dessert." Dipping the fork into the dish, she brought a small forkful of the cobbler to his lips.

Surprised by her gesture, he leaned forward and took the bite she offered into his mouth. He closed his eyes and savored the spices mixed with the peaches. "Mmmm, that's really good. I won't tell Becky your cobbler is better than her cookies if you don't." Grasping her hand before she could withdraw with the fork, he drawled, "You know you never gave the winner of the horse race his winning kiss."

"Oh, I don't know. I think the cowboy already received his congratulatory lip lock." She pulled back in a huff and started to pack away the picnic items.

Mitchell quickly sat up and reached for Rachel's busy hands. He had forgotten about Lucy. Obviously Rachel had seen Lucy's celebratory display, and she was upset. Was this a good sign she was distressed over the kiss he had received from the other woman? "Rachel, look at me." He stroked his thumb over the back of her knuckles. "Please."

Pausing, she quickly looked at him.

"Are you talking about the peck on the lips Lucy gave me? Lucy instigated the kiss, I didn't." He sighed and continued, "Please believe me when I say the kiss didn't mean anything to me." Lifting his hand, he drew his thumb over the softness of her bottom lip.

She eased slightly forward. "I guess I could find it in my heart to bestow a small kiss to the winner."

Leaning in the rest of the way, he met her lips with a gentle brush of his own.

"You are right. I don't think Mom's peach cobbler has ever tasted so delicious."

He watched as a becoming blush spread across her cheeks. Quirking his lips, he picked up his discarded plate and helped himself to more cobbler. "My compliments to the cook. This meal was delicious." After finishing the dessert, he sighed. "I was up early this morning. I think I'll just rest my eyes for a moment."

As his breathing slowed, Rachel's eyes skimmed his prone body from the top of his head to his boots. She fanned her face without thinking. He was such a fine specimen of a man. His muscular chest rose again and she looked away to observe the other couples sitting on the lawn enjoying the afternoon.

She smiled as she spotted Becky and Jim deep in conversation a few feet away. As her gaze moved on, she encountered Jake staring intently at her. His lips were formed in a mocking sneer, and he tipped his hat.

She quickly looked away. How long had he been studying her? Self-consciously Rachel smoothed out her dress. Heat flooded her cheeks as she realized Jake probably had witnessed the kiss she had just shared with Mitchell. Had Mitchell known Jake was watching? Did he initiate the kiss just to irritate Jake? Was she just a game to them both?

The afternoon lost some of its lustrous glow. She scooted across the blanket as inconspicuously as she could and propped herself up behind the nearby tree. Taking a steadying breath, she peeked back around the trunk to see if Jake was still watching. Her gaze encountered his unblinking stare and leer resting on his lips.

With a deep breath, she calmed her racing pulse. The charming gentleman from earlier had disappeared.

Chapter Twenty-Four

A warm breeze brought the fragrance of nearby flowers to her senses. Rachel brushed her nose. She frowned at the tickle at the tip that wouldn't go away. Her eyes flew open at the sound of a masculine chuckle.

Mitchell reclined beside her with a small flower extended from his hand. "Hey, sleepyhead, it's about time you woke up."

She stifled a yawn and eased away from the tree. Glancing around she noticed most of the people who had earlier been relaxing on the lawn had disappeared. "Goodness, how long was I asleep?"

Mitchell shrugged his shoulders. "At least an hour. You must have been exhausted."

How long had he been watching her sleep? Noticing the small flower in his hand, she eyed him and asked, "Were you tickling my nose?" She watched as he smiled innocently.

He handed the dainty flower to her. "Now you are rested, would you like to take a stroll with me around town?" He slowly eased up onto his feet and reached a hand down to help her up.

"Thank you," Rachel murmured. Glancing about she noticed all of the remains of their picnic were cleared away. Peeking out from below her lashes, she once again wondered how long Mitchell had sat watching her sleep.

"I believe there is a horseshoe throwing contest beginning soon. Would you care to come with me to watch?"

"I would love to."

Rachel couldn't remember an afternoon she had enjoyed more. Mitchell and his partner had come in second in the horseshoe tournament. She'd laughed at the antics of the grown men playing. Their clowning around indicated how much fun everyone was having. Once the tournament was over, they'd roamed about town enjoying different activities.

The sun was descending when they approached the makeshift dance floor set up for the celebration. She trembled at the nervous anticipation of being held in Mitchell's arms.

Rachel spied Becky and Jim threading their way to where they waited. She considered the glow radiating from Becky. She smiled as Becky bestowed a quick hug upon her.

"We've had such a wonderful afternoon. Jim and I have had so much fun!"

Jim stuck out his hand to shake Mitchell's. "Mitchell, do you have a moment? I would like to speak with you if I may."

A frown marred Becky's face momentarily as she watched her brother and Jim walk away. Turning back to Rachel she asked, "What do you suppose that is all about?"

If Rachel had to wager a guess, she suspected Jim was working up the nerve to ask Mitchell to court Becky. She smiled and kept the fact to herself. "I'm not sure."

Shaking off her confusion, Becky asked Rachel excitedly, "What have you and Mitchell been doing all afternoon?"

"I fell asleep at the picnic. Your brother must have been totally bored." She laughed. "Some stimulating company I am, huh? Not only do I send your brother to slumber land, but I also napped!"

Becky giggled. "At least I can say I didn't bore Jim enough for him to fall asleep in my company."

"Well, after our nap we both had a great time taking in the town and the different festivities. How about you, what activities did you enjoy?"

Rachel smiled as she listened to Becky's enthusiastic in depth description of each activity.

Becky paused for a breath and released a sigh. "I've spent such a wonderful day with Jim."

Rachel playfully patted Becky's shoulder. "So, do you have the hots for Mr. Jones?" If she didn't know any better, she would swear Becky was blushing. "Don't mind my teasing, Becky. I'm glad you are having fun. You really do like Mr. Jones, don't you?"

Coyly Becky smiled and leaned in to impart a confidence. "I wouldn't push him away if he wanted to give me a good night kiss."

People turned to stare as Rachel burst out in laughter. "Becky, you are scandalous."

Becky giggled, lowered her lashes, and asked softly, "How about you? Will you push my brother away if he wants to give you a good night kiss?"

She felt the beginning of a flush making its way to her face, and she gawked at Becky in disbelief. "Uh, I…" She swallowed in relief as she was saved from answering as the fiddlers started in on the first tune of the evening.

A soft touch at her elbow had her jumping. She turned to see Doctor Brown fidgeting beside her.

"Good evening, ladies. How are you this fine night? I hope you've had no repercussions from your accident, Miss Morgan."

"Good evening, Doctor Brown. I'm doing well. Thank you for asking."

Indicating the make-shift floor he asked, "Which of you lovely ladies do I get the pleasure of dancing with first?"

Studying the couples for a few seconds, Rachel realized the steps weren't too difficult. "I'll try since I'm the one who owes you." Smiling she took the doctor's arm.

After a few awkward moments, Rachel was able to catch on to the steps and smiled into the kind face of her partner.

Giving Rachel a sad smile in return he said, "My wife and I used to dance up a storm." His gaze settled over her shoulder with a faraway look.

"Did something happen to your wife?" She watched a sad expression cross the doctor's face.

Glancing back down into her eyes, he replied gruffly, "Yes. We were out for an evening stroll when someone celebrating down at the saloon shot his pistol into the air and the stray bullet found its way to my Martha."

Gasping in horror she exclaimed, "That's horrible. I'm so sorry! Did they arrest the man who did it?"

"Yes. The poor man hadn't even realized what he had done."

"How long ago did this happen?"

Swallowing with difficulty the doctor continued, "It seems just like yesterday, but it's going on the second year now. There isn't a day goes by I don't think of her." His watery gaze met her own. "I'm sorry, young lady. I didn't mean to go on. Thank you for listening."

Impulsively she leaned in and gave the doctor a quick hug. "I'm sorry for your loss. I lost my parents not very long ago."

The doctor patted her hand. "Thank you again my dear. Now I promised your friend a dance as well. I will try not to be as glum with her as I was with you. Have a good evening."

Gazing about, she stood and tapped her foot to the sound of the fiddles. Where was Mitchell?

"What do you say to a turn around the floor, pretty lady?"

Rachel turned and encountered Jake's hard threatening stare. A slight shiver ran down her spine. The man standing in front of her wasn't the charming man from earlier in the day. A slight alcohol odor flooded from his mouth as he exhaled. Alarmed she glanced around for Mitchell. A quick scan of the crowd didn't produce him. Swallowing nervously, she glanced back at Jake. "This dance seems to be almost over, why don't we wait until the next one begins."

His eyes swept over her bodice and a lewd smile contorted his face. "I can wait. I'm good at waiting."

She struggled to control the panic rising in her chest as she looked back upon the couples enjoying the lively tune. Out of the corner of her eye, she noticed Jake lifting something to his lips.

A few seconds later the small shiny object was

shoved under her nose. "Would you like to wet your pretty lips as well? Whiskey takes the edge off."

She tried not to gag at the potent smell permeating from the container. She held her breath as she realized it was a flask. How long had Jake been drinking? As unsteady as he was on his feet, she would venture to guess that while she had been taking in the activities, Jake had been getting sauced down at the saloon. Glancing apprehensively at Jake as he swayed unsteadily on his feet she replied, "No, thank you."

Jake saluted her with the hand holding the flask and drew another long draw from the container. "Suit yourself. The more for me."

As the lively tune ended, Jake placed his booze back inside his vest pocket, grabbed Rachel, and drew her flush against his frame. The fiddlers began a slow tune, and she squirmed as she felt Jake begin to draw her body even closer to his own. Her arms were powerless as he pinned them to his chest.

His stale breath fanned her face as he laughed at her attempts to put distance between their bodies. "What's the matter, pretty lady? You didn't seem to mind Reeves' advances earlier. Do you think you're too good for Jake Sanders?"

As the odor of alcohol wafted over her, she controlled the urge to gag once again. She had never been able to tolerate a drunk, and obviously Jake was one of those who became belligerent. "No, that's not it at all, Jake. I don't know you well enough for such... liberties."

A sudden frown creased his face. "Obviously you know Reeves well enough from the kiss I witnessed earlier today." His gaze lowered to her chest. "Have you let him caress those wonderful breasts? I've wanted to touch them since you had them on display yesterday at the pond."

She felt the blood drain from her face as his words sank in. She tried once again to put some distance between them. Even drunk Jake was able to keep a tight hold upon her. She hadn't been alone yesterday at the pond, the creepy feeling she had experienced was Jake spying on her. In slow motion, she watched in revulsion as Jake's finger touched the neckline of her dress and trailed down to caress her breast.

She gasped and found the strength to wrench away. Jake stumbled backward in surprise. Taking advantage of her opportunity, she fled the dance floor. Her pace quickened as she heard loud cursing behind her.

She apologized to couples as she bumped into them in her haste to escape. She scanned the crowd looking for any kind of assistance. Spying Becky and Jim by the punch bowl, she turned and made her way toward them. She had almost reached them when an arm from behind wrenched her around and jerked her to a stop.

"Not. So. Fast. Little darlin'." Through gritted teeth Jake pronounced his words slowly. "We're not through with our dance."

Her sharp cry for help was drowned out by the fiddle playing. She jerked her wrist from his grasp. His grip tightened, and she knew she didn't have the strength to overpower him. How was she going to get free from his grasp?

Pepper spray. She'd placed the container in her pocket. She fumbled in desperation for the small can. Clenching the small tube in her hand, she brought it out, extended her arm toward Jake's face, and gave two quick blasts into his eyes. "We. Are. Through!"

Stumbling back Jake growled, "What the hell?" Scrubbing wildly at his burning eyes he gasped, "You've blinded me you little…"

She staggered backward and fled before Jake finished cursing her. Tears filled her eyes as she blindly ran away. Glancing around frantically, she found a place to hide. Noticing a wagon, she ducked behind the rough wood panels and caught her breath. She closed her eyes when she heard footsteps a few seconds later. Her breath whooshed out from her lungs as she thought she heard Mitchell calling her name.

She choked back a sob. Her ears had to be deceiving her. She peeked over a wooden slat. She spotted a shadowed figure making his way toward her, and then she heard him call her name again. Rushing out from behind the wagon, she flung herself into Mitchell's arms.

His fingers gently tipped her chin until her gaze met his own. "Are you okay?"

She reached up to wipe a tear from her cheek and gave him a watery smile. "I'm getting there."

"What happened? The last I saw you were happily dancing with Doctor Brown." He smoothed a tear from her cheek. "Becky tried to tell me what happened, but she really didn't know herself. What did Jake do, Rachel?"

The soft timbre of his voice calmed her rattled nerves. "He'd been drinking." The arms cradling her stiffened, and she heard him mutter a curse from under his breath. She grabbed his arm just as he started to turn to go in search of Jake. "Please, don't."

He stared off into the darkened night, clenching

and unclenching his jaw. After a few moments he asked her softly, "Did he hurt you?"

She shook her head slowly and lifted the can she held in her hand. "I didn't give him a chance. I squirted him with my pepper spray."

He reached out and took the can. "What is this?"

She stole a look into his intent gaze and attempted to smile, but her lips failed to cooperate. "It's used to defend oneself. The contents blind your attacker." She knew she had chosen the wrong word when Mitchell became rigid beside her.

Growling he drawled, "Attacker?" He glanced over his shoulder searching intently for Jake. "When I find him, I'm going to kill him."

She gasped and grabbed his shoulder. "No, Mitchell, please don't. I don't want you getting hurt because of me. Please, would you just take me home?"

Mitchell warmed at her words. She had just called the ranch home. Gazing into her deep green eyes, he caught the shimmer of the last of her tears. Lifting his eyes, he glanced over her head to give the area one last quick scan. Reaching up he drew a calloused finger down her tender cheek. "Okay. I'll take you home if that's what you want. Let me find Becky and then we will be on our way."

Becky came running up and gasped, "Rachel are you okay?" She ran her hands up and down Rachel's arms trying to assure herself she wasn't harmed in any way. "I saw Jake grab you; he didn't hurt you, did he?"

"No, Becky, I'm fine. Just a little shook up, he scared me more than anything." She glanced about. "I hate to be a party pooper and dampen everyone's evening, but I would really just like to go back to the ranch now."

Becky gave a quick longing glance back toward the makeshift dance floor and shrugged her shoulders. "Of course I understand if you don't feel like staying."

Rachel felt horrible. She was ruining everyone's evening. "There's no reason you can't stay, is there Mitchell?"

Jim cleared his throat. "I can bring Becky home after a few dances. I promise not to keep her out too late."

Rachel saw the hope in Becky's eyes as she watched Mitchell stare off into the growing darkness thinking about the request.

He shook his head and glanced back into his sister's pleading gaze. "Jim, I trust you to get my sister home safely. I'll take Rachel home."

Becky broke into a huge grin and threw her arms around her brother's neck. "Oh, thank you, Mitchell." Giving a quick kiss to his cheek, she turned to Jim, "Come on, let's go have the dance I promised you."

"You just made her day, Mitchell."

He smiled. "You are probably right and Mr. Jones's as well." He grasped her hand, "I need to find Toby. Tell him what's happened. Will you be okay if I leave you at the wagon? I'll be right back."

A few moments later, they located their buckboard. "Go ahead, Mitchell, I'll just wait here." At his pause of uncertainty, she said, "Go on, I'll be okay. Just…don't be gone long."

Rachel scrambled up onto the seat a few minutes later and stared at the evening shadows with uncertainty. What had she gotten herself into? She thought back to Jake and his comments. She knew she had better be on her guard. Jake had made his intent clear with his slurred words. He meant to have her. She shuttered as she recalled his unwanted advances.

A movement caught from the corner of her eye had her jumping slightly in the seat. "Hello," she asked tentatively.

"It's just me, Rachel. I'm sorry I didn't mean to startle you." Mitchell swung gently into the wagon and picked up the reins. "Toby will make sure Rebel gets home safely. He also voiced his concern when I told him what happened and is going to keep his eye out for Jake."

"That's nice of him. I will have to thank him the next time I see him." She realized she'd become ingrained in more than Becky and Mitchell's lives. She absently rubbed her hands up and down her arms.

Mitchell transferred the reins to his right hand and put an arm around her shoulders. "Are you cold?"

Snuggling to his side, she said softly, "No, no I'm fine."

They rode in silence for a while as Mitchell maneuvered the wagon out of town. Fixing her eyes on the moon, she trembled slightly at the shadows the beams were casting upon the objects along the road. The drive into town this morning hadn't looked this sinister. It was all Jake's fault she was imagining danger where none lurked. Grimacing at her own overactive imagination, she turned in her seat to study the tree in the bend of the road as its hulking height mocked her.

"Would it make you feel better to talk about what happened tonight?"

The softly spoken question broke the silence and

she jumped at the intrusion. "Sorry, my mind was years away." Shrugging she said, "I'm not sure I want to talk about what occurred. You may go all Rambo on Jake if I tell you what all he said and did."

He frowned. "Go Rambo? I'm not sure I understand."

She clasped her hands and wrung them as she explained. "I guess what I'm trying to say is I don't want you to fly off the handle and beat Jake to a pulp. Becky had told me how you reacted to Jake kissing her on the cheek."

He recalled the night he had found Rachel. He had lost his temper when Becky had explained Jake's visit to the ranch. Would he have ever met Rachel if he hadn't been on his way back from town? He sat silent for a moment. Trying to coax himself to relax, he glanced down at her upturned face and smiled. "I will try not to fly off the handle, or go Rambo, as you put it."

She bit her lower lip and debated on how much she should tell him. From the grim look on his face, she wondered if she should sugar coat things just a little. Breaking eye contact, she studied her hands, "Jake was so charming this morning. Did you see how he handled himself when he had to kiss the pig?" She glanced at his tense profile and saw him shake his head. "He charmed everyone, including me. So I didn't see the harm when he asked me to save him a dance this evening." Giving a derisive snort, she asked, "How did I let myself be drawn in by his charm?"

She continued when her companion remained silent. "I just didn't realize by the time the dance began he would be inebriated and be a totally different person.

He wanted to hold me just a little tighter than I felt comfortable with, and that's when he got a little angry with me." She shrugged her shoulders. "I guess that's everything in a nutshell."

She could feel his anger radiating from his stiff frame. She wished she could see his expression clearer.

"Are you sure you've told me everything?"

She startled when he finally spoke. How did he know she wasn't telling him everything? She fidgeted. "That's all I can remember at the moment."

She heard him inhale deeply. "I've seen Jake drunk many times. He gets mean, and his treatment of you doesn't matter if you are a man or woman." He turned his head to glance in her direction. "Now you know why I didn't trust Jake around Becky. I've seen him abuse the women at the Silver Spur on too many nights. Unfortunately, his temper is legendary."

A surge of jealousy threaded through her body at the mention of the Silver Spur. Just how often did he visit his little saloon flame? "Guess he is a true Dr. Jekyll and Mr. Hyde!" He scowled and quirked an eyebrow in silent question. "The saying means he has two very distinct personalities, good and evil."

He nodded his head. "That explains Jake perfectly."

The shadows from the buildings on the ranch came into view. She shifted on the wagon's seat and tried not to shudder at the eeriness the darkness created. All of the ranch hands seemed to still be in town, even the bunkhouse lay silent. Moving a little closer to Mitchell, she glanced from under her eyelashes to study his darkened profile. Had he realized yet they would be all alone at the ranch? She shivered in anticipation.

Pulling up in front of the ranch house, Rachel jumped as a loud bang rent through the night. Gazing back toward town, she saw the first of the fireworks being shot into the nighttime sky. Closing her eyes, she could mentally visualize the crowd as they oohed and aahed over the colorful bursts as they lit the sky.

As the last of the display disappeared from the sky, Mitchell leaped down from the wagon and turned to help her down. He ignored the hand she had extended and instead reached up, encircled her waist, and brought her down to stand in front of him. Gazing into her eyes he murmured, "You know I never got my dance you promised."

She smiled. "Mr. Reeves, I do believe I'm available."

Humming a tune she had heard earlier in the evening, she placed one hand on his shoulder and the other on his lean waist. She could feel the heat emitting from his chest as he drew her closer and waltzed around the yard. The darkness didn't seem so scary cradled in his arms.

His tawny amber stare reflected a desire that had her stomach turning summersaults. Her humming stopped abruptly as she caught her breath. Awareness crackled between them as their bodies slowed and stopped.

His head descended slowly, and his kiss caught the sigh escaping her lips.

The brush of his mustache tickled until his firm lips settled unyieldingly on her own. All coherent thought raced from her mind as he softly nibbled, teased, and feasted. His mouth left her own, blazed a fiery trail across her cheek to her ear, and nibbled gently on her lobe. A slow burn began in the pit of her stomach as he whispered in her ear and took another nibble of her lobe.

He paused. "You smell so good."

His husky breath spread down her neck as she tipped her head back to give him access to her neck.

He released her hands and gently pulled her closer to his frame.

She could feel his body's reaction to their closeness as she naively rubbed against him. A groan tore from his lips as she slowly wrapped her arms around his body and inched them upward to furrow into his hair. His Stetson fell unheeded to the ground. She couldn't believe how soft and sexy his hair felt beneath her fingers as she ran them through the silken mane.

Passion. Fireworks. She heard him moan. He drew back and gazed into her eyes. She felt him drawing away mentally and physically. She missed his warmth immediately. "Did I do something wrong?"

His hand shook as he threaded it through his hair. "It's not you, Rachel, it's me." He looked around at the darkened ranch. "Things were getting a little out of hand, and I shouldn't take advantage of us being alone. I know better."

Rachel slowly backed away and bit her swollen lower lip. "I guess we shouldn't do anything you will regret in the morning." Why did he have to be the voice of reason? Fighting tears, she blurted, "I've seen you with the saloon girl." Swallowing hard she continued, "I understand I'm not the type of woman you usually desire. I'm sorry I made a pest of myself." Tears spilled as she turned and fled into the house.

"Rachel, that's not…" The shutting door broke off

what he intended to say. "That's not what I meant at all," he muttered.

He bent to retrieve his hat and beat it against his leg. What a mess! He stared at the house. Should he try to talk to her? Explain? Hell, he didn't even know why he acted like he did. How was he going to justify his actions?

He sighed, grabbed the reins of the waiting horses, and led them toward the barn to unhook the wagon. He shook his head. The night was going to be long.

Rachel leaned against the bedroom door and took a deep breath. She crossed the room to light the lamp. As the dim glow illuminated the room, she swiped at her tears. What a fool she was. First, with the inhibited display of her passion, then second with the words flung at Mitchell before storming into the house.

She paced over to the window. What should she do? Mitchell would be the only reason for her to stay in this time. If he didn't want her, then should she be trying harder to find a way back to where she belonged?

She sat on the edge of the bed and pondered her dilemma for a moment. Holding back a sudden yawn, she lowered her head to lie on the soft pillow and stared at the door. How could she have thought she had found the man for her? Swiping away a fresh start of tears, she slowly closed her eyes. She hoped tomorrow things would appear clearer.

Chapter Twenty-Five

Soft sunshine reflected about the room as Rachel awoke. Leaning up on her elbow, she looked out the window. Birds were happily singing in the distance. Goodness. She'd slept away most of the morning.

She drew a curl from eyes and groaned. She hadn't bothered putting on her nightgown last night. Her new dress had wrinkles that had made themselves at home in the fabric. She attempted to smooth the creases as she swung her legs over the bed and stood.

She retrieved her shirt and jeans. She needed the comfort from the familiar articles today. Pausing while buttoning her top, she heard voices and laughter coming from outside. Her curiosity got the better of her and she leaned over to take a peek. Moving the curtain aside just a smidge, she gazed out the window.

Mitchell stood with his back to her with a boot propped casually on the lower rung of the corral's fence. He tipped his hat up and pointed toward one of the horses in the corral. The three men he was conversing with nodded and turned to carry out whatever request he had issued.

She stepped quickly away from the window when he suddenly glanced back toward the house. She placed a hand to her pounding heart and peered around the curtain again. Had he seen her staring?

Whirling away from the window, she retrieved her

purse from the top dresser drawer and rummaged through the contents until she found her pick. Slowly she worked the tangles out of her hair and contemplated what she would say to Mitchell this morning.

Should she play it cool and pretend nothing had happened between them the night before? Or should she demand some kind of answer for his actions? Sighing she placed her pick back into her purse. Hearing the crinkle of plastic, she reopened her purse to examine the contents. She pulled out the Snickers bar. Why hadn't she remembered she had chocolate last night? She took a quick sniff of the chocolate after opening the wrapper. Oh, this is just what the doctor ordered.

She closed her eyes in true ecstasy. The small bite in her mouth exploded. Chocolate, caramel, and peanuts had never tasted so satisfying. She eyed the rest of her treat and decided she had better save the rest for another time. Reverently she wrapped the candy bar back up and placed it back inside her purse.

She couldn't hide in her room all day. She needed to take the bull by the horns! The house was silent as she paused in the front room and glanced into the kitchen. A fresh plate of biscuits sat on the table, but Becky wasn't anywhere to be seen. Picking up a biscuit, she quickly buttered it and strode toward the front door. Taking a bite, she scanned the yard and porch. Still no sign of Becky. With a lift of her hand, she shielded her eyes and glanced toward the barn. Mitchell still stood by the corral and as he spotted her, he waved her over.

Ignoring the butterflies flitting in her stomach, she made her way across the yard to join him. She couldn't quite bring herself to meet his gaze as she muttered a good morning.

She felt his gaze studying her intently. Did he notice the slight shadows under her eyes?

He lifted his hand and grazed a thumb along her cheek. "Rachel, I need to talk to you about what happened last night."

Was that regret she heard in his voice? Guilt for what happened or remorse for what didn't happen? She finally lifted her gaze and met his. Longing blazed bright from his tawny eyes as he intently studied her.

She turned her gaze away. "Where is Becky this morning? She got home safely didn't she?"

He jerked a finger over his shoulder. "They got home late last night. Becky convinced Jim to stay in the bunkhouse instead of travelling back to town. She's out front seeing him off."

"Oh." She mentally kicked herself for the stimulating conversation. "You called me over. Did you need me for something?" Her cheeks reddened as she thought how the question sounded.

He cleared his throat. Turning back toward the corral, he pointed at the horses gathered there. "We've just brought in a few of our horses from pasture."

She patiently waited for him to continue. What did the horses have to do with her?

She frowned. "I thought since you lost your horse and was missing your mount so much you might like to pick one you can ride. While you're staying with us."

Her eyes misted. What a bighearted gesture. She examined the horses running and nipping at each other in the corral. What did she do now? She'd never explained to him her Mustang wasn't exactly a horse. A hysterical giggle bubbled up, and she squelched it.

She could tell he waited for her answer. She nibbled softly on her lower lip. He looked away to study the horses.

"Maybe my horses aren't the high quality you are used to, but there are some gentle mares in the bunch." He stopped and let his statement hang in the air.

Gasping, she reached a hand out and placed it on his chest. "Oh, Mitchell. It's not that," she stammered. Feeling the warmth from his chest on her hand, she quickly withdrew it. "I've never had a horse before."

He shook his head. "I'm confused. The night I found you, you said you had been thrown from your mustang."

His confusion was justified. She didn't quite know how to explain. "Technically, you are the one who asked if I had been thrown from my mustang. I went along with your explanation because what you said made more sense than me traveling through time." Studying the frown beginning to form on his face Rachel continued, "My Mustang was a car powered by a motor and gasoline, not a horse. My vehicle had four tires not four legs."

He hid his uncertainty from her. She knew her words were complete gibberish.

He nodded his head as if he came to a decision. "Well, since you are a true green horn, we will probably need to make sure we find the gentlest one." He studied the horses a moment before pointing. "How about the black and white paint there? She's one of the mildest one's in the bunch."

Oh, what a pretty little thing. Her eyes watered. She was turning into a virtual weeping watering pot. "You really want to give me a horse?" His nod of

168

confirmation was hard to discern through her tears. Her gaze swung back to the black and white paint. She was smaller than the others, which seemed less intimidating and she was beautiful. "Does she have a name?"

He chuckled. "Why is that the first thing you women ask?"

She shrugged her shoulders. Her mind raced with excitement. What was an appropriate name for a horse?

"Do you want to meet her?" He lifted the latch to the gate, reached over to pluck a rope off the top rung of the fence, and started toward the little mare. Slowly he approached murmuring soothing words. The mare turned her head and pricked her ears listening intently to his deep voice. Slipping the rope slowly around her neck, he gently patted her on her neck. "Come on, girl; there is someone who wants to meet you."

She climbed onto the lowest rung of the fence and waited. Once the pair stood in front of her, she leaned over with her hand outstretched. The mare gently raised her nose and sniffed at her hand. She giggled at the feel of the horse's soft nose nudging against her palm. The big brown eyes studied her intently. "Oh, aren't you a beautiful girl." She ran her hand down the bridge of the soft nose. Tilting her head, she asked, "Now the question is, what are we going to call you? Your name shouldn't be something corny, but something hip."

She reached out to stroke a hand along the mare's neck.

Mitchell smiled and asked, "Are you expecting her to answer?"

She laughed as she recalled the time she'd caught him talking to Rebel. "Touché!"

"See, now you know I'm not the only one who

carries on a conversation with his horse. Just comes naturally, doesn't it?"

"What are you two doing?"

Startled, she turned to see Becky standing behind them eyeing each of them curiously.

"Check it out Becky. Mitchell gave me a horse."

Becky's eyebrows rose and she smiled. "He did, huh?"

Mitchell dipped his head and shuffled his feet. "Um, I will just take your mare and put her in the barn for you."

Becky's gaze swung from her brother's retreating back to Rachel's gaze following his movements. She smirked, "So, did you get a good night kiss last night?"

She tore her gaze away from his backside to where Becky stood with a silly smirk on her face. "Did you?" Turn about was fair play, after all.

A dreamy expression transformed Becky's features. "Yes. Did you know Jim asked Mitchell for permission to court me last night?"

Squealing with delight Rachel jumped off the fence and wrapped Becky in her arms for a huge hug. "Oh, Becky, that's wonderful." She stepped back a step to examine Becky's face. "Isn't it?"

Becky still wore a faraway look as she murmured, "Oh, yes." She fanned herself with her hand. "I had such a wonderful time last night. We danced almost every tune played." Pausing she chuckled. "You should have seen the expression on Jim's face when another cowboy asked me to waltz."

She laughed along with Becky. "I bet his look was priceless." Giving into the urge, she gave Becky another enthusiastic squeeze. "I'm so happy for you."

Untangling herself from the hug, Becky leaned back to give her a stern look. "It won't work this time, distracting me." She tapped her foot impatiently. "You never answered me. Did you get a good night kiss as well?"

Busted! Rachel sheepishly gazed at her, "I was hoping you had forgotten you had asked. I'm not sure I really want to discuss this, since you are his sister." Becky was the closest thing to a friend she had at the moment to discuss her predicament. Should she take a chance and discuss the situation with Becky?

"I'm on your side, you know. I think you and Mitchell would make a wonderful couple." Like a slow motion movie, the scene from the previous night flashed through her mind. She shook her head. "Oh, Becky, I'm glad you think so, but I'm not sure your brother thinks or feels the same."

"Why would you think that?" Becky glanced toward the barn. "What did he do?"

A sigh burst from her lips. "It's not exactly what he did, but more like what he didn't want to do that has me convinced he's not as into me as I am into him." She continued at Becky's questioning look, "We did kiss. Boy, did we kiss! But I don't think he found it as enjoyable as I did." There, she had said it. "Combine the fact he thinks I'm crazy, only spells relationship disaster."

"Rachel, that is ridiculous. I know my brother, and I know he really likes you. I'm not sure he thinks you are crazy. Give me a reason why you think that."

She twisted her hands in indecision. How much should she explain? Should she just blurt out she's from the future? She wasn't sure she could take rejection from Becky as well. "Becky." She stopped to gather her thoughts and stared at Becky's expectant face. This explanation may take awhile. She noticed a stack of hay bales a short distance away. She took Becky's hand, guided her over, and sat down. "I'm not from here. Of course, I'm from here, but I'm not from this time." Becky's confused expression didn't change, pausing she collected her thoughts and tried again. "Becky, I'm from the future. Somehow, I'm not totally sure how, I traveled back in time." She reached out and took both of Becky's hands in her own. "That night Mitchell found me and brought me back to the ranch is the night I traveled back to your time." She released her hands and nibbled on a fingernail as she met Becky's unblinking gaze and waited for a reaction.

Becky stared unfocused at the barn and nibbled on her lower lip deep in thought. After a few moments, she nodded her head as if reaching a decision. "Well. Are you going to stay now you are here?"

She was shocked. "You believe me?"

Rising from the bale, Becky started walking toward the house. She shrugged her shoulders. "I'm not sure what to believe." Stopping she turned back toward Rachel. "I just know you are good for my brother. The more important question I have at the moment is are you going to help me make lunch?"

With a laugh, she threaded her arm through Becky's. "I think I may be able to help you with that task."

They had almost made the steps to the front porch when they heard the sound of a fast approaching horse. Both turned to see a man rein in his mount. "Where is Mitchell?"

Rachel felt Becky stiffen beside her.

"He's in the barn, Bob. What's wrong?"

The cowboy dismounted quickly and started toward the barn. Over his shoulder he explained, "I was out checking the fence line to the north. There is some fence that's been cut and down. I wasn't able to find the cattle."

Rachel saw Mitchell emerge from the barn in time to overhear Bob. He whipped his hat off his head and muttered a curse. "I'll get Rebel saddled."

Becky rushed into the barn after him. "Do you want me to find Toby?"

Mitchell paused in hauling a saddle over Rebel's back. "Yes. I want to talk to him. Beck, I also need for you to get me some food and supplies put together for me to take with me? I'm not sure how long this will take." Tightening the cinch on the saddle Mitchell cursed again. Someone was doing a damn fine job of trying to ruin him.

He would ask Toby to stay behind. He wasn't about to leave the girls unattended again. Not after the way Jake had acted with Rachel at the dance the previous night.

He noticed Rachel standing in the barn doorway wringing her hands.

"Can I do anything to help?"

He led his horse from the stall. His stomach quivered with dread. Would Rachel be here when he returned? "Please. Don't leave."

He watched as her eyes widened. He'd guessed correctly. She was contemplating leaving.

Damn he wished he didn't have to go. He leaned down and captured her lips in a quick kiss. He pressed his forehead against Rachel's. "We need to have a serious talk. But I have to take care of this matter first."

She nodded and backed away toward the house. "I'll go help Becky get supplies together."

Moments later Mitchell hurried into the house and headed to his bedroom. He reappeared with a saddlebag flung over his shoulder. He took the sack they had packed for him and gave Becky a quick hug.

Becky clung to her brother and whispered in his ear, "I don't like this, Mitchell. Please be careful."

Kissing his sister's cheek, he whispered, "I don't like what's happening either. You take care as well. Toby will be here to help you and Rachel."

He turned and gazed into Rachel's eyes. He cleared his throat. "Take care of yourself."

He watched as a blush rushed into her cheeks. Her eyes lowered before she murmured, "You too."

He stood undecided for a moment before he dropped his saddlebag, supplies and wrapped her into his arms. His lips crushed down on hers in a quick demanding kiss. He eased back and whispered, "Stay."

Chapter Twenty-Six

Two days later Rachel found herself busily hauling water to wash her laundry. Her arms ached as she dumped the steaming water into the tub. Sweat trickled down her face as she bent to her knees. Laundry in her time was a piece of cake compared to this endless chore. She'd hoped the activity would take her mind off the fact they hadn't heard from Mitchell.

She frowned as she absentmindedly rubbed at her clothing. The foreboding feeling she felt when he had ridden out hadn't diminished in the two days that had passed. She swiped an errant curl from her eyes as she thought of a song to sing to soothe her turbulent emotions.

Chet sat a short distance away panting. He tilted his head and cocked an ear as Rachel hummed. His brown eyes stayed focused on her as he laid his head on his paws. Suddenly his head jerked up and he rose.

Rachel stopped humming to glance over at Chet. "What's the matter, boy?"

A low growl emerged as he stood looking down the lane. She lifted a hand to shade her eyes from the morning sun and glanced to see what had captured the dog's attention. A man on a horse was riding in. Standing tentatively, her heart jumped into her throat. Was the rider Mitchell coming home?

Her excitement died quickly once she recognized

the rider. Fear moved in to take over. Jake reined in his mount and tipped his hat in greeting.

Jake's dark intent eyes scanned her from the top of her head to the bottom of her feet before offering a smile. "Good morning, Rachel." Another quick flick of his eyes over her body had her shuddering. "You are looking mighty pretty this morning."

How could he sit up there on his horse and act as if nothing had happened the last time they had seen each other? She stiffened with anger. "What do you want, Jake?" Her eyes widened as she realized she had asked the angry rude question aloud.

Jake shifted in his saddle and his dark eyes hardened. In a softly controlled voice he asked, "Now, sweetheart, is that any way to talk to a man who has come a courting?" Swinging off the back of his horse, he slowly sauntered toward her.

At his approach, she backed up until the back of her knees hit the washtub she had been bending over just a few moments before. A wave of helplessness descended. She felt her skirt pocket. Worse yet, she'd forgot her pepper spray.

Chet emitted a growl from low in his throat.

Jake scowled at the dog briefly before returning his focus to her. "What's the matter, Rachel?" He chuckled evilly. "Reeves ain't here to save you, is he? Or are you just scared on how you may react to a real man taking you in his arms?" His hands snaked out so quickly to grab her by her waist she didn't have time to avoid them.

She struggled to breathe normal as she asked calmly, "What makes you think Mitchell isn't here?" His arms were like steal bands. Her brain raced as she tried not to panic. She needed to keep him talking or she was going to be in deep trouble. The smell of sweat and grime clung to his body. She concentrated on not gagging.

"You're not very good at lying are you, my sweet Rachel?" He leaned in closer to inhale her scent. Lifting a strand of her hair, he caressed the lock with his fingers. "But, you know, that's okay. I know Reeves isn't here because I helped make sure he wasn't."

She gasped. "You! You're the one who took the cattle?" She struggled trying to break free, but his hands dug in like talons.

"Easy there."

Chet eased closer and barked at Jake.

"Shut up, you mutt!" He kicked out at the dog and hit him squarely in the side. Chet flew a short distance away.

She watched in concern at the unmoving dog. A breath of relief eased out as Chet slowly got up, whimpered, and skulked off to hide under the front porch. She controlled the tears threatening to fall.

Jake turned back. "There isn't any use fighting me, my sweet Rachel. I always get what I want in the end." He smiled with a wickedness she hadn't seen before as he studied her mouth. "You know I never got to sample those lips at the dance. I'm thinking it's about time I did."

As his head descended, she turned her head to the side, and his lips landed on her neck instead of her quivering lips. His chest was an unmovable wall as she shoved him away. She shivered in revulsion as his lips nibbled on her neck before traveling to the shell of her ear.

His arms were like two steel bands, the force of his embrace almost cut off her air as she struggled desperately. Whispering huskily, he bit her ear. "Things could be good between us. Can you feel how much I want you? Tell me you want me as much as I want you."

She was feeling faint and couldn't catch her breath. "Please Jake, I can't breathe, you're holding me too tight." He shifted and eased his hold. She took a deep relieved breath and tried to think. Shifting her weight, she drew a knee up to place a blow to his private regions.

He jerked back. "Try it, sweetheart, and you will regret it."

"Jake, please, don't." She tried once again to dislodge herself from his arms with a shove against his chest.

"Don't what, sweetheart? Don't stop?" He smiled, and his mouth once again started to descend to hers. As Rachel turned her head away, Jake grasped her chin firmly. "My kisses are just as good as Reeves, if not better." A gleam of satisfaction fell across his face as his lips settled firmly on her own.

She stood stiffly as he coaxed a response from her. His tongue flicked out and ran along the seam of her top lip. The tears Rachel had tried to control ran unchecked down her cheeks.

A loud click sounded from a short distance away. Jake stiffened.

"Let her go, Jake, or I swear I will put a hole through your sorry hide!"

He threw his hands into the air, releasing her. Backing up slowly, he turned to stare at Becky. She had a rifle pointed directly at his chest. Chuckling he asked, "What's the matter Becky, are you jealous? Don't worry I have enough to go around if you are willing to wait your turn."

"Move away from her, Jake." Becky held the rifle steady and sure.

Jake stood silently for a moment eyeing Becky. "You know there isn't any cause for you to be troubled. This is between Rachel and me."

Becky frowned and didn't back down. "No, I disagree with you, Jake. You made this my business the night you tried to hurt Rachel. I won't stand by and watch you hurt my friend."

"Damn it, Becky, put the gun down." He softened his tone. "I've never done anything to hurt you, Becky. Why don't you just go on about your business?" He eased his hands down from the air.

Becky briefly shifted her gaze from Jake to Rachel. "Are you okay?"

Rachel took a side step away from Jake, wiped the tears from her face, and nodded.

Winking at Becky, Jake grinned. "See, everything is okay."

Irritation filled Rachel at his calm dismissal of the situation. Impulsively, she took the few steps needed to step up to Jake and slap his face. "I want you to keep your hands off of me."

Jake's surprise turned to instant anger as he reached up to his stinging face. "You little…" He drew a fist back in retaliation when he heard the distinct sound of another rifle cocking in readiness.

A gravelly voice shouted, "Mitchell may not be here, but I am." Toby stood a short distance away with another rifle leveled at his chest.

Becky shuffled forward. "Get off our land, Jake. I don't want to see you back here again. Ever!"

Jake's gaze swiveled between Becky and Toby. His body radiated fury. He swiped at his lip where Rachel had slapped. He examined the blood on his fingers before rubbing them together. "I suggest you ladies watch your backs." Hitching his head toward Toby he stated, "He's not always going to be around to protect you. Who knows what would happen then."

"Enough!" Toby shouted. "I suggest you ride out of here like the little lady told you to do."

Jake turned his head and spit. He glared at Toby as he backed up and picked up the reins dangling on the ground. Tipping his hat, he smiled sweetly at Rachel. "A pleasure once again, Miss Rachel. Your lips are as divine as I had imagined. Until the next time I can sample them, I wish you sweet dreams." Swinging up into his saddle the smile vanished as fast as it had appeared. "Don't forget what I said. Watch your backs."

With a swift hard kick of his heels, Jake turned and urged his horse down the lane. Not once did he glance back to see if he was in any danger of being shot.

Rachel trembled uncontrollably. Her bones felt like jelly. She sank to the ground. The encounter with Jake had scared the bejeebers out of her.

Propping the rifle up against a nearby tree, Becky rushed to Rachel's side. "Are you okay?"

Rachel glanced from Becky to Toby and shook her head. "I don't think I feel so good." She rubbed her hands up and down her arms trying to ward off the chill that had taken up residence within her body. "I want to thank both of you. I'm not sure I could have fought him off by myself." She pointed at the rifle leaning against the tree. "Could either one of you teach me how to use that?" She swallowed the hysteria that was threatening. "Or maybe how to shoot a pistol?"

Becky reached out and put a calming hand on Rachel's shoulders. "We would be happy to teach you how to shoot anything you would like." She leaned in to give her a hard hug. "I'm just glad I heard Chet barking, or I wouldn't have known something was wrong."

"Oh, Chet!" Rachel scrambled to her feet and ran over to the porch. Leaning down her anxious gaze searched for the scraggly pooch. As her eyes adjusted to the dimness, she saw the dog rolled in a ball in the far corner. "Chet?"

Rachel released a relieved sigh as she saw the dog's tail start to wag at her voice. "Come here, boy." He inched toward her with his tail between his legs. Once the dog came out, Rachel's hands made quick work of checking his body for any damage Jake may have caused. Grabbing his scruffy face, she rubbed her face against his head. "Thank you, you are a brave dog for trying to help. I think you will be okay."

Chet licked her hand. His soulful eyes locked with her own before he turned to shuffle back under the porch.

Sinking back onto her heels she looked at Becky. "I could use a Margarita or a good stiff drink."

"I'll have to check to see if we have any spirits. Let's get you inside. Maybe you can rest for a bit. The laundry can wait."

Once inside, Rachel sat down heavily on the couch.

Her legs still didn't want to cooperate with her. She watched as Becky returned with a small glass in her hand.

"Here drink this. I found a small stash of whiskey in the pantry. Mitchell must have put in there. This should help calm your nerves a little."

She shook away the images replaying in her mind. Lifting her hand, she swiped at her lips trying to rid the feel of Jake's lips and tongue.

Becky held out the cup once again for her to take. "Try not to think about what happened. Here. This really should help."

She sniffed the contents. The smell was overpowering. She'd never sampled whiskey before. What she wouldn't give for an Italian Margarita.

She took a swallow of the brew and gasped. Her throat and belly caught fire as the whiskey travelled to her stomach. "Why do I have to attract the weirdos like a magnet?" She took another tentative sip and glanced at Becky.

Becky tilted her head. "Weirdos? I'm not sure I know what that word means. Do you mean you attract the wrong type of man?"

With a tilt of the glass, she finished off the whiskey. The liquor definitely was working its magic. She felt warm and relaxed. "The men I like usually don't give me a second glance. The ones I try to avoid," she shrugged and left the statement incomplete.

"Mitchell likes you."

She accepted the reassuring pat on her back Becky offered, but really didn't want to argue. Could she dare to believe her? Because Lord help her, she had fallen in love with him. Rising somewhat unsteadily, she handed the empty glass to Becky. "I'm going to go lay down. I think I will feel better after I rest a moment."

"Go lie down. Don't worry about your laundry. I'll hang your things on the line for you."

"Thank you. I appreciate the help." She shut the bedroom door and let the tears she had been holding in check to fall. Sobbing, she eased onto the bed. What a mess. This situation was more frightening than when she realized she wasn't where she belonged. She wished her mom or Angie were here to help her through, but they weren't. Laying down, she hugged the feather pillow. Closing her eyes, she was asleep within seconds.

****

Becky waited a few moments before quietly making her way down the hall to peek in to see if Rachel was resting. Shutting the bedroom door, she headed out to find Toby. She shivered. What would have happened if Toby hadn't been around?

Becky paused on the front porch. Chet lay sprawled nearby. Poor old boy. He'd put in quite a fight today. She bent and gave him a soft pet. "What a little hero you are. We couldn't have fought Jake off without you. What a good boy." She rose and glanced about the yard for Toby.

She found him a few moments later by the barn whittling on a stick.

He paused in his task and scowled. "Is Rachel okay?"

She sat down on a bale of hay next to him and studied the project in his hand. "She's resting." Glancing back toward the house she tried to control the shudder that shook her. "Jake really shook her up. I guess I understand why Mitchell didn't want him hanging around me. He's not a nice man. I hadn't realized."

Toby eased the piece of wood in his hand back under the blade of his knife and smoothly drew the sharp edge down. "Sometimes actions show the truth about a person."

She glanced in the direction Jake had ridden. "He'll be back. We need to get word to Mitchell that Jake was here, don't we?"

He nodded his head. "Yeah, he will be back. An old man, a mangy mutt, and two women won't stop the likes of him."

"You are not an old man, Toby." Becky laughed as Toby pointed the stick he held. "Okay, maybe just a little seasoned."

Shaking his head, he chuckled. "You sure know how to make a body feel good." He took the knife and stabbed the blade into the ground. "We do need to get word to Mitchell, but I'm not sure I want to leave you ladies here by yourselves."

She nodded her head in understanding. "Would the situation improve if I went to tell Mitchell?"

He spit. "No, Miss Becky, I don't believe so." He gazed at the sun in the sky. "If I go now, Mitchell could be back before the sun goes down."

A shiver raced down her spine. "We don't even know where Mitchell is. You could end up searching awhile before you find him."

He nodded and gazed off into the distance. "I have an idea where to look."

"All right. We don't have much choice. I'll have the rifle loaded and ready for trouble." She took his rough hands in her own. "Please hurry and be safe."

He nodded. He rose and strode toward the barn. "I'll move as fast as these seasoned old bones can carry me."

She ran her hands up and down her arms and called after him, "Good luck! I'm praying you find him fast."

Chapter Twenty-Seven

Mitchell paused in repairing fence to wipe his brow with the back of his gloved hand. He hadn't expected the damage to his fence to be so extensive when he had ridden out two days ago. Each time his thoughts wondered on who would have done such a thing; they kept coming back to Jake Sanders. He couldn't shake the feeling Jake was involved.

The sun was high in the sky and beating down on him. He unbuttoned his shirt, shrugged out of it, and hung it on a nearby post. They had been working on this line of fence since early morning. This spot had been the worst patch. He had sent some of his men out to find the cattle. He had yet to hear from them.

He glanced over to where his ranch hand, Buck, worked. They'd repaired quite a bit of fence. He hoped to finish soon. Sighing, he glanced down at his feet. The truth of the matter was he was missing Rachel, her laughter, just the sight of her. He needed to tell her how he felt. The truth was he was scared. What if she didn't feel the same way? Or a more farfetched reason to be terrified is the claim she's from the future. Would she just one day disappear, and he would never hear from or see her again?

"Buck. Let's take a break. This fence isn't going anywhere."

Buck picked up his canteen and took a huge

swallow. "You won't hear any arguments from me."

Mitchell smiled. "Didn't figure I would. We've had a hard morning." He reached for his saddlebag and brought out a biscuit. Taking a bite, he sat under the nearest tree. The low limbs provided partial shade as he leaned his head against the rough bark.

His mind wandered back to the ranch. He hoped Rachel hadn't left. He had asked her to stay. Had she? He had seen her intention clearly written on her face the morning after the dance. What would he do if she chose to leave? Closing his eyes against the thought, he struggled for a second or two against the pain that thought had caused.

"Boss?"

Startled out of his reverie he looked at Buck. He wasn't looking at him, but off into the distance. Noticing the sound of a horse approaching, Mitchell eased to his feet. He cursed silently when he realized the rider was Toby. Something was wrong. Toby wouldn't have ridden out here otherwise.

As Toby reined in his horse, Mitchell studied Toby's relieved expression. Bracing himself for what news Toby brought, Mitchell asked, "What's wrong Toby?"

Toby looped the reins over his saddle horn and swung down from his horse. "Jake was at the ranch this morning slinking around." Toby swallowed hard and caught his breath, he wasn't looking forward to telling Mitchell about the scene he had witnessed when he had arrived in the yard.

Mitchell's hands clinched by his sides as Toby confirmed his fears. He was convinced now Sanders was the one behind the damaged fence and the missing cattle. Struggling to control the anger that flared, Mitchell pounded a fist against the tree. Jake had made certain Mitchell would be away from the ranch house and out of the way. He inhaled deeply as he waited for Toby to explain. At Toby's struggle to find words, he asked, "What happened?"

Toby cleared his throat. "Rachel was out this morning doing laundry when Jake showed up and made unwanted advances toward her. If Becky and I hadn't intervened, I would hate to think what might have happened to Miss Rachel."

The joy of hearing Rachel was still at the ranch was quickly overshadowed by the rest of what Toby said. Anger made his gut churn. Slowly his frustration bubbled out in a low menacing growl. Turning abruptly, he paced over to the fence where his shirt hung and jerked it off the post. He strode to the makeshift campfire where his bedroll and saddle lay. With quick jerks, he packed his belongings into his saddlebag.

"I've got to get back to the ranch. If I know Jake, he probably watched you leave the ranch and knows Rachel and Becky are alone." Mitchell paused in his packing when Toby groaned. Reaching up, he placed a gentle hand on Toby's shoulder and murmured, "It's all right. Things will be okay."

He finished stuffing his belongings into the saddlebag and strode over to where Rebel grazed. He flung instructions to Toby from over his shoulder. "I would like for you to stay here and help Buck finish the repairs." He cut Toby's protest off with a question, "Was Rachel hurt?"

Toby shook his head at the softly spoken question. "Becky had the rifle pointed at him by the time I got up to the house from the barn. Rachel was shaken up, but not really hurt. Jake, he warned us, said he knew you weren't around, and we needed to watch our backs."

"That no good son of a... He planned this." Mitchell made short work of saddling Rebel and swung up into the saddle. As he shifted in the saddle, he muttered a few more choice words. What would have happened if he hadn't left Toby behind? Patting Rebel's neck to soothe both him and the horse, he muttered, "Come on boy; we're heading home."

With a firm hold on the reins, Mitchell issued final instructions. "Toby, the repair to the fence is almost done. This is the last bit needing fixed. Come back as soon as you and Buck get done." He gazed off into the distance for a few seconds. "I hope the others will be able to find the cattle and be back soon."

Toby looked up at him and laid a hand on Rebel's neck. "I don't like this. Not one bit. I still think I need to come back to the house with you. Who knows what trap Jake has set for you? I think you are going to need all the help you can get."

He shook his head. "I smell an ambush as well, Toby, but this is something that has been brewing between me and Jake for some time. Help Buck finish the repairs."

Toby cursed lightly under his breath. "All right, but you be careful. I didn't see which direction Jake was heading when he left the ranch."

Mitchell tipped his hat, swung Rebel about, and started home. Thoughts of the broken down fence and missing cattle soon fled from his mind as he focused on getting back. The idea Becky and Rachel were at the ranch by themselves had his whole body shaking with a chill he couldn't dispel. How was he going to get word to the sheriff on what had been happening over the last couple of days? He groaned. He should have sent Toby into town after the sheriff. Where was his brain?

As soon as he knew the ladies were safe, he needed to rectify his error. The sheriff needed to dig deeper into Sanders' business. Was Jake acting alone, or were his orders coming from higher up? Mr. Waters had been bugging his family for years about buying them out.

Mitchell rode as fast as he could through the trees until he came to a clearing. The area seemed quiet and serene. Too calm. Where were the birds that were chirping happily not a few moments before? Apprehension crept up his spine. Something wasn't right. He scanned the land for any sign of trouble. Nothing seemed to be amiss, but not seeing danger didn't mean the possibility didn't exist. "Come on, boy," Mitchell urged Rebel. The faster he got across the open meadow back into the trees the less of a target he would make.

A short distance from the trees a noisy buzzing sound whizzed by his left ear. He leaned over his horse's neck and stiffened as he prepared for the next shot to hit its mark. Kicking Rebel in his sides, he motivated him to move a little faster. The report of the rifle echoed about a few seconds in the air before he felt a bullet slam into him. He fell and lay stunned on the ground as a wave of pain radiated from his left shoulder. A dust cloud settled around him as he lost consciousness.

Chapter Twenty-Eight

Drawing the curtain aside, Becky gazed upon the yard looking for any kind of movement. As soon as Toby had ridden out to fetch Mitchell, a quietness had fallen that was about to drive her crazy. She flipped the curtain closed, lifted the rifle, and resumed pacing. What could be taking them so long to get back? Had Toby been able to find Mitchell? Pausing in her stride, a noise reached her ears. She held her breath and listened intently. Was that the sound of a horse approaching? In a few steps, she was back at the window peering out into the yard. A horse stood near the porch pawing at the ground. A gasp escaped as she realized the rider less mount was Rebel, and he was alone.

Grasping the rifle firmly, Becky slowly eased the front door open and stepped outside. She quickly scanned the surrounding structures and trees. Tentatively stepping down the front steps, she reached for the reins dangling on the ground. Rebel snorted and tossed his head as Becky ran a calming hand down his neck. "Whoa, boy. That's a good fella." She felt Rebel's neck muscles bunch and slowly relax as she stroked his neck. Her gaze examined the horse, looking for injuries. Noticing a dirty mark on the saddle, she reached out a tentative hand to run her fingers across the dark spot. Peering closer, she realized the stain was dried blood. Tears pooled in her eyes as her hand flew to her trembling lips. "Oh Rebel, what's happened?"

Panic churned and bubbled inside her as she took a steadying breath. Mitchell was fine! He had to be. Shaking herself mentally, she quickly tied Rebel up to the front porch rail and raced back up the steps into the house.

Her heart raced as she slammed the door. Almost losing her footing, she gazed about the room for something to prop under the knob.

"Becky, what's the matter?" Rachel rubbed the sleep from her eyes as she walked into the room.

Becky burst into tears. "I don't know what we are going to do." She wrung her hands as the panic she was trying to control slipped. "There was blood! Blood!"

Rachel frowned as Becky paced. In a few strides, she was across the room and grasping Becky's shoulders. "What blood? You aren't making any sense, Becky. What are you talking about?"

Becky motioned toward the door weakly. "Rebel. His saddle, blood."

Becky was sobbing uncontrollably now. Dread settled in the pit of Rachel's stomach. She didn't understand what Becky was ranting about, but obviously, her raving had to do with Mitchell's horse. She took a calming breath and tried to interpret what Becky was trying to tell her. "Rebel showed up here?" Becky nodded and bit her lip to try to control her sobbing. What else had Becky said? Something about Rebel's saddle and blood. "There was blood on the saddle?" Becky nodded again and a bout of fresh tears rushed down her face.

Her hands shook as they dropped from Becky's

shoulders. She strode to the window and pulled aside the curtain. There had to be a reasonable explanation why Rebel was here. Riderless. She wasn't going to panic. Mitchell was fine. Damn it, he had to be fine. She hadn't come all this way to find a man to love to lose him now.

Love? Yes, she loved him. She had been denying and fighting her feelings for days. What would she do if something happened? Releasing the curtain, she angrily swiped at the tears trailing down her cheeks. "He's fine," she shouted into the quiet room. "We're not going to panic! Do you hear me?" Turning, her gaze met Becky's. "We need to remain calm." Wiping the last trace of tears from her face, she cleared the alarm from her mind. Jake! He was the one responsible for this. Her lips firmed as she realized she had to be right. "Becky, I think Jake did this. He wants to scare us to do something stupid."

Becky sobered. Her eyes flashed with anger. "Jake? Even Jake wouldn't stoop this low. Would he?"

She bit her lower lip and nodded. "He would be my first choice as a suspect. He admitted he was the one who tore up Mitchell's fence. Why wouldn't he try to hurt Mitchell?"

Becky's eyes welled up with renewed tears. "Do you think he…" She swallowed. "Do you think he killed my brother?"

With determined steps, she walked over to Becky and pulled her into her arms. "We can't think that way. Mitchell is fine. We need to keep our thoughts positive. Jake will win otherwise."

They took a few moments to cling to each other to gather a calm and strength they both needed.

With a shuddering breath, she drew away from Becky. "We've got to have a game plan. Do you have anything brilliant up your sleeve?"

Becky chewed on her bottom lip and glanced out the window. "It will be dark soon. Do you think Jake will be expecting us to go looking for Mitchell? He's probably watching the house." She stopped talking suddenly and glanced at Rachel. "We both need to go looking for Mitchell so you are not here by yourself. Because we both know that is what Jake is hoping for. You to be left alone."

Before Becky had finished her statement, she began shaking her head. "You don't understand. Becky, I don't know how to ride a horse. I would just hamper you. I can't go with you."

"Now is not the time to be joking around, Rachel," Becky stated forcefully. "What do you mean you can't ride a horse?"

She shook her head. "Oh, Becky, I wish I was joking, but I'm not."

"I don't understand." Becky's hands fluttered in irritation. "Why would my brother give you a horse if you don't even know how to ride one?"

Rachel could understand Becky's annoyance. If she had been in Becky's shoes, she would be just as confused. Shrugging, she explained, "I hadn't expected Mitchell to give me a horse. I think he did so because I told him I missed my Mustang." She sighed, "Except the Mustang I was missing was a car, not a horse." She watched as Becky tapped her foot impatiently waiting for her to clarify. "A car is a means of transportation that runs with a motor. Two totally different types of horse power."

"Oh. I believe I've heard of those. They are something new." Becky nibbled her lip. "I'm gathering from our conversation earlier you don't know how to shoot a rifle either, do you?"

Her gaze followed Becky's finger to where she pointed. Suddenly her mouth was dry as dirt. Shaking her head, she looked back at Becky. The situation wasn't looking too good from any direction. "No."

Becky released a groan and picked up the rifle. "I'm going to have to leave you here. I don't think there is any other way. I will give you a quick lesson, and then I'm going to go find my brother." They both looked into each other's eyes worriedly not wanting to voice their concerns or their worst fears that they may not find Mitchell alive.

The next few minutes blurred in her mind as Becky took the time to show her how to load, unload, and shoot the rifle. The instructions seemed simple and easy, but she would have felt better if she had actually had the chance to fire the rifle. The time constraints that they were working against hung heavily unsaid between them. A bead of sweat made a trail down the side of her face as she listened intently to Becky's instructions. Oh how she wished calling nine-one-one to ask for assistance was an option.

While Becky went into Mitchell's room to find some old jeans to wear, she retrieved a few supplies for Becky. Becky was rolling up the legs of the denims she wore when Rachel came back with a small sack of supplies. Handing the bag to her, she glanced out the window to see the shadows of dusk beginning to settle.

"I packed the whiskey from the pantry, some extra clothes, bandages, and a knife inside the bag." She closed her eyes and said a silent prayer for Becky's safety and for Mitchell's safe return as well. Please, Lord, let him be okay.

Becky sighed. "I need to leave. I still think you should come with me."

"I would only hinder you instead of helping if I came along, and we both know it." She watched as Becky struggled with her decision to go. "Becky, Mitchell needs you. You can't stay here and babysit me."

"I know, but I don't want anything to happen to either one of you." Both were close to tears again. "I will take Rebel, maybe he can show me where Mitchell is quickly, and we can get back here before anything happens here at the ranch." Before something happens to you was left unspoken as Becky gazed at her keenly.

She grabbed Becky's arm. "Please. Be careful!"

"I will, and I need you to be careful as well!" Becky crossed to the front door and slowly opened it. "Bar this door after I leave."

She nodded. "Becky, I…" Her voice trailed off. She couldn't get the words past her clogged throat.

Becky looked at her in understanding. "I know."

"Love him," she softly whispered as the front door clicked shut. Hurriedly she rushed over to lock the door and shoved a chair from the kitchen under the knob. Leaning over, she eased the curtain aside in time to see Becky stop in the yard to pet Chet on the head and issue him an order to stay. A few moments later, Becky grabbed Rebel's dangling reins and swung onto the horse's back. Quietly the horse and rider left.

Chapter Twenty-Nine

Mitchell groaned as he opened his eyes. What had happened? He tried moving and winced as he rolled over to his back. A dull pain radiated from his left shoulder as he sat up. He eased back down and stared at the darkened sky. Stars twinkled brightly as he cleared his thoughts. He had been on his way to the ranch to be with Becky and Rachel. His lips firmed in anger. He had been bushwhacked. How could he have been so careless and stupid?

He winced as he tried again to sit, gritting his teeth as pain reverberated through his shoulder. A wave of dizziness threatened as he sat awkwardly cradling his arm. He commanded himself not to be sick and pulled his shirt aside to examine the wound on his arm. A fresh trail of blood started as he pulled the shirt aside. The bullet had gone through the fleshy part of his arm.

He ripped a strip of material from the bottom of his shirt and wound the fabric around his forearm to stop the flow of blood. How much blood had he lost, and how long had he been unconscious?

He squinted into the dusk scanning the area for Rebel. Softly he whistled for his horse. He listened intently for a moment before he realized there was no answering sound or movement.

The nighttime breeze rustling the meadow grass was the only noise that reached his ears. He swore

197

softly under his breath. Grasping his arm, he slowly rose to his feet. He swayed a bit and tried whistling again for Rebel. Gathering his bearings, he started in the direction of the ranch.

****

Becky eased up in the stirrups to stare into the night. The going had been slow. The darkness had been a hindrance until the moon finally rose big and bright casting enough light on the land to see the ground in front of her. Worry wrinkled her brow as her eyes strained to make out objects. Was Rachel doing okay back at the ranch? She hated the fact she had to leave her behind, but she had to find Mitchell. As the minutes ticked by, she became more and more anxious to find her brother.

She reined Rebel in as she approached a small stream. Where could they cross safely? The horse jerked impatiently on the reins. She gave his neck a quick pat. "Okay, boy, which way do we need to go?"

He snorted, turned, and started across the stream. Moonbeams bounced off the trees lurking on the other side, casting eerie shadows. If Becky hadn't been so concerned about her brother and getting back to the ranch, she would have been scared to death.

As they continued into the night, her eyes grew heavy. How long had she been riding? Suddenly Rebel stopped and let out a soft snort. Jerking to awareness, she squinted trying to make out what had caused Rebel to pause. "What's the matter, boy?" Listening carefully to the night noises, she couldn't discern anything unusual. Wait. Did she just hear a groan?

She slid out of the saddle and scanned the area as best as she could. Whispering softly she asked,

"Mitchell, is that you?" Tilting her head, she listened. Not another sound was forthcoming. Disgusted, Becky turned and leaned her head against Rebel's side. She was so tired. A few moments passed as she closed her eyes and rested for a moment.

Her head whipped up as another sound not fitting into the night emerged. The deep-throated noise echoed again in the night's stillness. The moan hadn't been her imagination. She dropped to her knees extending her hands out frantically searching the grass. Moments later, she located the still form on the ground.

"Oh, Mitchell." She rolled him to his back. Leaning, she listened to his even breathing. What a relief. He was alive, but how badly was he hurt? Blinking back grateful tears, she whispered, "Oh, Mitchell. I'm so glad you're alive. I was so scared."

He opened his eyes and attempted a smile. "Hey Beck. I'm glad to see you too."

Her tears fell unheeded and dropped onto his face. "I am so glad you aren't dead."

"Well, I soon will be if you continue to cry on me. Are you trying to drown me?"

She chuckled and wiped at her tears. "Oh, Mitchell, Rachel and I were so worried when Rebel showed up to the ranch with blood on his saddle. What happened to you?"

"I was stupid. I let my guard down, and someone got the better of me and winged me."

"You're shot?" The moon had disappeared behind a cloud, and she couldn't see his features clearly. Once the light reemerged, she could tell his shirt had been soaked by blood and was stiff from drying. She grimaced as she thought about what her life would've been like if he wasn't there.

She had a hard time when her parents passed. If something happened to Mitchell, she didn't know what she'd do. She shook the thought from her head. There was no room for those thoughts. Her nostrils flared as her irritation and anger grew. Who would have taken a shot at her brother? Could Rachel be right? Was Jake the one behind this? "If I was a wagering person, I would bet Jake Sanders is the one responsible for doing this!"

"I don't like when you jump to conclusions Beck, but I'm not going to argue with you on this one."

She peeled back his shirt to examine his wound. "Looks like the bullet went through. I can have this stitched up in no time."

He winced as Becky continued to examine his arm. "Guess I'm lucky I have a sister who is a wonderful seamstress."

"Yeah and I won't let you forget the fact." His chuckle followed her as she retrieved the supplies Rachel had packed. Sitting crossed legged, she opened the bag and brought out what she needed. "Are you cold? Should I start a fire? Or do you think I shouldn't chance making one?"

He gave a disgusted snort. "Whoever did this is long gone. You had better start a fire so you can see what you are doing. I would hate for you to sew something together that doesn't need mending."

She emitted an offended huff. "Don't you be ungrateful, Mitchell Reeves! Do you see anyone out here coming to rescue your sorry hide?" She rose to her feet. "I'm going to find some wood."

The search proved more difficult than she had

imagined. The moon was playing peek-a-boo behind the cloud cover that had formed. She should have brought a lantern. The thought had never occurred to her when she was rushing about the house. At least Rachel had the foresight to pack some matches. A short time later, she sat back in satisfaction as a small fire came to life. She glanced over at her brother to see how he was fairing.

She bit her bottom lip and reached for the bottle of whiskey. This wasn't going to be easy. She'd never sewn human flesh before. She stiffened her resolve and gently nudged his good arm. "Mitchell? I've got the fire going." She waited until his eyes focused on her. "I have some whiskey. Maybe you should take a swig for good measure before I begin."

She waited as he lifted the bottle to his lips and took a deep swallow. With shaking hands, she threaded a needle.

His eyes met hers. "Okay. I'm as ready as I'm going to be."

She grabbed the bottle, took a big swig, and started coughing. The liquid encouragement burnt a fiery trail down the back of her throat. She wiped her burning eyes before pouring liquor over the needle and wound. Once her eyes cleared, she concentrated on her sewing skills.

She cringed at his indrawn breath and small gasp. She stiffened her back and continued. She wiped a stray hair from her eyes with the back of her hand. Her stomach revolted as she continued to stitch. She was glad the bullet had torn through his flesh instead of being lodged. She wasn't sure she could have handled digging a bullet out.

Perspiration clung to her forehead as she finished. Dabbing at the wound with a cloth soaked in whiskey, she inspected her handy work by the low glow from the fire. Not bad for her first attempt.

She wrapped his arm and leaned back. "Mitchell. I'm done." She glanced at her brother. The ordeal had taken a toll, and he appeared to be asleep. The situation could've been so much worse. She lifted a trembling hand to wipe her brow and stared into the flames of the dying fire. She would let him rest for a bit. She just prayed a fever or infection didn't set in.

Chapter Thirty

Rachel nibbled on her thumbnail as she paced the front room. She was restless and felt so helpless. What would happen if Becky didn't find Mitchell? She had been pacing the floor ever since Becky had ridden away. She shuddered as her imagination began to work overtime. Countless stories of the old west and the brutality that some people suffered in that time kept prancing through her brain. She silenced her errant thoughts as she closed her eyes and said a thoughtful prayer. Mitchell and Becky were going to be fine. They just had to be.

She jumped as she heard Chet emit a low growl from his position on the porch. The sound evoked a tremor to trickle down her spine. Whirling, she grabbed the rifle resting against the couch. She strode across the room and leaned against the wall. The gun shook as she held the weapon against her chest. She mentally considered all of the windows and doors in the house. Had she secured them all? Leaning over the table, she blew out the lamp she had lit earlier in the evening. Darkness settled over the room. She hadn't heard another sound from Chet. Should she be worried about the scruffy dog? She raised the nearby curtain and scanned the dark yard for signs of movement.

A slow burning sensation erupted in her stomach. This nervous anticipation was going to make her sick.

Was that movement she had caught sight of over by the barn? Could she trust what her eyes were seeing, or was her imagination working overtime once again?

Her breathing echoed harshly in her ears. She swallowed and pointed the gun at the door. Come on, you sucker, she thought, try to come to get me. Hysteria was building inside of her. She felt like Dirty Harry and asking someone to "make her day." Oh Mitchell, where are you? I need you!

****

Mitchell awoke abruptly. What had disturbed his sleep? He shifted and tried rolling to his side. He groaned as he rolled onto his sore arm. Sitting up, he looked at his sister sleeping by the dying fire. Glancing down at his shoulder, he examined the bandage she had placed on his wound. "Becky?"

Becky was alert and scrambling to his side in seconds. "Are you okay? Do you still hurt?" She lifted her hand to feel his forehead.

"What are you doing?"

"I just wanted to make sure you didn't have a fever."

He placed a hand over her own that rested in her lap. "I'm feeling a lot better. Thanks to you."

"You don't know how anxious we've been. This day has been trying."

"Did you leave Rachel at the ranch?"

"I had too. Did you know she doesn't know how to ride a horse?"

Mitchell swore and released her hand. "We've wasted time. We need to get back. I've a bad feeling."

"Are you sure you can ride?"

He threw her a disgusted look. "For God's sake,

Becky, I don't have time to convalesce! Rachel's in trouble."

"I know that, you stubborn goat! I just don't think I can handle you falling off your horse and breaking your fool neck." She placed a hand under his good arm. "Let me help you. You'll fall on your butt if I don't."

"Sorry. I didn't mean to snap." He wove his fingers through his already disheveled hair. "I'm a little irritated with this whole situation."

Becky linked her arm around his waist and started to lead him to Rebel. He paused and shuffled closer to the dying embers of the fire. He kicked dirt over the ashes.

"Mitchell. Stop it. I'll take care of the ashes. Let's get you on Rebel." Becky led him over to the horse and waited patiently for him to put his foot in the stirrup. She gently shoved his backside as he swung up into the saddle.

"I'll be just a moment." Becky grabbed the canteen attached to Rebel's saddle horn and poured the contents onto the fire. She stirred the embers with a nearby stick. "I think that should do." Turning, she hitched her foot into the stirrup and pulled herself up behind him.

He grunted as she jostled him. "Are you ready?"

Becky gently wrapped her arm around his waist. "Please be careful. We don't want you reopening your wound."

"I will, but the sooner we get back home and find Rachel safe, the happier I'll be."

Chapter Thirty-One

Rachel's eyes lowered. Then wrenched open. She was exhausted! Fatigue oozed from her body. She needed to stay awake. Jake was counting on her to make a mistake. Like falling asleep. Glancing about the moonlit room, she searched for something to occupy her mind. She didn't dare light a lamp to read a book. Constantly biting her lip hadn't worked to keep her awake either. Easing up from the couch, she slowly approached the window. How many times had she found herself looking out the window, hoping to see Becky and Mitchell returning? At least thirty minutes had passed since Chet had put her nerves on high alert.

Maybe Becky was just being paranoid. Nothing was going to happen. She peeped out the window and spotted Chet's shape lying on the top step of the porch. His head suddenly jerked to attention. A low growl emerged from his throat. Her heart skipped a beat. The growl turned into several disturbingly loud barks. Swallowing nervously, she leaned back from the window. Maybe he was barking at a rabbit invading his territory. A few moments later, she heard his barking end with a yelp. The yard became eerily silent. Was he all right? Had Jake come back and killed him?

A footfall sounded on the wooden stairs outside. The sound was faint, but she knew someone had just stepped onto the front porch. She held her breath. The footsteps became louder the closer they came to the front door. Leaning heavily against the wall, she placed a hand to her chest and tried calming her rapidly beating heart. The rifle. Where had she left it? She squinted as she searched the darkened room. A scream tore from her throat as the glass shattered from the window mere inches from her head.

Heart pounding, she whirled away from the flying shards. She needed to escape! Her knees collided with the couch, and she fell to the floor. Her hands burned as glass ground into her palms as she crawled blindly across the room.

A startled cry escaped as the front door splintered. Wood particles flew about the room. Scrambling behind the couch, she caught a quick breath before eyeing the distance between her and the back exit. Edging a few inches, she hoped the darkness hid her from view. With a quick spring, she lunged to her feet and made a run for the door.

She had almost made her escape when her hair was caught firmly and jerked from behind. A painful yelp escaped as she heard a voice drawl behind her, "Not so fast, pretty lady. You're not going anywhere."

She swore and turned to glare at Jake. "Why are you doing this?" Tears of frustration and exhaustion pooled in her eyes.

His grip briefly tightened on her hair. "Why?" He chuckled crazily. "I gave you a chance. I want you! I get what I want."

His hot breath on her neck sent a shiver of fear down her spine. "I still don't understand. Why me? I'm nothing special."

He brought a handful of hair up to his nose and

breathed deep of the strands fragrance. "There is something about you. You're something special to me."

Something special to me. She'd always enjoyed that George Strait song until this moment.

Dropping her locks, he grabbed her arm and jerked, "Enough! Let's go, nice and easy. I would hate to have to hurt another hair on your beautiful head."

He pulled her across the room and shoved her down on the couch. "Light the lamp."

She winced as her scratched palms made contact with the fabric on the couch. "The matches are in the drawer of the desk. Light the lantern yourself." She gulped. Where was her bravado coming from?

He growled. "Lady, I don't think you grasp the situation you find yourself."

She raised her chin. "Probably not, but I'm not going to go easily."

"Don't move!" He shuffled over to the desk and rifled through the drawer. A flare suddenly lit the room, and he brought the wick up to full brightness and turned to look at her.

The intent look in his eyes had her squirming. His dark eyes held no humor or gentleness. Her throat constricted. Was there a way out of this mess?

He glanced about the room. "Where the hell is Becky? Where is she hiding?"

She hid her surprise. He didn't know Becky had ridden out. She pursed her lips so tight they ached.

"Becky! Come out," he shouted. He advanced toward Rachel and said angrily, "Answer me. Where is she?"

She heard him grinding his teeth in the short space that separated them. She closed her eyes and slowly opened them. She'd never been a good liar. Would she be able to bluff and let him think Becky was hiding somewhere close? Should she anger him more than she already had? Eventually he would realize she was alone. Struggling with the words she muttered, "She's not here."

He leaned down into her face, "Speak up, I didn't hear you. Where is she hiding?"

Rebelliously, she glared into his dark eyes. Through clenched teeth she answered, "I said, she's not here."

An evil grin spread across his face. A chuckle escaped. "Well. Well. That bit of news just made my evening. Guess that means you are at my mercy. Doesn't it, pretty lady?"

She leaned away from his sneering face. How she wanted to wipe the smirk off his face. Squaring her shoulders, she stammered, "Becky left hours ago. She went to fetch Mitchell. They both will be back here shortly. You had better not be here when Mitchell gets back. I'm sure he will shoot first and ask questions later."

The bark of laughter that escaped him took her by surprise. What had she said that could be construed as funny? His lips curved upward as he perched a booted foot upon the couch. He reached a steady hand into his coat and brought out the makings for a cigarette. "Most unlikely you will receive any help from Reeves. You see, I shot Reeves." He withdrew another match from the drawer and with a flick of his wrist lit the end of his finished cigarette. "He won't be riding to your rescue. Or anyone's."

She choked on the cloud of smoke unfurling from

the cigarette. Dead? No! She didn't believe him. She wouldn't. "Are you sure? Did you personally examine his body?"

A brief look of uncertainty crossed his features then vanished. Through clenched teeth he stated, "Let's get one thing straight. Reeves is dead! I don't miss what I aim at!"

A surge of hope flooded her body. He hadn't taken the time to make sure Mitchell was dead. That meant there was a good chance he was alive and well. How far should she push Jake? If she angered him further, what would he do?

His booted foot dropped from the couch and he ground out his unfinished smoke. "Get up! I've had enough of your mind games."

Her eyes met his boldly. "Why should I? You know I don't want to go with you." Her words were fearless, but she was feeling anything but brave as he stared her down.

He drew his Colt from his holster and waved the weapon under her nose. "Missy, my patience is gone. I said get up!"

She could feel the blood draining from her face as he brandished the pistol a few inches from her face. "Put that thing away. I'm getting up." She felt her limbs tremble uncontrollably as she eased to her feet. "Where are you taking me?" She could feel her heart hammering within her chest as she waited for him to answer.

He ran the barrel of the gun down her cheek. "Now if I told you, that would ruin the surprise, wouldn't it?" Pointing with the weapon he declared, "Go and be a good girl and pack a few of your things."

She couldn't think of any other time in her life more frightening than this moment. Even the night she time travelled didn't compare to the terror she was feeling. She had to be insane when she asked him challengingly, "And if I don't, go pack a few of my things. What will you do?"

He cocked his gun, and the sound echoed about the quiet room. "Then I'll make you."

Her eyes widened. Surely, he wouldn't actually shoot her if she didn't follow his instructions. Sidestepping him, she turned and headed toward the bedroom. She couldn't take the chance he was bluffing.

He followed her closely down the narrow hall, his presence daunted her every step. She glanced over her shoulder before opening the bedroom door. There had to be a way out of this mess.

She chewed on her bottom lip as she thought of a way to stall. "What exactly do I need to pack?" When Jake didn't respond, she turned and found him staring at the bed.

What was he looking at? Her gaze landed on her discarded nightgown. She rushed over and grabbed the garment. She wasn't sure what he was thinking, but she was sure she didn't want to encourage any fantasies he may be having about her.

He turned his heated gaze upon her. "As much as I would like to see you in that nightgown and have the opportunity to unveil your delectable body, we don't have the time for such pleasure."

She stood like a stone as his gaze turned form passionate to one of anger.

"Hurry up! You're wasting time on purpose."

She huffed. She wasn't the one who had taken the

time to ogle a piece of clothing. Her feet felt like lead weights as she crossed the room to the dresser. A few minutes later, her purse was stuffed. Her gaze caught on the small container of pepper spray. With a small sleight of hand, she deposited the spray into her skirt pocket.

An impatient sigh escaped his lips. "That's enough, we need to travel light." He still held the gun and indicated for her to leave the room.

"I need to grab my coat; the night has gotten colder."

Jake nodded his head.

She grabbed the green leather coat from the back of the rocker. The chair rocked back and forth as they left the room.

The situation seemed so surreal. Was she dreaming all of this? The time travel? Mitchell? The love she felt for him?

She startled as Jake's voice interrupted her thoughts. "Grab some extra food from the pantry."

She tried to bite her tongue. Really she did. The flow of sarcastic words burst forth from her mouth, "Someone wasn't prepared for this little caper. You wouldn't have made a good boy scout."

His hand rose as if to slap her but stopped inches from her face. "Enough! Last warning. My patience is gone. I won't stop myself the next time."

With a flinch, she stumbled a few steps back from him. What had she been thinking? Was she trying to get herself killed? Turning Rachel made her way to the pantry.

After placing a few items in a sack, he waved his gun toward the front door. "Let's go, we've wasted enough time."

A cool breeze hit Rachel as she stepped into the night and she shivered. "Wait. I need to put my jacket on."

Jake took the sack of food from her and tied the bag to his saddle horn. Turning, he eyed her. "Hurry up then. I don't have all night."

She smiled. A slug would move faster than she was at the moment. She shook out her jacket and pulled the coat on. She wasn't sure what else she could do to stall. She was running out of ideas. Suddenly she remembered Chet. "What did you do to Chet?"

The confusion on his face was clear. "Chet? Who the hell is Chet?"

"The dog. You didn't kill him did you?"

He snorted as he placed his pistol back into his holster. "Hell, that mangy mutt deserves to die. He's a nuisance. But I didn't kill him."

Now that the gun was holstered, she may have a chance of getting away from him. Hefting her purse off her shoulder, she waited for her chance to slug him. Studying the lurking shadows, she debated on which direction to run.

She made her way down the front steps. Jake turned to untie the reins of his horse from the porch and she pounced. Swinging her leather purse up with all of her might, she clocked him under his chin. Not taking the time to appreciate her David and Goliath move, she sprinted toward the barn. Loud cursing trailed her into the shadows.

She paused when she reached the barn door. This would be the first place he would look. Flinging the door open wide she hoped he would take the bait and look for her in the barn buying her some time. She skirted around the entrance and gazed about to get her bearings.

The night cast eerie shadows everywhere. She could just make out a line of trees a short distance away. If she could reach those, she may be able to hide from Jake long enough for help to arrive. Taking a deep cleansing breath, she started running.

Just before she reached the grove, a loud curse ripped through the air. Jake must have realized she wasn't in the barn. He would soon be in hot pursuit. She picked up her pace, ignoring the stitch in her side. Reaching the first tree, she stopped to catch her breath. Panting she bent down to rest her hands on her legs. She had to catch her breath. If she got out of this alive and in one piece, she really needed to get into shape.

How long did she have before Jake would look for her here? She peeked around the rough bark and gasped as she made out the shape of a horse and rider slowly making their way toward her. Whipping her eyes forward, she calculated the distance to the next hiding spot and crept toward it. A stick snapped beneath her feet before she safely made it to the tree. She froze briefly before rushing onward.

Jake laughed from a short distance away. "We can play this cat and mouse game all night. I enjoy the pursuit. Makes the diversion a little more exciting. Don't you think?"

How far could she run without him seeing her? She was a sitting duck if she didn't attempt to try. She swore she could hear her own heartbeat as she dashed forward. She gasped as she heard the sound of pounding hooves in pursuit.

She stole a glance over her shoulder. Running in appropriate attire was one thing, but the skirt she was wearing made the activity difficult. Why hadn't she had the foresight to put on her jeans? Suddenly she tripped on her hem and sprawled on the ground. She attempted to scramble to her feet as she heard a horse snort a short distance away. She gave a yelp as she was knocked down from behind. His body slammed what little air she had left out of her.

Her lungs burned. She wheezed in a breath and choked as she sucked in a little dirt from the ground.

Jake leaned down to whisper in her ear, "You could have just told me you like to play rough, and I would have been glad to oblige. All you had to do was ask." He chuckled as she bucked him off her back. He flipped her effortlessly to her back.

She pummeled his chest with her fists. "Let me go," she bit out through clenched lips.

He grabbed her flaying hands and stretched them above her head. "Where did you think you were going?" Jake smiled as she attempted to wrack him in the groin with her knee. "I've fantasized many times about you being in this position. I like my women feisty."

She stilled under his weight when she realized she was making her situation worse. "Get off of me! I'm not your woman! I will never be your woman, and I'm not going anywhere with you."

His eyes roamed over her face and journeyed down her body. He smiled again as she squirmed in earnest. "Too bad we don't have the time for me to explore your delicious body." Easing off her body, he rose to his feet and dragged her up to her feet. Leaning in he whispered in her ear, "Don't try running again, or you won't live to tell anyone."

Trying to wrench free of his grasp, she tried once again to lift her knee to place a well-placed blow to his private area.

He clasped her arm and grabbed the dangling reins of his waiting mount. "No more foolishness. You're coming with me."

She dug her heels in the soft ground. "No!"

"All right. You want to do this the hard way; we will do it the hard way!"

She watched in amazement as he drew back a fist, he was going to punch her. She couldn't believe what she was seeing. That's the last thought that ran through her head before she fainted.

Chapter Thirty-Two

The first fingers of dawn were stretching across the sky when the ranch came into view. Becky struggled to keep Mitchell upright as he leaned farther over in the saddle. Her arms were weary from keeping a tight hold upon him. Just a little bit further. She hoped when they arrived everything would be okay and their fear for Rachel had been unfounded.

Rebel picked up his pace. She knew he was just as tired. The relief at being home was short lived as she stopped in front of the house. Things were too quiet. Where was Chet and his welcoming bark? Letting out a quick whistle, she hoped the dog just hadn't heard them ride into the yard. She twisted in the saddle and gazed about. The hair on the back of her neck stood at attention. Something was wrong.

Her knees buckled as she slipped awkwardly off Rebel. She leaned against the horse's side for a minute. Reining in a calming breath, she straightened. She gently prodded Mitchell's arm. "Mitchell, wake up; we're home."

Mitchell jerked awake with a start. He straightened in the saddle before looking toward the house. "Is Rachel okay?"

"I'm not sure. I haven't been inside. Something doesn't feel right. Do you think you can manage to get off Rebel by yourself? Or do you need my help? I'm so tired. I'm not sure I could catch you if you fell." She stopped talking when she realized she was rambling.

"I think I can manage on my own. I'd hate to have me smashing you on my conscience." Taking his time, he slowly lowered himself from the saddle.

"Do you need any help?"

"No. I'm good." He had only taken a few steps before he stopped.

She almost tripped into him at his abrupt stop. "What? What's the matter?" Her gaze travelled to where he stared. On the ground lay Rachel's leather satchel. She swallowed hard and peered at the house. Shadows had been hiding the shattered window and busted door. Her stomach took a nosedive. Her fears had been justified. Dread settled as she prompted Mitchell to climb the front steps. "Let's check inside. Maybe Rachel was able to get an upper hand on Jake."

The front door swung on one hinge as they crossed the threshold. Alarm raced up Becky's spine as she took in the broken glass and splintered wood littering the floor. The rifle she left for Rachel to use as protection lay forgotten on the floor by the couch.

Mitchell growled his frustration. "I'll kill the bastard!"

Becky placed a calming hand on his arm. "Let's think sensibly. Being unreasonable won't help Rachel's situation."

Mitchell sighed. "I know. I just feel so helpless." He rubbed his tired eyes. "Beck, I need to find her. Who knows what that monster will do if I don't."

A chill chased down her spine. She didn't even want to mull over what Jake had planned. "You also need rest. You're about to fall over."

"I can't. Every second I waste here Jake slips farther away."

"You can. Just sit a moment on the couch while I find food to take with you. Please."

Glass crunched beneath his boots as he made his way to the couch. As he lowered himself he whispered, "I love her, Beck."

"I know, Mitchell." She watched her brother lean his head back and close his eyes. "Just rest for a minute. I'll hurry."

She rushed into the kitchen. The pantry door stood open, and she stepped over a stray can as she surveyed the shelves. Jake must have helped himself. A fresh wave of anger settled in as she scurried about.

She watched Mitchell sleeping for a moment. He hadn't moved a muscle since she had left him. She hated to wake him. Gently she shook his arm. "Mitchell."

He came awake instantly and sat up with a start. "How long did I sleep?"

"Just a bit."

Rubbing his face, he stood up. "I need to be going. Who knows how far behind I have gotten by sleeping just the short time I did."

She offered him a clean shirt. "Let me re-dress your wound before you go."

Chapter Thirty-Three

Mitchell reined in his impatience as Becky cleaned his wound and put on a fresh bandage. He flexed his arm. The injury was tender, but the pain he had experienced earlier had eased. "Thank you, Beck. The trail is getting cold. I need to go."

He inhaled deeply as he descended the front steps. Bending he examined the footprints in the yard trying to discern which direction Jake may have taken Rachel. There seemed to be some kind of scuffle before they led off in the direction of the corral.

Trailing after the prints, he inspected the ones he found down by the barn. His gaze rose to look at the stand of trees a small distance away. Rachel may have given Jake a hard time before he finally was able to take advantage of her.

He took several deep breaths fighting off the wave of dread wanting to emerge. Now was not the time to panic. He strode back to the house and retrieved Rachel's satchel. He glanced at Becky as she waited on the porch. "I think Jake took Rachel into the mountains." He gave a fleeting look at the closest range. "When Toby arrives back today, I need you to send him to town after the sheriff. He needs to let him know what has happened the last few days."

She clenched her hands together and nodded. "Are you sure Toby will be back to the ranch today?"

"He should." He took his hat off and hit it against his leg. "When Toby goes into town, I need you to go with him. I want you to stay there until I return."

"But, Mitchell, I'll be fine staying here at the ranch."

His gaze locked on her own, "Please Becky, don't argue with me." He swallowed and continued, "I need to know you are safe. Okay?"

Becky rushed down the front steps and hugged her brother fiercely. "I promise. Please take care of yourself. I don't want to have to come to your rescue again."

He chuckled. "I will keep that in mind. I'll try to keep a better eye out this time. Thanks, Becky." Swinging the bag of supplies and Rachel's satchel over his shoulder, he turned to leave. Rebel nudged his shoulder. He gave the horse's soft velvet nose a quick pet. "We didn't even get the saddle off did we boy? I'm sorry, but we don't have the time to rest. I hope you are up to this." He quickly tied the bags to his saddle horn. Lifting his leg into the stirrup, he mounted quickly. Giving Becky a quick wave, he rode from the ranch, his mind already on his search for Rachel.

Becky settled onto the porch chair and leaned her head back. A soft whimper broke through her pensive thoughts. Leaning up she scanned the area. "Chet?" The dog emerged from under the porch and limped slowly up the porch steps. The tears she had been fighting to contain since they had found Rachel missing pooled in her eyes and spilled over her lashes. She softly sobbed as she gently picked the dog up and gave his scruffy neck a gentle hug. Chet whined and licked her ear. "Oh, boy, you don't know how happy I am to see you."

Cradling the dog closely to her body she went inside and lay on the couch. Chet didn't stir as she closed her eyes, sent a brief prayer up before she fell into an exhausted sleep.

Chapter Thirty-Four

The throbbing in Rachel's head kept rhythm with the sound of hooves hitting rocks. Moaning, she opened her eyes but quickly closed them again at the view they encountered. She was riding a horse, but she'd envisioned her first ride differently. Jake had slung her over the saddle on her stomach like a sack of potatoes, and she rode sideways, her head hanging low. The horse was traveling along a very narrow path next to a deep gorge. The drop was easily a few hundred feet. How long had she been hanging over this horse with the blood rushing to her head? She felt faint and a little bit nauseated. "Please, let me up. I think I'm going to be sick." She contained a squeal as she felt Jake's hand roam up the back of her thigh and rest on her backside.

Reining in the horse Jake snidely remarked, "As you can see, I can't really let you off the horse at the moment. Not unless you want to take a spill down into the canyon."

She clenched her teeth as he kneed the horse and started up the path again. Barfing on his leg would serve him right! She mentally groaned as the horse slipped on the path and regained its footing. She was going to die. On the back of a horse.

She imagined herself somewhere else. After a few moments, her eyes flew open when she realized Jake had reined the horse to a stop. Had he decided to throw her off into the ravine after all? She breathed a sigh of relief as he removed his hand from her bottom.

Jake swung himself off the horse and slowly lowered her to the ground, purposefully sliding her backside down the full length of his frame.

A wave of dizziness had her crumbling to the ground.

Jake stood a few feet away, studying her.

She brought her hands up to rub at her throbbing temples. After a few moments, she started to feel better. Rising on shaky legs, she glared at him and raised a hand to throw a punch. "What the hell do you think you are doing? I don't believe I gave you permission to manhandle me."

His eyebrow quirked as he deflected the punch easily. "Who said I needed to ask for permission?" He pulled on a strand of her hair. "So, you do have the temper that goes with the red hair." Leaning in close he whispered, "Just remember to save some passion for later."

She took an uncertain step back managing to yank her hair from his grasp. What had she been thinking? Hadn't she learned she shouldn't be mouthing off or trying to strike him? Maybe she did have a death wish. This man wasn't someone to anger intentionally.

She gazed about taking inventory of the surrounding area. The gorge was just a few feet away, now was not the time to try to get away from Jake.

The sun was past its zenith in the sky indicating she'd been passed out for a good part of the day. Raising a trembling hand, she rubbed at her throbbing left temple. The nausea had receded, but her headache had not.

"Come on; if you are feeling better, we need to keep moving." He made a grab for her arm, but she dodged his grasp.

"Where are you taking me?"

His second attempt at grabbing her arm was successful. "Never you mind where we're going." She struggled as he clutched her waist and hoisted her up into the saddle. At least this time she was sitting up and facing forward. He swung up with ease behind her in the saddle and encircled her waist with his arm. Leaning forward she could feel his breath on her ear as he whispered, "Now isn't this a lot more comfy?"

Irritated, she jerked away to escape his mouth on her neck. She felt his thigh muscles bunch as he nudged his horse forward. Sitting stiffly, she watched as the trail stretched endlessly before them. If she had been in any other kind of situation, she would have enjoyed the view as they rode.

A few moments passed before she tried again to get an answer from him on his plans. "What are you planning to do with me, Jake?"

An evil chuckled rumbled in his chest. "Darling, if you can't figure that one out then you are not as smart as I made you out for."

She had to get away and soon. Her mind scrambled for a solution to her dilemma. Angie and her had enjoyed many backpacking excursions in these mountains, but that was with a backpack full of food and supplies. Could she last a day without the proper equipment? Did she have a choice?

She jerked from her musings as Jake stated, "I think Reeves will be more than willing to sell his ranch to Mr. Waters to get you back, don't you?"

If possible her spine stiffened further. "That's what this is all about," she asked in shock. "This is about getting your hands on Mitchell's ranch?"

She felt him shrug his shoulders. "Not my hands, exactly. Mr. Waters wants Reeves' ranch. I'm just following orders." He trailed a finger down her stiff back. "You just happen to be part of the package deal. Of course, I intend to have my fun with you before I actually agree to hand you back over to Reeves. I'm sure he will be more than happy to sign over his land to Mr. Waters to get you back."

An unladylike snort burst from her lips. "Dream on."

He halted the horse and drew her chin around with his finger. "What does that mean?"

She wrenched her chin free. "I said dream on. Boy are you screwed if you were planning on me being your trump card." She laughed. "Isn't this just rich? Mitchell isn't going to sign over his ranch because of me."

He prodded his horse forward. "I saw how he looked at you when you picnicked together at the July Fourth celebration. I think I have played my cards very well."

She firmly clamped her lips shut. He couldn't have seen any kind of affection from Mitchell that day. Mitchell had been too busy locking lips with his saloon girl and telling her no later in the evening.

They rode in silence the rest of the afternoon and into the evening as the sun slowly eased behind the mountains.

She shifted, trying to get a better position on the saddle. Her bottom ached. She was getting sore in places she didn't even know existed. When were they going to stop for the evening? Or were they going to at all. She was afraid to ask.

When he finally reined his horse in for the night, she sighed in relief. Her backside had lost feeling a couple of hours ago. Jake swung a leg over and alighted off the horse with ease. He didn't show any signs of suffering with the same problem she was having. Turning he wrapped his hands around her waist and brought her down off the horse. As her legs hit the ground, they gave out from under her, and she grasped his arms to steady herself.

"See, I knew you would come around." He clutched her closer to his body.

She jerked away from his arms and stumbled. "Don't flatter yourself. My legs gave way. I wasn't trying to snuggle with you."

He shrugged, turned, and dug in his saddlebag. "That's a shame sweetheart. You will change your mind." His gaze he tossed her way was fierce. "Or I could change your view for you."

She froze when she saw what he had pulled from his saddlebag. "What are you going to do with that," she stammered. She took a step backward as he advanced with a rope.

"Well, up to this point you haven't been very cooperative, and I don't want a repeat of last night. I need to gather wood for a fire." He untangled a little more of the rope as he continued, "So, I thought I would save myself the headache of having to chase you by tying you up."

"I'm sure that's really not necessary. I promise not to run off while you get firewood?"

He shook his head and chuckled. "Nice try. I don't

believe you."

She fought back as he dragged her hands together. He looped the rope easily around her wrists. Dragging her to a nearby tree, he helped her sit down before looping a length of the rope around her middle tying her to the sturdy trunk. After he felt she was secure, he turned to make his way into the trees.

"Jake," she shouted. She heard his footsteps halt a short distance away. "Please, I need to go. You know, do my business."

A moment later, she heard his retreating steps once again. "You can wait. I won't be gone long."

She groaned as she listened to his footsteps diminish. She tugged on the rope, testing the knot he had tied. He hadn't left any wiggle room. The twine held firm. Was there any hope of her getting out of this mess? Leaning her head back against the tree, she gazed up into the night sky. Too bad her pepper spray was no longer in her pocket. She must have lost the container in her struggle with Jake earlier.

Her thoughts turned to Mitchell as she watched the stars twinkling above. She hadn't had time to even ponder if Becky had found him alive. Had Jake succeeded in killing Mitchell like he claimed? Wait, if Jake had killed Mitchell, why would he be using her as a pawn for his land. Hope filled her entire being. He had to be alive, but had he washed his hands of her? Or would he come after her? A tear journeyed down her cheek as she thought of never seeing Mitchell again.

She lifted her arm to wipe the tears as she heard rustling nearby. She wasn't going to give him the satisfaction of seeing her cry. Glancing back toward the trees, she saw him emerge with an armload of firewood.

"Could you please untie me now? I really need to go!" She was close to doing a jig.

He ignored her as he went to work building a fire. He had a small blaze going in no time. Okay, so the cowboy was good at tying ropes and building fires. He needed to work on his social skills though. Her bladder was going to burst!

The warmth from the fire seeped into her limbs. She hadn't realized how cool the night air had become since the sun had descended behind the mountains. If he had left the fire building up to her, they would probably still be waiting for the first spark.

She jumped as she felt Jake touch her hair. She had been so deep in thought she hadn't heard him approach. "Do you still need to go to the privy?"

Trying to jerk away from his disturbing touch, she replied sarcastically, "No, I've already wet my pants! What do you think, you jerk. Of course I still need to go."

She felt the rope around her waist loosen. "Feisty little thing, aren't you?" He reached to loosen the knots holding her wrists. "I'm going to keep a close eye on you. You had better not try anything."

Edging around the tree she replied, "Scouts honor. You don't have to come with me. I promise I won't try anything."

He watched silently as she backed away into the woods. "Don't go too far. If I hear you running away, I may be tempted to shoot you!"

Ducking behind a huge tree, she peeked around the trunk to make sure he couldn't see her. Fumbling with her skirt she quickly squatted and relieved herself. She jumped as she heard him call out to her, "Are you finished?" With trembling fingers, Rachel stood and adjusted her skirt. She leaned around the tree. "Just hold your horses! I haven't gone to the bathroom all day. I'm almost done."

"Well, you had better 'potty' quick, girlie, or I will be forced to come and lend you a hand."

She cringed as she heard him let loose a loud laugh. Her heart tripped rapidly as she studied the dense forest and mounting evening shadows. She patted her jacket pockets hoping for a miracle.

Her left pocket yielded a tube of Dramamine. The motion sickness medicine was from her last flight home to visit her parents. She didn't enjoy flying.

Turning the tube, she noticed the words less drowsy formula. Dang. Why couldn't she have bought the heavy-duty stuff? How many pills would make Jake drowsy? Hastily she opened the tube to see how many tablets were inside. She held her breath as she examined the contents. Only one tablet missing. Excitement bubbled in her chest. This was her chance. She dumped the tablets into her hand and prayed she'd get to use them. She quickly buried the tube.

Jake paused in his pacing to observe her coming out from behind the tree. "I was beginning to think I was going to have to come in after you." Reaching for her hands, he wrapped the rope securely around her wrists and tied the end of the rope through a belt loop on his jeans. Pulling another length of twine out from his back pocket, he leaned down to tie her ankles. Indicating the secured line tied to his jeans and around her feet he stated, "I thought this was necessary, just in case you had any thoughts of running away."

She tried not to show her disappointment. She gave

herself a mental pep talk about staying calm and waiting for the right opportunity. Lowering herself to the ground by the warm fire, she asked calmly, "Can I help prepare the food?"

He squinted at her suspiciously. "Naw. Don't worry your pretty head. I've got supper covered."

Rolling her shoulders, she shrugged. "I'm fine with having a night off from cooking." She watched as he opened a can of beans and dumped them into a pan balanced on the fire. Opening her hands, she sneaked a peek at the tablets. She shuffled them around. They were starting to get soggy in her sweaty palms. The Dramamine wasn't going to help if she couldn't find a way to get him to take them.

She looked up to see him crossing to his saddlebag. Her spirits lifted as he pulled a bottle of whiskey out. Here was her chance. "Hey, Jake, do you mind if I have a small swig to warm up my bones a little?"

He lowered the bottle from his lips and wiped his mouth with the back of his hand. Slowly he made his way toward her. Squatting down, he held the bottle out for her to take. "I don't mind sharing. Have more than one swig if you want."

She eyed him over the top of the glass as she brought the liquor to her lips. She wished she could have wiped the opening, just touching the lid of the bottle where his lips had been was discomforting. She pretended to take a swallow of whiskey and faked a cough as she drew the container away from her lips. "Oh, that is some good stuff. Sure hit the spot."

He rose and made his way back to the fire to stir the pan of beans. Making sure his attention was elsewhere, she quickly stuffed the tablets inside the neck of the whiskey bottle. Sneaking a glance at him, she swirled the bottle trying to dissolve the white tablets quickly.

Catching movement from the corner of her eye, she promptly lifted the bottle again to her lips and pretended to take another sip.

With a smile, he squatted in front of her. "Hey easy there, we want to have some for later. I enjoy a woman who enjoys whiskey as much as I do." Reaching for the container, he enjoyed a long draw. She breathed a sigh of relief when she didn't notice any tablets at the bottom when he tipped the bottle as he drank.

She jerked back in surprise as he suddenly brought the whiskey back to her lips. Rubbing the lip of the bottle against her mouth, he tipped it until she had no choice but to take a drink. The sip she took burned a fiery trail down her throat. As he drew the bottle away a little bit of whiskey spilled out from the seam of her lips and ran down her chin.

He watched the spilled liquor run a course down her chin, leaned forward, and slowly licked the trail. She swallowed hard. She hoped she had put enough Dramamine in the whiskey to knock him out and soon. She tried to control the panic building within her, the night of the dance flashed in her mind. How could she have forgotten how he acts when he has alcohol? Her plan had better work.

He laughed before tipping his head back and taking a long drink. He eyed her over the lip of the bottle. "Oh yes sir, we're going to have lots of fun."

Her gaze didn't waver from his as she smiled. "I think you are burning the beans."

"That's not all that's going to be burning,

sweetheart."

Relieved his focus swung back to their supper, she released a groan. She watched over the next few minutes as he alternated between stirring the beans and taking swigs of the whiskey. Would he pass out from the Dramamine or from his consumption of the liquor?

A glint of steel caught her eye as the fire bounced off the blade of a knife. Just what she needed. She watched as Jake rose, shuffled unsteadily as he spooned some beans onto a plate, and brought his offering over.

She lifted her bound hands. "I'm not sure how I'm supposed to eat those with my hands tied, and I know I don't want you spoon feeding me."

Frowning in indecision, he put the plate down and leaned down to loosen the ropes on her wrist enough for her to eat without his help. His words slurred slightly as he told her to eat while the beans were hot.

Shoulders rigid with tension, she scrutinized him. He sat down hard across from her as he lost his balance. Shaking his head, he picked up his own plate. Neither said a word as each devoured their meal.

In between bites, she watched in pleasure as he finished the bottle of whiskey. This had to work! She placed her empty plate aside and waited. He shook his head from side to side and put his plate down as well. Rising precariously to his feet, he approached her. "Time to tighten back up the rope." His words slurred. Elation filled her. He should soon be out like a light. He grabbed her hands and tightened the rope quickly.

Stumbling, he kicked the now empty whiskey bottle as he settled back down against a log and stared at her. Seconds ticked by as his eyes got heavier and heavier. Finally, he gave up the battle and slumped ungracefully on the log.

Rachel wanted to give a shout of joy as a soft snore rent the air. The Dramamine had finally kicked in. She crawled forward and cringed as dirt ground into her already sore palms. She grabbed the nearby knife and glanced at Jake to make sure he wasn't aware of her movements. She worked furiously clawing at the thick strands of twine binding her wrists.

****

Mitchell stretched his legs and stood tall in his stirrups. He gazed up the trail into the night. The sun had disappeared behind the mountain range just minutes before, and following the trail he had picked up was becoming difficult. Firewood would be hard to find if he didn't stop soon and gather some in the fading light. Patting Rebel on the neck, he swung out of the saddle. He couldn't take the chance of harming his horse by traveling farther in the dark.

He squinted as he tried to make out any evidence of a flicker from a campfire in the distance. Disappointment flooded his being when he didn't see any signs. How far was he behind them and was he too late to save Rachel from whatever Jake's intentions were?

He led the horse off the trail to a small clearing. Rebel snorted as Mitchell began the routine of removing the saddle. A shooting pain exploded through his sore shoulder as he lifted the saddle from the horse's back. He winced and stumbled into his horse. "Sorry, boy. I guess we've both had a hard day."

Dropping his burden on the ground, he rotated his shoulder to ease the stiffness and pain. His gaze landed on Rachel's satchel, still hanging from the saddle horn.

What contents did the strange object hold? He rubbed a hand over his chin as weariness invaded his whole body. With a slight stagger, he turned to gather wood for a fire.

Five minutes later, he emerged with his arms laden. Soon he had a blaze going and stared into the flames. He massaged his sore shoulder and tried not to reflect on the fact Rachel was out in the woods alone with Jake. He leaned against his saddle.

His gaze once again encountered Rachel's satchel. He rubbed a hand down the leather before placing the bag in his lap. He pulled a tab down and looked into the large compartment. He withdrew a square object to study by the firelight.

Inside there was a likeness of Rachel. He ran a finger over the colorful image. Across the top Colorado was written in bold letters. His roving finger stilled as he read the numbers on the card. September Twenty, Nineteen ninety-two. That was a date in the future. Had Rachel been telling the truth? She had travelled through time.

Next, he pulled an envelope from the satchel. Inside were colorful images of Rachel smiling or laughing. He had once seen a photographer with a giant wooden box creating images, but the pictures taken were nothing like the images he held in his hand. Shuffling through, he saw Rachel standing with her arms around an older couple with her dimples flashing as if she didn't have a care in the world. The next she leaned against a huge strange green metal object. What could that possibly be?

He replaced everything and leaned back to study the stars. He closed his eyes and lifted up a silent prayer. Please, don't take her away from me. I've just found her, Lord, and I would like for her to stay here with me. Within minutes, he fell into a deep exhausted sleep.

Chapter Thirty-Five

Rachel shifted to ease the dull pain that had descended into her limbs. She hated having numb buns. Exhaustion threatened to take over her body. How long had she been trying to saw through the rope? She dropped the knife into her lap and flexed her fingers. They tingled as she worked some feeling back into them. The fire Jake had built had burned down to embers ages ago. She squinted at her handy work to see what type of progress she had made.

She straightened trying to ease the tension in her back. She fought the tears of frustration that threatened. Come on, Rachel; now isn't the time to fall apart, she silently coached.

After listening for a few moments to Jake's snoring, she started to saw at the rope again. She hoped she could eat away the fibers soon or drugging Jake would be for naught. What a mess. How did she land herself in these predicaments? She shook her head and lectured herself about throwing a pity party. That wasn't going to help matters any. She needed to remain positive! The situation could be worse. Jake could have tied her to a tree with her hands behind her. Escape would have been impossible if he would have had a little foresight.

Sweat broke out on her forehead, and she shivered in the late night air. The nighttime sky twinkled at her as she glanced up to gauge the time. She had no clue how long she had before morning. An excited gasp escaped her lips as the ropes binding her wrists broke free. Success! She shoved the knife into her skirt pocket and checked to see if Jake had stirred. She rotated each hand to get the circulation flowing. A jolt of pain shot through her left arm. She bit her lip trying to reframe from whimpering at the excruciating pain.

She stared at the frayed rope in the dim night. She'd finally sawed her hands free. Her fingers trembled as she made short work of freeing her feet.

Sharp needles shot up her legs as she stood. Both feet were asleep. She crumbled back to the ground and crawled away on all fours. The debris from the forest floor sliced into her lacerated palms. She bit her lip to keep from crying out.

Taking the time for a fleeting look at Jake, she scrambled behind a tree. Would he come to at any moment and try to shoot her for escaping? From her hiding spot, she tried to calm her racing heart and gazed into the darkness, wondering which way she should go. Which direction had they come? Damn. Why hadn't she been paying closer attention when Jake had stopped for the night?

She needed to make sure she was heading down the mountain and not up. Going back the way they had come was the most logical choice for her to make. She knew Jake would think so as well, but she didn't have much choice. She probably wouldn't survive if she went further into the mountain range.

The tingling in her feet and legs eased. She struggled to stand. She glanced around the tree and headed in the direction she believed would lead her down the mountain. She would try to stay off the path so her footprints wouldn't be easy to follow.

She crept a few feet before she stopped. Once Jake awoke, he would be hot on her trail. She couldn't leave his horse. With a quiet turn, she retreated to where the horse stood. A soft nicker greeted her. She stroked the flame on the horse's nose and whispered, "I sure wish I knew how to ride. I'm sure it isn't hard, but my fear is holding me back. If not for my fright, I would be riding you out of here instead of letting you go." She untied the reins and gave a slap to the horse's rear.

The resounding noise echoed briefly among the surrounding trees as the horse took off. Her stinging palm protested. Her poor hands.

She followed the horse as quickly as she could through the woods. Surely, the horse knew his way down the mountain. Didn't horses head for home if given the chance? Rebel had returned to the ranch. Without a doubt, Jake's horse knew where his meals came from.

A low hanging branch almost smacked her as she stumbled about. She needed to stay alert. The semi-darkness hanging thick amongst the trees cast eerie shadows. She suppressed a slight shiver. The forest was oddly silent. She was exhausted but had to keep moving, or Jake would definitely catch up with her.

As the darkness gave way to pre-dawn, she staggered slightly. She was beyond tired. She gasped and stopped abruptly. Directly in front of her was the deep ravine they had travelled the previous day. Elation rose within her as she realized she was on the right path.

She gazed about looking for any sign of Jake

following her. Once she was on the trail by the gorge, there would be no escaping if he happened upon her. She tilted her head as she listened intently. A lone bird sang a happy tune from a tree branch high above, but that was the only sound that registered. Carefully hugging the bank of dirt on the opposite side of the cliff, she slowly made her way down the trail.

****

Mitchell came awake with a start as he heard a shuffling noise close to his head. His stiff arm didn't cooperate at first as he reached for his pistol. The cocking of his weapon echoed in the early morning as he shifted to aim. He chuckled as he watched a fat porcupine beat a hasty retreat into the trees. Easing the hammer back, he rose into a sitting position.

The first fingers of dawn were creeping across the sky as he rose to his feet. He had slept better than he had expected. Rotating his shoulder, he tried to ease the stiffness from his gunshot wound. Unbuttoning his shirt, he slowly eased the fabric back. Carefully he removed the bandage to examine the wound. The skin was red and puckered, but as far as he could tell, there wasn't any infection and the wound was healing nicely. Placing the bandage back in place, he adjusted his clothes and moved to break camp.

After a breakfast of cold biscuits and beef jerky, he checked to make sure the fire from the night before was out before he turned and strode toward Rebel. Giving the horse's nose a stroke, he softly whispered, "We'll find her today, buddy. We've got to!"

He groaned as he lifted his saddle. A few seconds later, he retrieved Rachel's satchel and looped it firmly over the horn. Fingering the leather, he pondered over the items he had discovered inside the night before. Didn't he have to believe her story about being from the future now?

He leaned against Rebel's side and stared off into the distance at the mountains. Would Rachel disappear as fast as she had appeared? A finger of fear travelled down his spine. Twisting the reins in his hands, he mounted. He couldn't let her disappear.

Chapter Thirty-Six

A fine sheen of sweat had appeared on Rachel's forehead as she made her way down the trail. Man, she hated heights. The ravine's drop off gave her the chills every time she happened to glance over the edge. "Don't look down, don't look down," she muttered in a singsong chant. How had they gotten through this part of the trail without Jake's horse spooking and dropping them over the edge?

Her crossing seemed to take ages, before she finally made the other side. Her breath came in pants as if she had run a marathon instead of walked down the path. With a glance back at the trail, she breathed a deep sigh of relief. Still no sign of Jake.

Maybe she could chance staying on the trail. She hurried down at a fast clip. The morning chill had finally dissipated. The jacket donned earlier to chase away the chill now started to suffocate. She took her coat off and tied it about her waist. She ran her tongue over her chapped lips. Man she was parched. She sure could use a drink of water. Why hadn't she thought of taking the canteen when she had crept away?

The ravine she passed probably meant there was a stream nearby. She ventured off the trail into the tall grass in search of a river. It seemed like hours before she heaved a sigh of relief as she heard the trickle of water.

She cautiously stepped from the protection of the trees and eyed the stream in relief. Clear water rushed happily over stones. A large boulder called to her a short distance away. She sat, closed her eyes, and let the song of the trickling brook calm her frazzled nerves. The stress of the last twenty-four hours eased somewhat.

Leaning down, Rachel studied the water. Would bacteria be a concern like it was in her time? They always boiled the stream water before drinking. Did she really have a choice? She didn't want to become dehydrated. Cupping a handful of water, she cautiously sipped. The cool liquid tasted like heaven.

After drinking her fill, she rinsed her palms and chapped wrists in the fresh water. Overhead the sun beat down upon her, relaxing her. Lying down on the boulder, she stretched lazily and closed her eyes. Maybe she could afford to rest her eyes for only a moment.

She jerked awake and sat up abruptly. How long had she slept? The sun was higher in the sky. She jumped to her feet as she berated herself. Fool. How much precious time had she wasted? Her legs trembled as she scrambled off the rock and started back up the hill to the trail. Almost to the top, she stopped when a loud noise rent the air. Crouching down low in a field of skunk cabbage, she waited to see what the loud noise had been. Her heart stopped beating when she heard the sound of thundering horse's hooves.

Trying to make herself as small as possible, she parted the grass and gazed back up the trail. When she finally spied who was coming, she sank even lower to the ground. Jake! Damn it! He'd found his horse and was in hot pursuit.

His gaze was focused intently on the ground, following her footprints. She had been so worried about falling off the trail into the ravine she had forgotten to cover her path. What a fool!

An eternity passed as she watched him dismount and examine the ground closely. He was only a few feet away. She didn't dare move. He'd realize soon her footprints led off into the woods. She needed to act fast if she was going to stay out of his clutches.

She crouched lower as a hiss passed from his lips. He glanced into the forest, and she felt he was looking directly at her as he scanned the foliage and beyond. Staying as still as a statue was hard, but if she moved, he would have her tied up again, and that wasn't something she wanted to experience again anytime soon.

Rising, Jake paced back and forth on the trail before turning back to look into the trees. She was so caught. Slowly she started to inch her way backward attempting not to make a sound that would draw attention to her whereabouts. Her breathing sounded loud to her ears. Could he hear her?

"Dammit to hell, woman, I know you're there!"

His outburst startled her enough she jumped and paused in her backward motion. She separated the grass and peeked out. He mounted his horse and started down the trail.

She couldn't believe he wasn't following her. Astonishment had her shaking her head. She eased to her knees and quickly brushed off the debris clinging to her blouse. Rising to her feet, she hid behind the nearest tree. Surely, it wasn't going to be easy to be rid of Jake.

He would be back. She was sure he would figure out soon there weren't any more footprints farther down the trail.

As quietly as possible, she descended the mountain. She needed to stay as close to the trail as she could, but far enough away in the thick foliage so Jake couldn't follow her on horseback. She paused to scan the area. She should level out and not go any farther downhill if she didn't want to get lost. Paranoia had her glancing over her shoulder to make sure Jake hadn't spotted her. Seconds later, she came upon the stream. How deep in the forest would it take her if she would follow it?

She trudged along about half an hour before she noticed the change in direction of the stream. Kneeling, she scooped up a handful and drank deeply. With a splash to her face, she listened to the rushing water. Earlier the noise had calmed her, now all she could think about was Jake close on her heels. She bowed her head and tried to focus. She couldn't afford to follow the stream any farther, or she would be utterly lost with no chance of rescue.

How far had she gotten away from the trail? Was Jake up there waiting? She rose and began the trek back up the mountain. She just hoped she hadn't wandered too far.

Winded, she paused. She had gone farther than she thought. She tensed as she heard a twig snap not far from where she stood. Bolting behind the closest tree, she peeked around to see what made the noise.

She heard a growl. Was that a bear? No. Worse. Seconds later, she heard Jake yelling in the woods, "I know you're not far, Rachel. I will find you!"

She eased back behind the tree. She let out a pent up breath. He wasn't far away. Think. What should she do? Her heart fluttered wildly as she glanced about for an avenue of escape.

Her gaze fell upon a fallen log a few feet away from where she stood. Looked like her next hiding spot presented itself. She cast a fleeting look around the tree. She couldn't see him, but she knew he was close. Crouching low, she made her way to the log. This cat and mouse game couldn't last forever, but she was going to give it her best shot.

The closer she got to the log, the more she realized the tree looked hollow. Was it big enough to hide inside? Scrambling the last few feet, she dropped to her knees and peered within.

Darkness greeted her gaze. Could she hide completely within? Before she could change her mind, she crawled into the narrow space and wiggled until her feet were hidden from view. The log proved to be spacious enough she didn't feel cramped. She wouldn't think of the critters sharing the space with her until later. She was just happy she had found a place to hide from Jake. Forcing herself to breath normally, she waited.

Her heart skipped a beat when a few minutes later she heard the sound of someone running nearby. "You know you will die out here if I don't help you, don't ya?" Jake called from only a few feet away.

She thought of the two evils she faced, Jake or being lost in the forest. Neither appealed to her, but she had a better chance of survival by being lost in the forest.

She jerked in her tight space as he yelled. The

pleasant, pleading voice he had used moments ago was no longer present. "Dammit, woman! I'm through messin' with ya. If you don't come out in the next few minutes, I'm going to shoot you the next chance I get."

She rolled her eyes and tried not to laugh. Yeah like that threat was going to get her to come out of her hiding spot. Snuggled within the log, she breathed a little easier when she heard him move away. Her forehead dropped wearily to rest on her outstretched arm. Exhaustion flowed through her body. The short nap she had taken by the stream seemed like ages ago. Her eyes burned from fatigue and grit. She waited, hoping Jake would give up soon.

****

Mitchell moved up the trail, keeping his eyes on the tracks he'd been following all morning. He knew he was on the right path. The tracks were too fresh not to belong to Jake. At the sound of another horse, he pulled up sharply on Rebel's reins. A short distance away a bay stallion stood tethered munching on grass. Joy filled his being. Wasn't that Jake's?

Easing out of his saddle as quietly as possible, he led Rebel into the foliage and tied him off. He backtracked up along the trail to make sure this wasn't a trap. He found a boulder to hide behind as he waited to see what was going on. He was closer to the animal and recognized it as the one Sanders' had ridden in the Independence Day race. Where was Jake, but more importantly where was Rachel?

Footsteps echoed through the trees a slight distance away. The sound was almost as loud as a herd of cattle stampeding in his direction. He crouched low behind the boulder. His eyes narrowed as he silently watched

Jake come into view. Sanders kicked at a rock and started cussing up a storm. "Damn women!" As Jake turned away, the cussing wasn't as clear. Sneaking to the side of the rock, Mitchell eased his way around until he was behind Jake. Pulling his gun quietly from his holster, he clicked back the hammer.

Jake was cussing so loudly he didn't hear him ease up behind him. Mitchell growled, "Get your hands where I can see them, Sanders."

Tensing, Jake slowly turned to study the gun Mitchell had trained on him. He quickly masked the stunned expression on his face and smiled. "Why Reeves fancy meeting you here. What brings you out this way?"

He kept a steady hand on the pistol. "I'm not stupid Sanders. You know exactly why I'm here. What have you done with Rachel?"

"Miss Morgan? I don't understand. Why would I know where she is?" Jake spanned his hands slowly around. "Do you see anyone with me?"

He eyed Jake suspiciously. Was Jake innocent? Could he have accused him unnecessarily? He didn't like the gleam in Jake's eyes. "What have you done with her?"

The sly expression slipped a little from Jake's features. "Mitchell, I haven't seen Miss Morgan since the dance. Why would you think I would have seen her, especially clear out here?" A look of feigned horror filled his face. "Is she missing?"

His hands shook as his anger grew. "Toby told me you had been out to the ranch. So don't tell me you haven't seen Rachel," He growled low in his throat. "Where is Rachel?"

"I don't know what you are talking about." He shrugged his shoulders nonchalantly. "What proof do you have I took her?"

Dread filled his gut. Jake was right. What real proof did he have to prove Jake had taken Rachel from his ranch? A thought suddenly occurred to Mitchell. "If you didn't take Rachel, then why were you cussing women just now when you were coming out of the forest?"

Jake's smirk disappeared "Doesn't a man have the right to cuss a woman if he wants?"

"Why do I not believe you, Sanders?" He motioned with his gun for Jake to move. He edged closer to Jake's horse and pulled the rope hanging from the horn loose. "Put your hands behind your back, Jake. I'm going to tie you to a tree and have a look around. Don't want you pulling any of your tricks on me."

Jake glared but finally turned and put his hands behind his back. "You're going to regret this Reeves. You don't have anything on me."

"Maybe so, but I would rather play it safe than not."

A few seconds later, Jake was secured to an aspen. He glanced in the direction in which Jake had come. What had Jake been doing in the forest? Had he left Rachel down there somewhere?

He followed the path of flattened grass Jake had left behind and started down the mountain.

"Hey, where ya going Reeves? You're not just going to leave me here are you?" Cussing, Jake struggled with his bound hands. "Reeves," he yelled.

Mitchell ignored Jake as he yelled after him and continued to follow the trampled trail. Jake had come quite a distance through the foliage. His mind began churning with questions. Could Jake be telling the truth when he had told him he hadn't taken Rachel? Could his instincts have been wrong regarding Jake?

A feeling of hopelessness settled in his bones. Was Rachel hurt somewhere out here? Trying not to panic he asked, "Oh, Rachel where are you?"

Chapter Thirty-Seven

Rachel jerked awake as she heard someone muttering nearby. She cursed as she realized she'd missed her chance for escape. Jake had returned while she had closed her eyes for but a moment. He was sure to find her now. A scream clawed up her throat and tried to emerge as she realized there was something crawling up her arm. Probably a creepy bug like the one she had feared. She hoped whatever it was wasn't poisonous.

Silently she waited taking shallow breaths. Jake had left before because he hadn't found her, she prayed he would give up soon. She gasped softly when she heard a voice.

"Oh, Rachel, where are you?"

Was she dead? Had a poisonous bug bitten her after all? Her exhaustion had finally gotten the better of her. Because the voice wasn't Jake's, but Mitchell's. Dare she trust her ears?

"Mitchell?" Her voice came out a strangled crackle. Shifting, she peered back around her feet to the opening of the log. She couldn't see anything.

"Rachel? Was that you making a noise?"

A cry of relief tore from her throat. Oh, thank you, Lord, thank you! She struggled in the log in earnest. Her brain hadn't been playing tricks on her. She *had* heard Mitchell's voice.

Slowly she wiggled backward. The log she had thought huge now closed in around her. She started to panic. What if she was stuck permanently and couldn't reach Mitchell before he gave up looking for her? She started whispering his name over and over like a chant. Each time coming out stronger than the last.

"Rachel, my ears aren't deceiving me are they? Was that you?"

She contained a sob as she yelled. "Oh, Mitchell I'm in the log. Please help me. I think I may be stuck."

"Rachel, honey, you are going to have to keep talking so I can find you."

She paused in her wiggling. Had Mitchell just called her honey? The panic that had filled her body slowly ebbed. She began the slow journey of inching backward from the log. Mitchell had found her. Jake hadn't killed him, and he had come for her and if her ears hadn't deceived her, he just called her honey.

Mitchell systematically searched from one fallen tree to another. His mind hadn't been playing tricks on him. Had it? He had heard Rachel's sweet voice.

Approaching one of the bigger fallen trees, he peered around the end to discover a pair of boot heals sticking out. The surge of elation he felt was indescribable. He dropped to his knees as all of his energy left his body. Suddenly he realized tears were streaming down his face. Wiping at them he chuckled. "Oh, Rachel, you do get yourself into the tightest spots, don't you, girl?"

He heard a chuckled sob from inside. "Mitchell! Just help me out of here, would you? I think I have a bug crawling up my shirt!"

He studied the log and wondered how she had

gotten into such a tight spot. He smiled and shook his head. "If you can wiggle back just a little farther, I should be able to pull you out.

He heard her groan in frustration. "That's what I have been doing. I'm just getting a little impatient I haven't made too much progress."

"Start wiggling, sweetheart. I will help you out."

Chapter Thirty-Eight

First honey and now sweetheart. Rachel's heart swelled with an emotion she couldn't name. Throwing around those kinds of words surely meant he had some kind of feelings.

Her shirt crawled up as she wiggled backward again. At least she hoped the bug finding his way up her shirt would be dislodged. A slight shiver swept through her at the thought.

"Rachel, I think you are far enough out for me to give your feet a good yank. I'll have you out of there in no time."

Mitchell's firm hands gripped her ankles as he pulled. A few seconds passed before she popped from the log. She gasped in a breath of fresh air. Her gaze searched and found Mitchell's warm amber eyes.

Her gaze soaked in the sight of him. He had never looked as handsome as he did at this moment. Throwing a smile his way, she replied huskily, "Hey there good looking, fancy meeting you here."

Kneeling down and scooting closer, he grasped her head firmly and gave her a firm kiss on her lips. "I'm so glad to see you, even with the dirt, bugs, and who knows what else covering you."

"Bugs," she squeaked. She ran her hands down both her arms and shivered at the thought of creepy-crawly's. A few seconds later, her eyes met his gaze.

"How much did you miss me, cowboy?" Her smile slipped from her face as he remained quiet and continued to study her intently. Her heart tripped. Had she read too much into his sweet words earlier? "Mitchell?"

When he finally spoke, his voice cracked with emotion. "I'm having a difficult time finding the words to tell you how much I missed you."

She eased to her knees and met his serious look with one of her own. She leaned in close and grazed his lips with her own. "What about now, cowboy? Any words coming to mind?" At the negative shake of his head, she leaned her weight against his chest and eased both their bodies to the ground. She delivered a slow lingering kiss. She nibbled along his jaw line. "Can you tell me now, cowboy?"

She squealed with surprise as he flipped her to her back. His lips greedily sought out hers. The kiss was deep and hungry, and she met each thrust of his tongue eagerly. Breaking free, he eased away and studied her full well-kissed lips. A groan escaped as her tongue darted out and licked her lips.

She chuckled huskily. "Okay, you have convinced me actions are just as good as words."

He laughed and leaned in for another kiss. His lips trailed over her dirt-smeared face and nipped softly at her ear. "Lady, I love you so."

She stiffened in his arms at the softly spoken words. What did he say? She pushed at his chest until she could look into his glorious eyes. "What…did you say?"

A crooked grin appeared. He leaned in once again to nibble on her earlobe. "I don't think there is anything wrong with your hearing. I think you heard me." His tongue gently swirled in the shell of her ear. "I said I love you." His teeth brushed her earlobe before moving farther down to graze her neck.

She closed her eyes and swallowed hard. "Do you know how long I've waited for you to say those words?"

Reluctantly he tore himself away from lavishing her neck and leaned back to watch as tears filled her eyes. Studying her knowingly he finally answered, "Years."

Her tears fell as she nodded. "Well over one hundred years to be exact." Reaching up with her arms, she encircled his chest and hugged him fiercely.

He eased out of the hug and drew a finger up to wipe at the trail the tears. "I found your satchel. I saw some of the items you have inside." He swept his Stetson from his head and ran an unsteady hand through his hair. "I'm sorry I didn't believe you."

She leaned her forehead against his chin and smoothed her hands over his chest. "I don't blame you for not believing me. I'm not sure I would have believed anyone spouting such nonsense myself." Her gaze locked onto his amber eyes as she scraped his lips with her own. "I love you, Mitchell. Can you please take me home, and in case you are unclear on what I mean, I mean your ranch."

"Are you sure?" He placed his hat on his head and rose to his feet. Drawing her up by her hand, he dragged her up and against his body. "I like hearing you call the ranch home. You plan on staying here, don't you?" At her look of confusion Mitchell clarified, "You're not going back to the future? Are you?"

Her hands flittered up to caress his chest. "Oh, Mitchell, I have no idea how I got here, but I pray I don't get taken from you now we've found each other." She stopped stroking his chest when he grimaced. "What's wrong?"

He reached up to unbutton the top two buttons of his shirt and moved the bandage aside to show her his wound.

Rage filled her eyes, "I'm going to have Jake's hide for this. He did try to kill you."

He grasped her shoulders. "Jake shot me? I had my suspicions, but I didn't have any proof."

"Oh, I have proof. It'll be my word against his, but I have his confession. He was bragging to me about how he doesn't ever miss what he aims at and he told me you were dead." Her eyes misted. "It tore me up to have to listen to him brag about you being dead. I'm so glad you are going to be okay." Unconsciously she buttoned his shirt.

He gathered her hands in his own and placed them over his heart. "I'm glad I'm okay as well, Rachel, with all of my heart." Leaning down, he kissed the tip of her pert nose. "Jake is tied to a tree up by the trail. The faster we get him delivered to the sheriff, the faster we can get home." She gasped as Mitchell grasped her hand firmly within his own.

He paused, turned her hand over to examine the red angry cuts and scratches. "Oh sweetheart, I'm sorry." Slowly he lifted her hand and placed a gentle kiss to her palm. Shyly she lifted her other hand for him to kiss as well. "Better?"

At her nod, he softly linked his fingers with hers and turned to make their way back up the mountain.

She relished the feel of his hand linked softly with her own. A bubble of happiness consumed her as she glanced at his profile. She was on cloud nine. She'd lost so much to get here, but she had also gained so much.

As they reached a clearing in the trees, he stopped abruptly. Wrenching her hand from his, he exclaimed, "Get down, now!" He shoved Rachel to the ground just as a shot echoed throughout the trees.

The air rushed out of her body as he knocked her to the forests floor. He landed hard on top of her, shielding her body with his own. The bullet that whizzed by had been close. Too close.

An evil chuckle slashed through the air and a sarcastic voice called out, "Now isn't that sweet. I'm glad you were able to find her, Reeves." Jake cocked his pistol once more. "This way I won't have to continue looking for her later after I have taken care of you. But, I kinda feel bad about you having to die together."

No, Rachel's brain screamed! Things weren't going to end this way, not if she had anything to say about it. She hadn't come all this way to find a man to love to be robbed of his love this way. Nothing was going to take him away from her, except maybe old age.

As Mitchell grasped her body and rolled them into the trees another shot whizzed by. "Stay down," Mitchell hissed into her ear.

"I thought you said you tied him up."

He swore softly. "I did." He rubbed his shoulder.

She placed a hand to still his action. "I hope you didn't re-open your wound when we rolled."

"I can't think about that right now. We seem to

have a more important problem to think about." He took a quick peek around the tree. "Stay here. I'm going to try to circle around him."

She grabbed his arm halting his departure. "Please be careful." She watched worriedly as she observed him silently creeping away.

"Come on out, Reeves. Come out and face me like a man!"

She gritted her teeth and peeked through the blades of grass covering her. She couldn't let him face Jake alone. Mitchell was going to be pissed at her for not staying still, but she had to try to help. Crawling on her elbows and knees, she started to inch forward in the opposite direction Mitchell had taken.

Mitchell squinted through some low hanging evergreen limbs. Where was Jake hiding, and could he easily squeeze a shot off? He finally spied Jake crouched behind a boulder with his pistol ready to fire.

He lifted his firearm and took aim. Before he could squeeze a shot off, he caught movement from the corner of his eye. He swallowed hard. Damn it! He watched in shock as Rachel moved from tree to tree making her way behind Jake.

He cursed under his breath and lowered his pistol. What was he going to do with that stubborn woman? Why couldn't she have stayed safely where he had left her? He had to do something before Jake noticed her.

Using a tree as a barrier, he yelled, "Hey, Sanders, you still there?"

The sound of a shot reverberated around him as bark flew slightly above his head. How many shots did Jake have left? If he kept up this cat and mouse game with Jake, would he use all of his bullets? He glanced around the trunk of the tree. He didn't see Rachel. Where was she?

"Do you have nine lives, Reeves? I should have made sure you were dead the last time I shot you. You're not going to be so lucky today. I'm going to make sure the bullet hits true."

Keep on bragging Sanders, he thought. We will see how this turns out. Pulling the brim of his hat down lower, he raced to the next tree. Another shot rang out.

"We can play this game all day. I have plenty of bullets, Reeves."

What the hell was Mitchell thinking? Jake's shouts echoed off the trees and rang loudly in Rachel's ears. Was he trying to get himself shot? Killed?

Maybe he was trying to draw attention to himself so Jake wouldn't know where she was. She needed to locate Mitchell's rifle. He must have left the firearm with his horse. Disappointment shimmied down her spine as she realized both horses were quite a distance away. There wasn't any way she could get there without being discovered.

Frantically she searched the ground. Was there any object she could use for a weapon? Spying a medium sized rock, she slowly bent to pick it up. She tossed the rock from one hand to the other. The weight wasn't much in her hands, but if she could put some force behind a blow maybe she could knock Jake out.

She listened intently as Jake continued shouting threats at Mitchell. Sidling around the tree protecting her, she crept up behind the boulder that concealed Jake. Forcing herself to breathe normally, she peeked around to see if Jake had detected her.

Jake's gaze was bouncing crazily from tree to tree.

He was clueless where Mitchell was hiding. From her viewpoint she could see a film of sweat coating his forehead. He didn't look as confident as before. She crept up behind him while he was distracted. Lifting her arms, she brought the rock down hard on the back of his head. Jake went down like a ton of bricks and lay unmoving at her feet.

She threw the rock as if it had scalded her skin. What had she done? Surely, she hadn't killed him with just one blow. Squaring her shoulders, she lifted her chin. What she had done was save both her and Mitchell's lives. Jake wouldn't have stopped shooting until both of them were dead and breathed their last breath. He was so still. Bending down she reached to check his pulse. She breathed a sigh of relief when she felt his steady heartbeat. She hadn't killed him.

Mitchell came bounding out of the trees. "Woman. What the hell did you think you were doing? Are you trying to put me in an early grave scaring me like that? Didn't you hear what I had asked you to do?" He pointed at the nearby tree line. "What part of stay there did you not understand?"

"I heard you. I couldn't just stay there while you made yourself a target. Where did you think you were going to end up if I hadn't tried to do something?" She glared back. "This isn't the time to yell at me. Please do something with him before he comes around! Then you can yell at me to your little heart's content."

His body radiated frustration as he stared. He shook his head and brought his fingers to his lips. A shrill whistle echoed through the still forest. Moments later Rebel came to an abrupt halt in front of them.

"I want to train my horse to do that. Can you teach

me?"

He retrieved a rope. His irritation rippled from his body. He knew she'd only been trying to help.

He stopped in front of her and lifted her chin with his finger. "Only if you promise me you won't take fool-hardy chances with your life."

"I'm sorry, Mitchell, but I disobeyed because I was worried about you. I'm not ready to lose you."

Mitchell nodded in understanding. "I need to make sure this rope is tied better than the last time. I don't want him escaping before we get him to town."

A few moments later Jake lay tied up and unconscious against a boulder. Turning away from Jake, he advanced toward her. Grabbing her around the waist, he hauled her up against his chest. "Don't you ever scare me like that again!" His voice was low and gravelly, but then he added on a pleading whisper, "Please."

****

Reaching up, she took his Stetson from his head and ran her hand through his thick hair. She watched as his eyes blazed with longing. She rose to her toes, grazed his lips, and looped her arm around his neck. "I'll try to behave since you asked me so nicely."

Groaning, he hauled her up close and gave her a fierce kiss. "Lady, I don't think you know the meaning of the word. You are driving me crazy."

Swallowing hard, she eased away from the warmth of his embrace. She observed him from under her lowered lashes. The passion she found in his gaze set her heart afire. There was no doubt in her mind how he felt about her. Glancing at Jake who lay tied up a few feet away she realized now wasn't the time to indulge in passion.

Mitchell cleared his throat. "I'll retrieve Sanders' horse. We need to deliver Jake to the sheriff."

She fanned herself with his hat as she watched him walk away. She shook her head. "That man knows how to exit. What a great pair of buns!" She perched the hat atop her head and started to hum. Life was good. The tune died in her throat as her gaze encountered a glare from Jake. A chill raced up her spine as she witnessed the evil glint that flickered in his eyes.

"How'd you do it? Get away from me?"

Rachel shrugged. "Pure determination."

"You know, honey, you should have given me a chance. I could have curled your toes if you would have just let me."

Seriously? "I never felt that way about you Jake. Mitchell is the one I love. He's the one that curls my toes."

Turning away, she watched Mitchell approach leading Jake's horse.

"Can you get Jake on the horse, or do you need my help?"

"I can handle it."

She watched as he secured Jake on his horse. Rebel stomped impatiently a few feet from her. Startled she turned and eyed him.

"It's your turn, Rachel. Do you need help up?"

She considered Mitchell's hand before turning to face the huge horse. She was going to have to learn how to ride a horse if she was going to be staying in the Wild West with Mitchell. She wasn't going to be able to walk all the way back to town. Giving Rebel's neck a confident pat she spoke softly, "Don't make me look like a fool, okay?" Rebel turned his head to watch her with big soulful eyes. "Does that look mean you're going to cooperate?"

She sidled up to Rebel's side and gingerly put her left foot in the stirrup and swung her leg over the saddle. "That wasn't so bad." She leaned over and gave the horse a friendly pat on the neck. "Thank you for not making me look like an idiot."

Mitchell smiled. "We may make you into a real horsewoman yet. You really look the part wearing my hat."

She tipped the hat and laughed. Her smiled slipped a notch when Rebel sidestepped as Mitchell mounted the horse behind her. She clung to the saddle horn as he shifted in the saddle. The nervousness at being on top of the tall horse soon altered to a different feeling as she felt his muscular thighs flex against her derriere as the horse began the downward trail.

The sensation of his hard body against her own was a total different experience from the previous day when she was forced to ride in front of Jake. Liquid heat pooled as her body gently rocked against his. Each step down the mountain was totally erotic and played havoc with her nerves.

They arrived on the outskirts of Durango early afternoon. She had been so distracted by her body's reaction to Mitchell's the time had flown. Curious onlookers watched their progress down the street.

Stopping in front of the sheriff's office, Mitchell dismounted, reached up to grasp her waist, and lifted her down from the saddle. The heated gaze that settled on her told her he was just as aroused by their intimate ride into town.

The sheriff strode out of his office and broke the spell lingering between them. "Reeves, I was just headed out to look for you. Your foreman Toby stopped by the office about an hour ago and explained what happened." The sheriff's gaze shifted to Jake. He studied him silently for a moment before he spoke again. "We rode out to Mr. Waters' ranch to question him about Mr. Sander's actions." The sheriff paused to make sure Jake was listening before he continued, "He claims Sanders here was acting on his own, not on any order from him."

"Do you actually believe that, Sheriff?" Mitchell stared intently into the Sheriff's eyes.

"No, Mitchell, but I don't have any solid proof."

Jake had been silent staring at the sheriff in shock. Suddenly he started to sputter like a wet hen. "That no good son of a …."

All eyes turned to Jake. The sheriff spit a stream of tobacco. "You have something to say, Sanders?"

Jake clamped his lips firmly shut and glared at the sheriff.

Rachel stood to the side softly petting Rebel's neck. She cleared her throat. "Gentlemen, can I put my two cents worth into the conversation?"

Every eye trained on her as she took a step forward. "Jake was quite willing to talk after he kidnapped me. He admitted Mr. Waters wanted Mitchell's ranch, and he was using me as a bargaining chip to get Mr. Waters what he wanted."

Mitchell rested a hand on her arm. "He told you that?"

She nodded and glanced at Jake silently daring him to rebuke what she said.

Jake shifted on his horse and looked at Rachel. "I will admit I took Rachel against her will, but the other stuff I did, Mr. Waters asked us to do."

The sheriff cleared his throat. "Like what kind of things, Sanders?"

A defiant looked crossed Jake's face quickly. "What are you going to give me if I help you?"

The sheriff turned to Rachel. "Well that all depends. How did you treat this young lady? Did you harm her physically in any way?"

She caught her lower lip with her teeth and gnawed softly. While it was true he hadn't violated her, he could have if she hadn't escaped, and he had made some pretty strong threats against her while he had held her captive. What should she say?

She studied Jake a moment contemplating. His dark gaze met hers unflinchingly. "Sheriff, he didn't violate me, but that doesn't mean he isn't without fault. I wish to charge him with kidnapping, assault, battery, and assault with intent to kill."

"Sanders. Those are some hefty charges. I'm not going to lie to you. You're in serious trouble and will be serving jail time." The sheriff paused to spit. "Now how much jail time is going to depend on you. Will you cooperate and tell us what you know about the cattle-rustling going on in these parts? We may be able to get some leniency from the judge if you do."

The defiance Jake had worn like a cloak melted away. "I'll tell you what I can." He shook his head in defeat. "Mr. Waters told me and some of his other hands to cut Reeves' fences and cause problems."

"What about the other ranchers in the area?"

Slowly Jake nodded his head. "Yeah, we were told

to cause problems with them as well, but we hit Reeves place the hardest because Mr. Waters wants his property since the land is adjacent to his own. I had help. I'm not taking the blame for all of it!"

The sheriff's face split into a delighted grin. "Is that a confession, Sanders?"

Jake shifted in the saddle. "Damn straight! If you need one."

"I'll need names besides Mr. Waters to round up all the culprits."

Jake nodded reluctantly. "I'll give them to you."

The sheriff turned to his deputy who had joined them. "I'll lock Sanders up. Boyd, I need you to go out to Mr. Waters' ranch and bring him in with whoever Sanders tells you to lock up. Take Clyde with you as well, you may need the help."

Mitchell reached up to help Jake down from his horse. "Thanks for the help, Sheriff."

"Thank you, Mitchell. You did all of the hard work by bringing Sanders in. You just let me know if you ever need a job. I might have one available for you."

Mitchell shook the sheriff's hand and turned to study her. "No thank you, Sheriff, I think I will stick with what I know. I'm a rancher." He walked over and held out a hand. "I would like the honor of becoming a husband though. Rachel Morgan, would you do me the honor of becoming my wife?"

She couldn't contain the excited squeal escaping her lips. She flung herself at Mitchell. She wrapped her arms around his neck and clung onto him. "I thought you would never ask."

Nuzzling her neck, he nibbled and chuckled. "Is that a yes, Miss Morgan?"

"That's a hell yes, Mr. Reeves!" Joy bubbled from the bottom of her feet to the top of her head as she hugged his neck tightly and lifted her lips for a kiss.

"Such language darling," he drawled. "We're going to have to work on cleaning that up, aren't we?" His lips settled firmly onto hers and she sighed. Now everything was right with her world. She had her cowboy.

"Mitchell! Rachel!" They both were nearly knocked over as Becky flung herself at them. "You're back. You're safe! I was worried about you both. What happened? Is everyone okay? Rachel, you're filthy."

When Becky stopped to pause for a breath, Rachel lifted her hands to form a T. "Time out, Becky. One question at a time, please."

Becky laughed and launched herself once again at her. Whispering into her ear she said, "I'll start with the most important question then. Has he told you he loves you and wants to marry you?"

Leaning back, she studied her face. "You know we are really going to have to work on your inquisitive nature. It wears me out. The answer to your question is yes."

She could see the wheels in Becky's head turning trying to remember what her questions had been. With a delighted cry, she asked excitedly, "When?"

Mitchell stepped in to take control of the moment by asking his baby sister, "When did I ask? Or when are we getting married?"

"Both!"

Placing his arm around Rachel's shoulders, he looked into her eyes, "As soon as I can find the preacher."

She stood speechless with her mouth gaping. "You mean you want to get married today? Now?"

Tipping her chin up with his finger, he stated firmly, "I love you, Rachel. I don't want to wait. As you had said earlier, we've been waiting years. Why should we delay?"

She glanced down at her filthy clothing and grimaced. "This isn't quite what I had envisioned my wedding apparel would look like on my big day. I look awful."

"You will always be beautiful to me, no matter what your appearance!"

"Excuse me, but maybe I can help."

Three sets of eyes landed on Mr. Jones who stood patiently on the walk. "I may have a dress that will fit Miss Morgan in my store." Turning to Mitchell he also supplied, "I may also have some rings to choose from for a token of your love." Jim's blue eyes settled on Becky. "I do have one request though."

Mitchell cleared his throat, "What's that, Mr. Jones?"

"Please. Call me Jim. I would like the ceremony to be a double wedding. That is if you wouldn't mind sharing your special day."

He glanced from Jim to his sister. Becky wore an excited expectant look upon her face. "Is that what you wish, Beck?"

She clasped her hands to her chest. "Oh, yes. With all my heart."

"Then, Jim, I suggest we make a trip to your store to make sure your sign says closed for the day."

Jim clasped Becky around the waist and swiftly kissed her upturned face. "Let's go find a preacher."

Chapter Thirty-Nine

The rest of the afternoon rushed by in a blur of activity for Rachel. She stood in front of the preacher scarcely two hours later all clean and dressed in a gown of soft ivory. The dress fit her perfectly. The bodice hugged her body in all the right places. Tiny buttons trailed down the back to rest at the tapered waist. She felt beautiful. Special.

The vows were murmured with voices filled with love. She glanced down at her finger as Mitchell slipped the gold band on her hand. The preacher pronounced them man and wife and urged the groom to kiss his bride.

Mitchell smiled down softly at her as he lowered his head slowly and lovingly caressed her lips with his. Leaning his forehead against hers he whispered, "I love you."

The preacher cleared his throat and began the ceremony anew for Becky and Jim. Clinging to Mitchell's hand, they watched as Jim gave his bride a lengthy kiss.

Once the vows were complete, Mitchell welcomed Jim to the family. Rachel gave Becky a hug and a kiss on the cheek. She whispered in Becky's ear, "I won't say no if he wants to give me a good night kiss."

Becky smiled remembering the words they had spoken the night of the Independence dance. "Nor will

I." Both chuckled.

"We need to get a move on if we're going to get back to the ranch before dark." Mitchell lovingly put his arm around her waist. A glint of desire showed brightly in his eyes.

She was sure her eyes mirrored the same longing. Linking her arm through his she turned to say her farewells to Becky and Jim. "We will have to get together soon." Grinning up at her husband, she added huskily, "But not too soon."

"I'll give you a few days before I come to get my belongings." Becky grinned shyly at Jim. A rosy glow spread across her face as she stared at her new husband.

Dust swirled about their feet as they made their way down the street to where Rebel waited patiently. "Should I change back into my dirty clothes for the ride home?"

Mitchell leaned in to give her ear a soft nibble. "No. I'm looking forward to helping my bride out of her wedding dress. Don't rob me of the pleasure."

She accepted his help into the saddle. He quickly tucked her dress about her legs, making sure they weren't exposed. He swung gracefully behind her and held her tight as they started down the street. The molten lava sensation from earlier returned and ran pleasantly through her veins. After they had left Durango, his hand slowly caressed her ribs on his journey to purposefully cover her breast. The heat from his fingers stroking her tender flesh through the fabric of the dress made her squirm. She leaned further into his chest and felt the heat from his breath upon her neck.

Her mind was screaming hurry, and as her lips

parted to voice the demand aloud, he urged Rebel into a gallop. If she had thought walking the horse was pure torture, it didn't compare to the rubbing of his thighs against her backside as they galloped toward the ranch.

As they approached the bend where Mitchell had found her those many nights ago, she placed a hand on his thigh. In understanding, he slowed their pace and stopped. "I'm not sure what happened that night, but I'm glad you're the one who found me."

He stared into her eyes and gently kissed her. "Me too."

The day was fading into twilight as they approached the ranch. Mitchell dismounted in front of the barn and gave her a hand down. "It'll only take me a moment to take care of Rebel." He brought her hand to his lips and placed a tender kiss against her knuckle.

She lowered her tingling hand slowly. "Where are Toby and the other hands?"

"I gave them a well deserved night off. Do you approve?"

"Oh yeah, Cowboy, I approve." Slowly she backed up. "I think I'm just going to go down to the pond and take myself a little refreshing dip." Crooking her index finger, she beckoned, "Come on down and join me after you've taken care of Rebel."

"Yes, ma'am." Tipping his hat with his finger, he grabbed Rebel's reins and led him into the barn.

She chuckled and started down the path toward the pond. Who would have thought she could ever be this happy? She whistled a soft tune. She stopped abruptly when she saw a shadow emerge onto the path in front of her. Sucking in a breath she started to scream until she realized the shadow was Chet. She rushed to his side and gave him a hug. "I thought you were a goner! I'm so glad to see Jake didn't kill you." Leaning back, she studied Chet's whiskered face. "I don't know if you are the reason for me being here, but if you are I want to thank you with my whole heart. I would have never met Mitchell if you hadn't darted out in front of my car that rainy night." She observed the dogs curved lips. Was that a doggy grin?

"Well, we know the truth, you and I. Mitchell and I were married today, and I wish to stay." Standing, she gave him a final pat on his head and renewed her whistling.

She paused at the top of the hill to gaze upon the serenity of the scene laid out before her. The moon was high in the sky and reflected serenely against the gentle waves dancing on the water. She inhaled deeply of the pine hanging in the air and smiled. She hoped the happiness she felt at this very moment would never end.

Her smile slipped a moment as she thought of her parents. What were they doing at this very moment? Were they still looking for her wondering what had happened? They would have liked Mitchell. She was sure of that fact. Staring into the darkening sky, she closed her eyes briefly and said a quick prayer for her parents.

She twisted trying to reach the buttons on her dress. The top two buttons came undone without too much of a problem, but from there she was having difficulties unhooking the rest. She heard his soft footfalls before she actually saw him.

His arms wrapped around her and he nestled her neck with his firm lips. His mustache tickled as it glided across her flesh. Goosebumps arose on her arms as the tingling sensation from his kisses travelled throughout her body. Sighing with pleasure, she laid her head softly against his chest.

"I expected you to be in the pond already." His voice came to her soft and sensual.

Chuckling, she murmured, "I tried, but I'm a prisoner of my dress. I can't reach all of the buttons. I need help."

"Hmmm, I've never been able to ignore a lady in distress." His hands smoothly left her waist and began unbuttoning her dress. She heard him draw in a breath and groan. He fingered the silky material of her green bra. "I don't know how many times I've envisioned you in this in my mind." As her dress dropped and he exposed her lacy boy shorts he continued, "and these," he ran a trembling hand over her backside, "should be outlawed." He took a small step back and eyed her exposed body. "Have I ever told you I like what the future holds for women's undergarments?"

With a sensuous smile, she shook her head. She reached up and released the front clasp of her bra freeing her breasts. His amber gaze smoldered with desire. That look was for her.

He reached out and traced a fingertip around a nipple. It puckered instantly like a flower petal blooming at the first kiss of dawn. Her breath hitched. Everywhere his fingers traced, a trail of fire followed in its wake pooling in her lower belly. She had never felt so alive.

"You are beautiful!" His voice was a mere whisper, but in the stillness of the night, she heard the words clearly.

With a shy smile, she reached for his buttons on his

shirt. "I believe you are a little overdressed, cowboy." She soon had his muscled chest bared to her gaze. Her hand trembled slightly as she ran a hand over the bandage on his arm. "Does your shoulder hurt?"

"A little."

Her eyes misted once she removed the bandage. She studied the angry wound. She swallowed the knot forming in her throat as she thought of how he could have been killed. Leaning in, she gave his sore a gentle kiss. "Better?"

She heard him suck in a breath. "Much."

She smiled and took a step back. His eyes remained trained on her as she slowly lowered her lacy panties. Her nails trailed slowly down his chest and paused at the button to his jeans. "Last one in is a rotten egg!" Turning smoothly, she dived into the pond emerging a few feet away. The moon reflected off the drops of water on her skin.

He leaned over, shucked his boots and denims with quick jerky movements. His eyes never left hers until he dived into the water.

She shivered as he drew her into his arms. He gently nibbled a trail from her lips to her neck and back.

She leaned back to provide better access. All lucid thought rushed from her brain. His touch turned her to jelly. A mass of tingling nerves.

She barely noticed when he lifted her from the water to carry her to the grassy bank.

He leaned in and whispered, "I love you, Mrs. Reeves."

"I love you, too, Mitch."

He quirked a brow. "Mitch?"

"My brain is mush. You're lucky I remember your

name."

He chuckled until she gyrated her hips timidly against his own. He sucked in a breath. "Easy. I don't want to hurt you."

She reached up, clasped his jaw, and drew his lips to her own. "Not likely."

The moonlight danced upon their glistening skin as they become one. Their bodies perfectly matched in a rhythm as old as time.

Rachel clung to his body with quivering limbs. Holy Moly. She corralled her thoughts. She brushed his bangs from his forehead. "I think I just found something I love more than chocolate."

A sexy grin lit his face. "Just remember I have a ranch to run."

She shivered as a breeze caressed her skin.

Mitchell frowned. "Cold? Let's go inside where I can warm you up."

With a giggle, Rachel took off up the trail to the cabin. He grabbed her arm before she made it through the door. Gently he swung her up into his arms and carried her across the threshold. His lips descended onto hers on the other side of the entryway. "Welcome home, Rachel."

Epilogue

Angie pulled into her grandmother's drive. She stared at the house with unseeing eyes. Her grandmother's message on her answering machine had been a little unclear on why she needed to stop by for a visit. With a shrug of her shoulders, she pocketed her keys and made her way to Grammy Jones front door.

"Angie, give your grammy a hug. It's so good to see you. I'm glad you came over to visit me."

Angie followed her retreating grandmother into the kitchen. "Have a seat. I've got some cookies baked up and some milk for you."

Pulling out a chair at the kitchen table, Angie grinned. "Just what I need, are they your oatmeal raisin ones?"

Her grandmother dimpled as she laughed. "You betcha, what other cookie am I known for?"

Grammy settled a small plate of cookies in front of her and sat down opposite of her. "How are you doing?"

She took a bite of cookie before wiping crumbs from the corner of her mouth. "I'm okay. I didn't really understand the message you left on my machine." Her grammy had said something strange. She had said she knew what had happened to Rachel. Which was bizarre. Rachel had disappeared about a month ago, and no one had heard or seen her since. If the police couldn't figure out what had happened, how would Grammy know?

She closed her eyes as the usual guilt settled in. What if Bruce and her hadn't asked Rachel out for pizza? Rachel wouldn't have even been out in the storm. Her eyes flickered open, and she sighed. Taking another bite of the cookie, she waited for her Grandmother to explain her strange message.

Grammy reached across the table and patted her hand, "You look tired, dear. Is everything all right with you and Bruce?"

She stretched her legs out in front of her and settled in for a long visit. "Bruce and I couldn't be better. I guess I'm just tired. I haven't been sleeping well worrying about Rachel and what happened."

"Oh, but I do dear! Know what happened that is. I've been cleaning house. Rachel is fine."

Should she even ask what she meant? Taking another bite Angie smiled. "I swear Grammy these cookies just get better and better every year."

Grammy laughed with glee. "An old family recipe you know that's been passed down. You know it wouldn't hurt for you to try your hand at making them so you can make them for your children when you start having them."

She could feel her cheeks burning with a blush.

Grammy chuckled. "It's good to see the honeymoon isn't over!"

She tilted her head and studied her grandmother. "I know there is more to this visit than to discuss your future great grandchildren. What have you been up to Grammy?"

"Come, come, I have something to show you. It's the strangest thing!"

She rose from the table and followed her grandmother to the stairs to the attic. Rays of sunlight filtered through the stained glass windows and scattered colored dust bunnies as she walked to where her grammy bent over an old trunk dusting it off. "Grammy, is it safe for you to be up here in the attic alone?"

She waved a dismissing hand her way. "Oh posh, it's fine!" She lifted the top on a nearby trunk. The hinges creaked with age as the lid settled open. Grammy shuffled through the items in the chest. "I don't recall seeing this here before today. I was just looking for something of your grandpa's when I ran across this."

Angie shuffled closer and peered over her grammy's stooped shoulders. The top item in the trunk was a very old ivory dress folded neatly. Easing down to her knees in front of the trunk, she ran a hand in admiration over the outfit. The material had aged well. She could tell it had once been a very pretty dress. She fingered the delicate lace sleeves. "Isn't this gorgeous? Look at all of these tiny buttons. Could you imagine trying to get in and out of this thing?"

Grammy continued to shift through the items until she drew out a package that resembled a book. "This is what I found to be strange, and I didn't know if you would know what it means."

Angie placed the dress lovingly aside and reached to take the package. Written in a delicate hand on the outside of the parcel were the following words: *Please give this and the items in this trunk to Angie, great granddaughter of Jim and Becky Jones.* She fingered the writing with shaking fingers. Strange, but the writing looked like Rachel's.

She flicked a quick look toward her grandmother before she untied the strings that bound the package. Gasping she sat down hard on the attic floor. A picture lay on top of the book. The photo was a family of five. But the biggest shock was Rachel stared at her from the photo.

Grammy studied the picture over her shoulder. "Isn't that Rachel?"

She nodded and struggled to keep from crying. The tears finally fell as she replied, "If it's not, she has a twin." Her fingers lovingly ran over the framed picture. Rachel's hair had lost its perm, but she was sure it was her.

Grammy eased to her feet and patted Angie on her shoulder before she turned to leave the attic. "I'll leave you alone, but let me know if you need anything." She didn't hear her grandmother leave. Her fingers trailed over the faces in the photograph one more time. She lay the picture aside and opened the book. An envelope yellowed with age fell to the floor. She retrieved it to see her name neatly printed on the outside.

The words in the letter made her gasp. The note was truly from Rachel!

Angie,

I'm hoping someday this letter will find its way into your hands. You are going to say I told you so after I tell you my story, but I'm glad you were right. You see the night I hit a tree when that stupid dog ran in front of my car, I traveled back in time to the year eighteen ninety-two. Okay, close your mouth you're gaping like an idiot.

Angie quickly snapped her mouth closed as if

Rachel was there telling her to do so. She stifled a giggle as she put her hand up to her mouth and continued to read.

It's hard to believe, I know, trust me I thought I was fast approaching the Looney bin when I first figured out what was going on. I met someone, as you said I would. His name is Mitchell Reeves, and he is wonderful. In the journal you hold in your hand, you will find out all about when we first met and the dangers we went through. I know, I know, it sounds like a Hollywood movie, but it's true.

I wish you and Bruce the happiest of lives, like mine has been. Tell my mother and father I love them and think of them often. Feel free to share the enclosed diaries with them so they know my family. I'm fine and I'm living a life I love, with a wonderful man who loves me.

Becky, Mitchell's sister, is a distant relative of yours. She's famous around these parts for her raisin oatmeal cookies, and they tasted so familiar when I first had one. I didn't realize until later when names started to click into place that she was a relative, thus why her cookies tasted so familiar. After all, I should know I visited your grammy enough with you to know.

The picture is my family. Mitchell, isn't he just the handsomest man ever? My oldest son is Andrew. Oh, and the twins' names are Angela and Bruce. Somewhat original don't you think?

Enjoy the things in the trunk, Angie. They are my gifts to you. The dress is my wedding gown and yes, those buttons are a booger to get out of.

> *With all my love,*
> *Rachel*

Angie sat in the attic for a long time tears running unchecked down her face. "Oh, Rachel I miss you so," she muttered. Slowly she shifted through the trunk. Miscellaneous items piled up around her as she lovingly caressed each. Placing everything back into the trunk, she tenderly opened one of the journals Rachel had placed inside the trunk.

She smiled as she read the first line. She breathed a sigh of relief as she gazed out the attic window. Rachel was fine. She needed to call her parents. Would they believe her? Heck, she barely believed the evidence herself.

With awe she clutched the journals to her chest and rose from the floor. She needed another one of Grammy's famous cookies. Her smile lingered as she made her way down the attic stairs. Life was good.

A word from the author…

I've been married to Nathan for twenty-seven years. We have two grown sons, Blake and Mason. Blake is married and Mason is attending culinary school. We have two fat spoiled rescue cats, Mango and Meera.

I have enjoyed writing since high school. I am a current member of the Wichita Area Romance Authors (WARA) club and Romance Writers of America.

Thank you for purchasing
this publication of The Wild Rose Press, Inc.

If you enjoyed the story, we would appreciate your
letting others know by leaving a review.

For other wonderful stories,
please visit our on-line bookstore at
www.thewildrosepress.com.

For questions or more information
contact us at
info@thewildrosepress.com.

The Wild Rose Press, Inc.
www.thewildrosepress.com

Stay current with The Wild Rose Press, Inc.

Like us on Facebook

https://www.facebook.com/TheWildRosePress

And Follow us on Twitter
https://twitter.com/WildRosePress